SCEADU

PRASHANT PINGE

SCEADU

Prashant Pinge

www.1889books

ISBN: 978-1-915045-37-9

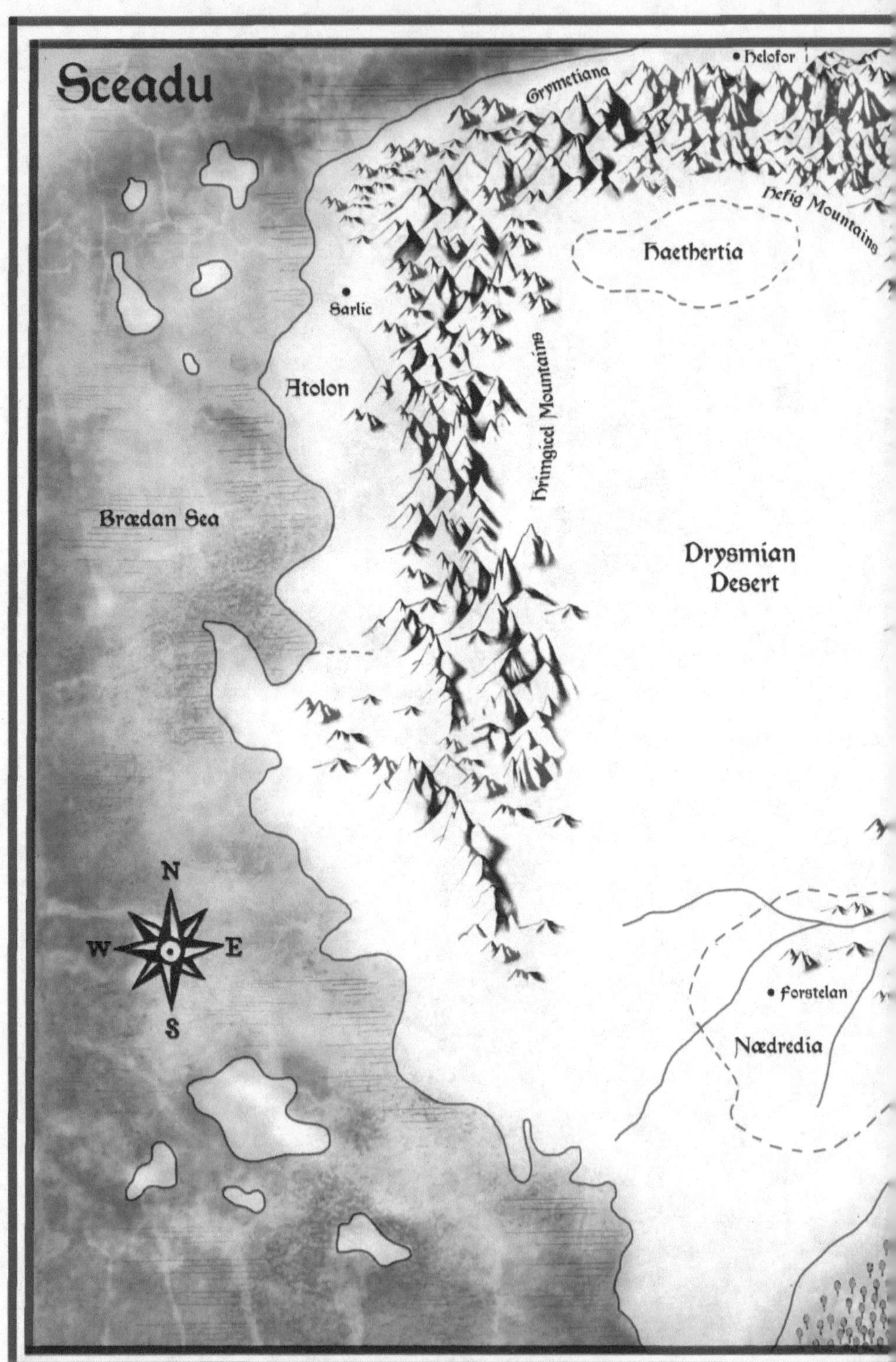

Sceadu
Grymetiana
Helofor
Hefig Mountains
Haethertia
Sarlic
Atolon
Hrimgicel Mountains
Bræcan Sea
Drysmian Desert
N
W
E
S
Forstelan
Nædredia

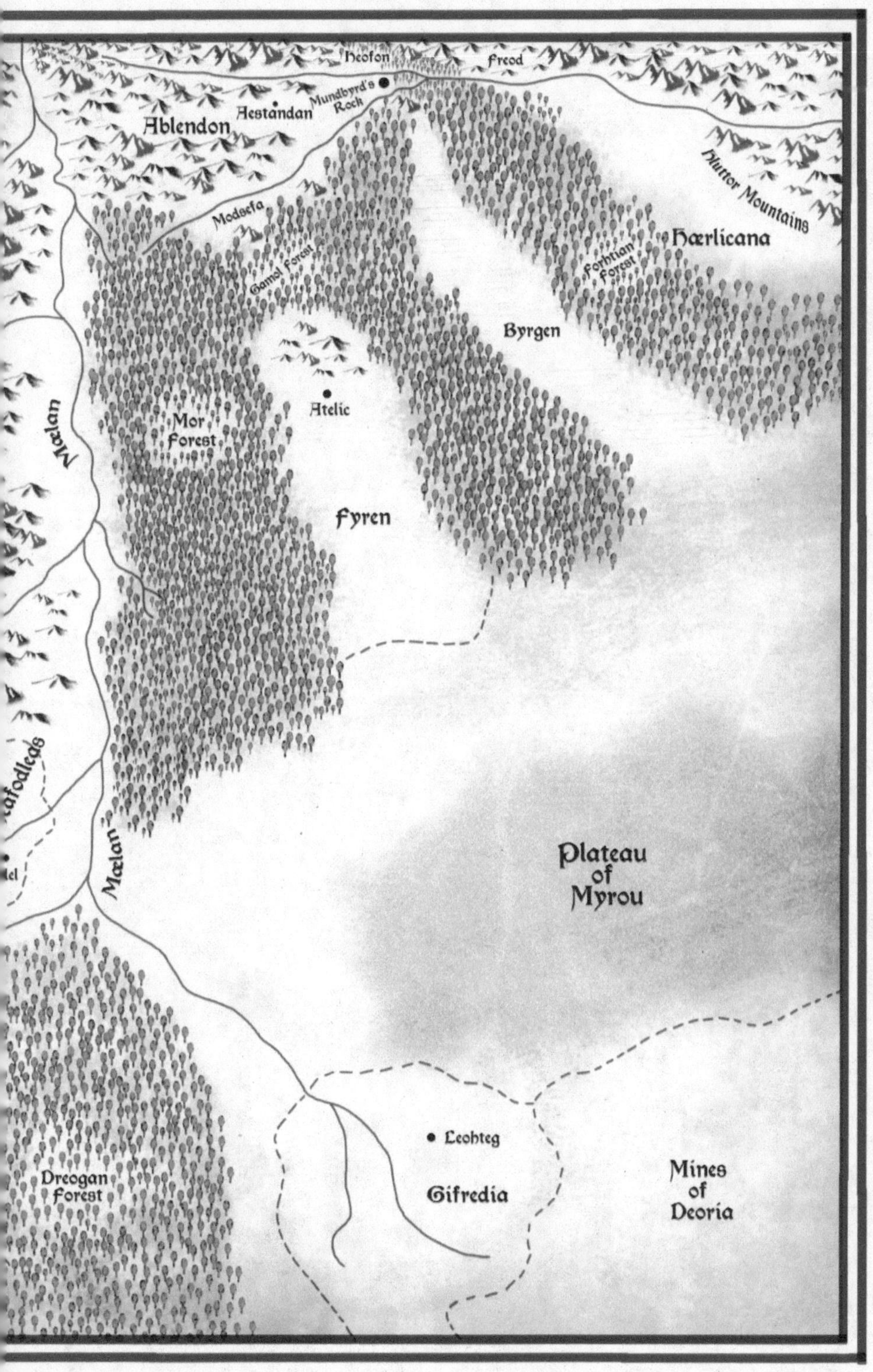

Ablendon
Aestandan
Mundbyrd's Rock
Heofon
Freod
Hluttor Mountains
Haerlicana
Modsefa
Gamol Forest
Forhtian Forest
Byrgen
Maelan
Mor Forest
Atelic
Fyren
afodleas
lel
Maelan
Plateau of Myrou
Leohteg
Dreogan Forest
Gifredia
Mines of Deoria

PROLOGUE – DESTINY'S PAWN

Almost four years to the day

A lone man stood carefully concealed behind the moss-covered boundary wall of a long-forgotten structure. The night was blacker than usual, draped with thick, grey-bellied clouds that had entombed the neighbourhood with a grim silence. Just what the man had hoped for.

Suddenly, a gust of blistering hot wind blew up the tails of his coat. The man pushed them down with a rather stoical gesture, crushing the cigarette butt against a broken pillar in the same instant. But his eyes remained steady, never moving off the deserted street.

Just then, the cloud cover eased briefly, allowing the tepid moonlight to slip through the indigo night. It fell harshly upon the man's face. The spell was broken, and he tottered back a few paces, clutching hard at the polished goblin's head that sat atop his cane. Behind him, his shadow danced nervously upon the dilapidated building.

The man pushed his back against the uneven bricks and reached for his hat, slowly easing the rim that had been eating away at his temple. He closed his eyes and then abruptly jerked his hand close to his face. The silver dial read six minutes past midnight. Only two minutes since he had last checked. The man dabbed at the beads of sweat that glistened on his day-old stubble. Exactly forty-five hours and thirty-one minutes had passed since the full moon had occurred. Which meant he only had two hours and twenty-nine minutes. And the seconds continued to tick away.

Across the street, the pink bougainvilleas rustled softly against the tall brick wall of the post office. The man dug his boots into the hard gravel. Had he done the right thing in selecting this building? Had he been wise in trusting the tramp? How much longer? The man bit his lip. Perhaps he should have gone himself, despite the incident. But it was too late now. He would have to be patient. After all, he had been patient for six long years. And he was so close now. So close.

The man fished out a slightly crumpled cigarette from his coat pocket and stuck it between his trembling lips. But despite repeated tries, the lighter refused to spark. He let it fall to the ground with a sigh. His quest had landed him in this godforsaken little town, and he had almost lost it all. But the game wasn't over. Not just yet. The man spat out the cigarette. There was something extremely perplexing though. How had the boy known? It had very nearly brought his long and arduous journey to a fruitless demise.

The man could feel the ivy swaying gently behind him on the ruins, part of a world where time no longer had any meaning. But it did to him. He pressed his taut fingers against the crumbling plaster. When would his wait be over? He raised his hand once again, almost mechanically, but stopped. Would the fool even find the building? Or had he changed his mind? Perhaps he was lying dead in a gutter in some dirty alley. No, the man thought fiercely. The money would bring him here. It would be enough to go on a drug binge for at least a few days.

The moon had once again found refuge behind the clouds.

"You there?" a voice croaked out of the velvety darkness.

The man scraped his elbow hard against the rough edge of the wall. But the searing pain never reached his lips.

"It's me… Mark." A pale shadow followed.

"Do you have it?" The words burned in the man's throat.

The haggard figure stumbled, and a messily wrapped packet fell out of his abscessed fingers. The man dived, grabbing at it with both hands. The packet landed with a gentle thud, followed by the dull clank of his cane. "Idiot," he hissed. "You've shot up, haven't you? I should send you without a dime."

"… a quick fix… but I got it," Mark mumbled, swaying like a reed.

"Quiet," the man snarled, thrusting his fingers into his trouser pocket. "Take these and be off." He pushed the bills into the tramp's quivering hands.

"… promised two hundred bucks," Mark protested, trying hard to count.

But the man hadn't heard a word. He simply stood still, staring at the packet that promised to change the course of his destiny.

There was a tap on his shoulder. "But you promised… "

The man swung around, his cane raised. But his grip tightened and his hand stopped. "It's more than five hundred," he said, clamping down his jaw. "Now get out of here."

Mark staggered away in his drug-induced haze.

The man drew in a long breath and put his cane to one side. For a brief instant, his mind wandered off to that gloomy winter evening many years ago, to the discovery he had made in a faraway corner of the country. But this wasn't the time for reminiscing.

The man gently loosened the strings and brought out the contents: an old book. He had the means now. From here on, his path would be one that few humans had trod through the ages. The brown wrapping slowly drifted to the ground.

The man suddenly jerked his head. But it was only Mark, still sauntering towards the street. The man's shoulders relaxed; he was in control, at least for the time being. There would be challenges ahead, grave ones. The boy had probably complicated things. But he could deal with all that later...

***

An incessant flapping noise cut through the harmony of the early morning sounds. The caretaker of the public library, on his usual short cut through the deserted Penrose property, stopped and listened. It seemed to be coming from around the building. He walked across cautiously and turned.

It was a strange sight that met his eyes. A book was lying face open on the ground, its pages repeatedly pounded by the early morning breeze. The caretaker picked it up hesitantly and turned it around. The library's mark was on the book. "Vandals," he muttered, when he saw that a few pages had been torn from the back.

Once at the library, the caretaker placed the book on the counter and stared at it from under his bushy eyebrows. There wasn't any point in returning it to the stacks. After all, what good was a book that had no ending? He dusted it clumsily and tossed it into a large dirty pile at the back, other books that had been removed from circulation. It really was a pity these words would never be read again. Or so he thought.

CHAPTER 1 – RELUCTANT CATALYST

Present day

Isabella sat at her old wooden desk, staring into the thick, yellowed pages of a book under a dull moth-ridden beam cast by the table lamp. But every time she blinked it seemed as if the words had played a round of musical chairs. And the moths, fluttering through the words at times and hovering over them at others, did not make things any easier.

She was about to turn the page when there was a tug at her feet. It was a very gentle one, almost imperceptible. Surprised, she glanced down, but there was nothing. Perhaps it's just my imagination, Isabella thought. She was about to shake her thick dark brown curls out of her face when she felt it again.

She pushed her head down and looked into the dark void with furrowed brow. Her skinny legs stared back. But before she could decide on whether she had actually felt anything, there was another tug, an unmistakable one this time. And another one. The truth suddenly dawned upon her. It was her shadow, trying to drag her into itself.

Isabella jerked back the chair, kicking hard at the floor. But her shadow snapped back, pulling at her even more viciously. She stomped upon it repeatedly. But the dark grey shape began jabbing at her feet and ankles. She pushed herself up and made a frantic attempt to run. But her legs refused to move, and she almost toppled forward.

All this while, Isabella's shadow had been growing larger and larger. Suddenly, it lunged out of the ground and swallowed her, like a python does its unsuspecting prey.

Isabella's slight frame shuddered as her hands reached for her throat. For a few moments, she grappled with an invisible force that seemed to be choking her. And then, the coughing started, in fits at first but soon with such intensity that her eyes burned. Slowly, silhouettes of familiar objects began to take shape. It was her bedroom.

She sat up with a start and dug her nails into the soft blanket. Only a dream, she mumbled repeatedly, bobbing her head up and down. Her thick curls were matted to her forehead and her entire body drenched in perspiration. It had all seemed so real.

A few minutes later, Isabella's heart finally stopped pounding against her ribcage. She took a few calming breaths and flicked on her bedside lamp. But just as her hands reached for the towel, so did her shadow, swaying ominously on the wall. She froze. Was it going to devour her? But all it did was mirror her movements, almost mocking her inability to escape its presence.

Isabella's hand shot out to switch off the lamp. And that's when her eyes fell on the book, staring back innocently from under her satchel. At that very instant, a nauseating feeling needled her from within, like rats were gnawing away at her intestines.

Eight hours earlier

"You've been awfully quiet today." Isabella's mother looked from across the steering wheel. "Still upset about your grade?"

"Did you read Mr. Doherty's remark?" Isabella said in a low voice.

"That's your physical education teacher, right?"

Isabella nodded and slumped in her seat. "Has the potential but does not try. But I gave it my best this year."

"I know you did, sweetie," her mother said, pushing back her daughter's curls. They promptly bounced back over her forehead.

"And I don't see any potential," Isabella continued, dangling her legs. "Perhaps Milo's right. I do have chicken legs."

Isabella's mother coughed gently to hide a smile. "Your brother's just teasing. And you really shouldn't be bothered. I mean, you did score straight A's in your other classes. Here we are."

A large 'Used Book Sale' sign had appeared, attached clumsily on the side entrance of the local library. Isabella squished her nose against the window. Nothing mattered any more, not even the blot on her report card.

Isabella ran up the steps and pulled open the door. She was instantly greeted by a blast of cold air, blended with the delightfully musty scent of books. But the sight was so mesmerizing there just wasn't any time to get lost in the fragrance. Row upon row of books, stacked untidily on long wooden tables, ran like a maze around the hall. And the narrow aisles were bursting with people, scurrying with lists and poking around for a bargain. She belonged here.

"Better hurry up. The sale closes in forty minutes." It was Isabella's mother.

"That's okay," she chirped, swivelling on her feet. "I'll be back tomorrow. The sale… "

"Today's the last day," her mother interrupted, pointing to a stencilled sign pasted untidily on the wall.

"But the newspaper ad said… " Isabella's lips quivered.

Her mother knelt beside her. "It doesn't matter," she said, dabbing her daughter's eyes. "You have enough time to buy all the books you want."

Isabella pulled back her tears, scrunched her teeth and stepped into the first aisle. She was immediately lost in a sea of legs. But she kept her chin straight and began burrowing through the books, keeping her elbows handy just in case. About half an hour later, she found herself juggling eight books.

Just then, a nasal voice droned out of the shabbily hung loudspeakers. "The sale will close in ten minutes. Please start moving to the cash counter. Thank you."

Isabella placed her precious stack on the edge of the table and pulled out her list. There was only one book to go. When she looked up, its unmistakable design was staring at her from between two forgettable thrillers just a table away. She trotted over with a smug smile on her face. Unfortunately, the book had also caught the attention of someone else. It was a thin woman with pencilled eyebrows in a striped dress that made her look even thinner.

Isabella pulled out the book, but the thin woman somehow lunged at it in her tall stilettos and managed to grab the other end. They both yanked hard, trying to get complete ownership.

The nasal voice echoed through the hall once again. "The sale will close in five minutes. Please move to the cash counter."

This seemed to spur the woman, and she put everything in her next tug. Poor Isabella tumbled backwards and mowed her elbow on the table behind, knocking something down.

The woman's lips curved into a smirk. "Sorry, girlie. Nothin' personal, but I've been lookin' for this for months now." With long strides, she made her way to the cash counter.

Isabella stood still, rubbing her elbow. Her face was burning up, but she fought back the tears.

"Are you done yet, Bella?" Her mother's voice had found its way through the aisles.

"In a minute," she shouted back, resting her back against the table and taking a few short breaths. At least she had the other books.

But Isabella had not bargained for this. When she turned, her stack had disappeared. In fact, the entire table had been emptied. The volunteers, irritated and frustrated after three long days, had started clearing the tables a few minutes before the sale actually got over. And they had mistaken her selection as just another pile. She could see them a little ahead, sweeping books carelessly into large cloth sacks. Her precious pile had been reduced to anonymity once again.

A few years ago, Isabella had fallen into a pond. For the few seconds she had been submerged in the murky water, she had been overwhelmed by an utter sense of helplessness. The same feeling had returned once again. The hall had gone blurry. All the noise was condensed to a buzz. And she no longer seemed to have any control over her limbs.

Isabella wanted to call out to her mother, but all she managed was to splutter a few incoherent words. She somehow clutched the table and pressed her hand against its cold surface. It felt empty, but at least it felt real. She slowly pushed herself forward, still holding onto the edge. A few deliberate steps later, however, her foot hit something on the floor.

Even before Isabella could turn her gaze downwards, a memory had been triggered, taking her back to the events that had transpired minutes earlier. The last book on her list. The thin woman. The struggle. And then she had lost the battle. But wait. Just before that, her elbow had hit the table and knocked something down.

At first, things were a bit hazy. But gradually, she could see the outline of a book forming by her feet. It was bound in rich, black leather, worn away at the edges, and had an intricate design embossed in silver, parts of which had greyed over time.

"S C E A D U," Isabella read out the title. It shimmered mysteriously in the myriad shadows around. She was about to return it to the stacks when a churning gripped her insides. Without knowing why, she pulled the book close to her chest. The other books didn't matter any more.

Isabella sat by her window, staring listlessly at the bright moon through the tangled silhouettes of faraway trees. The wall clock read three in the morning. But she had been awake for almost an hour now, waiting patiently for the unsettling feeling to subside.

For the third night in a row, Isabella had been subjected to the same dream. But there was something different about tonight. It had been the first time she had clearly seen the book, the same book which she was sure was lying just a few feet away.

Isabella pushed aside the satchel and picked it up. She slowly moved her fingers along the delicate grooves of the design. There was a distinctive feeling of tiny needles poking at her skin. As she snatched her hand away, the soft rays of the moon passed over the silver motif, causing it to shine like the slithery skin on a snake. Isabella could feel every fibre in her body begging her to stop. But she knew what she had to do. It was the only way to stop the nightmares. It had to be.

Isabella crawled into her chair and switched on the lamp. The time was sixteen minutes past three. Her mind wavered, but only for a moment. And then, with trembling hands, she opened the book.

Isabella waved off a moth from under the lamp and pushed herself up. She fidgeted with her curls for a few moments and sat back down. But the book had made such extraordinary claims that Isabella was up once again and pacing the floor. Could it all be true? She opened it again and flipped to the last page. It was really disappointing a few pages had been torn after that. But it did have what she needed.

Isabella blew into her hands. There was only one way to find out. She walked to the middle of her room. But before she could do anything, there was a loud thump from below.

Chapter 2 – First Awakening

he night was no longer dark when Isabella opened her room door.

"Must you be so clumsy?" a shrill woman's voice came from downstairs. "It's five in the morning."

"That's precisely why I'm so clumsy," a boy's voice droned.

The voices weren't familiar. Isabella got down on all fours and crawled over to the balusters. Her eyes grappled with the shadows until figures began to emerge out of the grey morning hues.

"Don't answer back. And be careful with that stupid backpack." It was a woman with an oval face, so much like her mother's, but creased beyond its years.

The lanky boy next to her let the backpack slide to the ground and righted the fallen red suitcase. So that was what caused the bump, Isabella thought with a sigh.

"Did we wake you, dear?" It was her mother.

Isabella was so startled she bumped her head against the bottom of the railing. She pulled it back and stood up with a sheepish smile.

"Honey, you remember your Aunt Sarah, don't you? From the photos? And this is your cousin, Ben. Your other cousin's still outside."

Isabella took a small step back and bit her lip. But before she could decide on how to respond, the front door opened and a tall, athletic boy dressed in casuals stepped in, dragging behind two suitcases.

"Will, where have you been all this while?" Aunt Sarah screamed.

"But… but mom, I was only paying the… " began the boy, but stopped as his mother suddenly covered her face and burst into tears.

Isabella wrapped her arms around herself. Something just did not feel right.

"There, there, Sarah," her mother said, throwing a blue woollen shawl around her sister. "You've had a rough night. Why don't you rest for a while?"

Aunt Sarah raised her tear-stained face. "Did you reach Carlos?"

"I'm not getting through. He's probably in some remote location in Indonesia."

"What… what do we do?"

Isabella's mother glanced up at her daughter's scared face. "We'll manage," she said calmly. "Uh… Will, why don't you go online and check for air tickets? We all need to be on the earliest flight to Denver. You can use my laptop."

Isabella sat down on the cold stairs as Will began his search. Ben had propped his head back on the couch and was staring at the ceiling. Aunt Sarah was fiddling with the shawl, but tears continued to pour down her cheeks. What had happened that had turned everything upside down? Nothing was making sense. She wished her father had been there.

"I'm going to get started on the packing. Bella, can you make some hot cocoa for everyone? Please use the microwave. And wake up Milo."

Isabella walked out of the kitchen with a tray a few minutes later.

"Thanks," Will said, as she handed him a cup. He swivelled around on the chair. "Aunt Emily, there's only one early morning flight to Denver. I see only two seats available. What should I do?"

"When's the next flight?" Isabella's mother asked, running down the stairs.

"Not until afternoon."

"That won't do. Book the tickets." She handed him her credit card.

Aunt Sarah sat up, panic-stricken. "But… but what about the children?" she cried. "We can't leave them behind. I won't have it."

Isabella's mother looked at the children. But when she spoke, her voice had an air of finality to it. "I'm sorry, Sarah, but it has to be this way," she said, reaching for her mobile. Minutes later, she looked up. "I've had a word with Mrs. Rothschild. She's agreed to provide meals for the next few days."

"It's done," Will said, handing back the credit card.

Isabella's mother stared at the pattern cast by the scanty morning rays on the faded carpet. She knelt down and squeezed her sister's hand. "Everything's going to be all right," she said, her grey eyes meeting Isabella's in the same moment. It will be all right, they pleaded.

But Isabella could feel a knot forming in the pit of her stomach.

"Milo," Isabella whispered, nudging him gently, "wake up. Mom's coming over."

Isabella had somehow dragged Emilio, her twelve-year-old brother, to the living room. He was now sprawled beside her with his eyes half open. "More cream cheese," he yawned, and closed his eyes completely.

Isabella dug her elbow sharply into his ribs, or more accurately, the layer of fat around them.

Emilio had been about to snore. Instead, his head shot up like a cannon, causing a loud grunt to escape his mouth. He clutched his sore side with one hand and was about to pinch his sister with the other when their mother walked up. Emilio pulled his hand back hastily but not before a quick glare that promised revenge later.

"You guys must be wondering what's going on," she said, sitting on the coffee table. "Grandpa's very ill."

Isabella's face went pale. Emilio was suddenly wide awake.

"I got a call just after midnight. That's why your aunt and cousins are here."

Isabella and Emilio glanced sideways. Ben seemed to be busy with his backpack while Will was browsing aimlessly.

"Anyway, we need to leave soon," she continued, checking her watch.

"Should we start packing then?" Emilio asked, dragging his rotund self off the couch.

Their mother got up with a sigh. "I'm sorry, Milo. We can't take the children along. There were only two tickets available."

"But that's not fair," he blurted out. "It's summer vacation, and I don't want to be stuck at home. Not with her."

The house suddenly fell silent. Emilio slowly uncrossed his arms and stared at his feet.

"We're not going on a holiday," their mother said, every word forced through her teeth. "Even your nine-year-old sister understands…"

Aunt Sarah slowly shook her head at her sister. "What your mom is trying to say," she said, walking over and tousling her nephew's thick dark brown curls, "is that we'll be busy with Grandpa. So can you please manage for a few days?"

"Okay." Emilio pulled his lips in and moved his eyes around the room, blinking hard to stop the tears.

Their mother's lips narrowed, but she walked out of the room without a word.

"Can you stop picking out the bits of strawberry?"

Ben pulled his sharp protruding nose out of the yogurt pot and looked at his mother. "The yogurt doesn't agree with my delicate constitution," he said matter-of-factly. "You should know that by now. It's been eleven years."

"Then why don't you just eat strawberries?"

He put down the cup and adjusted his horn-rimmed spectacles. "The yogurt coating tempers the strawberry flavour and at the same time moistens…"

"Oh, stop it," she cried, pulling out her compact and staring into the mirror. "Why do I even bother?"

"I was merely offering an answer to your question."

Aunt Sarah dabbed at the dark circles under her eyes. "There was a time when everyone said we could pass off as twins," she said, glancing at her sister as she poured out the orange juice. "And… and then… everything just went so horribly wrong."

Isabella's mother patted her sister's shoulder. "The past is gone. But we all need to keep our calm to deal with what lies ahead."

"You're right, of course," she replied, looking away. She snapped her compact and slipped it back. "It's… it's just been so tough ever since their father…"

"You have to be strong, Sarah."

Aunt Sarah choked back her tears. "This one," she said, pointing to Ben, "is out of control with his… with his… And the other one… do you know he got detained and interrogated at the airport for carrying a knife of all things? It was so embarrassing. He was lucky not to be arrested by the police. It would have been nice to have their father around. A knife of all things. It was so embarrassing. He was lucky not to be arrested by the police. And he just can't get his mind off girls."

Will almost choked on the cocoa. "Mom, you know that's not true. I mean… it just happened that one time at the mall. And anyway it was just a stupid camping knife."

"There's no reason to be ashamed, Will," Ben said, patting his mouth with the napkin. "It's a very natural reaction. Although I must confess you seem to be having a delayed hormonal response. I would say you're about a year late."

"You see what I have to put up with," Aunt Sarah cried. "And now… this thing with Dad…"

Isabella's mother suddenly clapped her hands. "It's time to head out. Boys, why don't you start moving the luggage outside? We leave in five minutes."

The awkwardness gave way to a sense of urgency. A few minutes and some tearful hugs later, the two sisters and the luggage were bundled inside the family car. "Now for some final instructions,"

Isabella's mother said, rolling down the window. "I know this is hard on all of us. But we have to make it work for Grandpa."

"How long will you be gone?" Isabella asked.

"I've taken leave for eight days, unless… but let's just say eight days for now. But you can always reach us by phone anytime. Now about your meals. There are leftovers in the refrigerator for today. Mrs. Rothschild will be coming every morning from tomorrow. I guess that's about it. You're all sensible children. So please behave in a responsible manner. And yes, one more thing. Will's in charge during our absence. I've given him enough money as well."

The tips of Emilio's ears burned red, but Isabella coughed gently. You'd better not anger mom, her eyes said. He pursed his lips and frowned. But that was it.

Chapter 3 – Scorching Decision

he neighbourhood trees had cast gloomy shadows upon the house. And the few rays of the sun that had struggled through were uncharacteristically subdued for a summer morning.

Isabella watched the car back out of the driveway and into the street. How could she even think of deserting her family at a time like this? But she had been gripped by a perverse curiosity ever since she had finished the book. She could feel a lump in her throat, but the glint in her eyes said everything.

Emilio came and stood next to her, a faraway look clouding his face. He mumbled something about using his cousins as a punching bag.

She slid her hand into her brother's. "Everything's going to be fine," she said, almost to herself.

"How can it?" he cried, pulling his arm away. "How can Mom put that Will in charge? This is my house. And you, why didn't you say anything?"

Isabella moistened her lips. She had been expecting this but had hoped it would happen later, much later. "Uh… he is the oldest."

"If that was the case, then I should have been made the class monitor."

"But you bully the other kids."

"It's called leadership," he replied, pulling in his stomach and stretching down his t-shirt in the same breath, "but you wouldn't understand." The t-shirt rolled back almost immediately, leaving his stomach wobbling out once again like a blob of jelly.

"How is pushing someone around leadership?" she asked, rolling her eyes.

Emilio tried to answer but ended up spluttering. He suddenly pinched his sister and walked away. "That's for earlier."

Isabella rubbed her arm. "Nothing but a bully," her voice trailed.

"Eh… what's that?" Will had just emerged from the guest room. "I'm all settled in. You've got a nice place here."

"Thanks," Isabella replied shyly, but Emilio walked past with a grunt and fell upon the couch.

"So, what's the plan?" Will asked, pulling out a soda from the refrigerator.

Emilio glared at him. "That's my soda."

"Why didn't you say so?" Will winked, throwing it at him. "I'll have another one."

"They're all mine," he shot back, fumbling with the ring-pull. The can fell with a dull thud on the carpet.

"Classic baboon behaviour." It was Ben, who had just wandered into the living room. "The younger male trying to oust the head of the troop. Don't you see, Will? He sees you as a threat. So, he's trying to assert himself."

Will grinned as Emilio's face turned a beetroot red. "Did you just call me a monkey?"

"Not at all," Ben said with a wry smile. "All I'm saying is that your behaviour is reminiscent of a baboon's. Will, can you pass me some yogurt?"

"Why you… you look like an insect," Emilio shouted.

Ben peered at his reflection in the glass window. "A praying mantis, to be precise."

"And… and your head is tiny."

"Of course, it is," Ben smiled. "Compared to your head, that is. And it also proves there's an inverse relationship between the size of one's head and one's intelligence."

Emilio suddenly jumped up and pulled his fists out. "You're messing with the wrong guy. I'm going to get you for that."

Ben scratched his chin thoughtfully. "If I have calculated this correctly, I believe the odds are stacked sixty to forty in my favour. I would like to draw your attention to my bony limbs and longer reach. Do you still want to have a go at me?"

Emilio's fists uncurled slowly. Was this a fight he could lose? Unlike the school yard, his opponent had not yielded. This was posing to be a huge dilemma. "Humph," he finally blurted out, "I don't fight with sissies. I'll fight him."

Ben yawned loudly. "Suit yourself. But I must warn you. Will's a black belt in taekwondo."

"Okay, that's enough talk about fighting," Will said, grabbing another soda and a cup of yogurt. "But I'm in charge. So, deal with it."

Emilio wasn't quite done yet. "This is my house," he said, kicking the couch hard.

Isabella had been suffering through this exchange in a shadowy part cast by the stairs. While a part of her was happy to see her brother get a bitter taste of his own medicine, she was beginning to feel a little concerned about the mauve spots on his cheeks. "Uh… Milo, they never said it wasn't. Can't we all just get along?"

Emilio swung around, pushing his hands on his hips. "I don't care what you think," he said, glaring at her. "So, butt out."

"Aunt Emily's put me in charge," Will said firmly. He opened the can and took a long sip. "So that's how it will be till they return."

Emilio could feel his lips quivering but words had never been his strong point. Unfortunately though, his brain had also sent a strict order against engaging in any physical misadventures. It did, however, offer him a consolation prize. Isabella, it slyly pointed out, was an easy prey.

But Will had sensed his intentions. He stepped in front of her. "Really?"

"Humph," Emilio snorted, "I don't need you. You're all losers anyway." And he marched upstairs to his room with his nose in the air.

"I'm… I'm really sorry," Isabella piped.

"Don't be," Will replied, picking up the remote and sliding on the couch. "By the way, are we doing anything? I'm getting bored."

Ben ran his hands through his straw-coloured hair. "Typical," he yawned. "We just got here. Do you want to finish doing everything on the first day?"

Will crossed his legs on the coffee table with a sigh. "It's going to be Netflix for me then."

"I suppose you'll be watching The Vampire Diaries. That programme is killing your brain cells."

Will shrugged as Ben pushed open the guest room door. "Yes," he nodded at Isabella, "he's always like that. But you'll get used to it soon enough. So, tell me, would you like to do something?"

Isabella didn't answer immediately. She really liked her older cousin, but her mind was made up. "Perhaps later," she smiled, wondering whether there would be a later. She felt a little guilty immediately and added, "Please call me Bella. All my friends do."

The alarm rang with piercing alacrity at two in the afternoon. Isabella felt like a mad elephant had been let loose inside her skull. Her tiny arm shot out instantly, groping around for the upturned top of the alarm clock. Alas, it was safely tucked away behind the lamp on her desk. She was about to drag a pillow upon her head when a barrage of memories from earlier that day flooded her mind.

Isabella kicked away her blanket and stumbled out of bed. Had it all been a dream, she wondered, reaching out to tap the annoying alarm clock. But just as she did, her fingers grazed something. Isabella buried her face in her hands. It was the book, waiting patiently for its owner to come through on her promise.

But things had changed. All the bravado and excitement of the early morning hours had ebbed during her sleep. And a rational voice had replaced all the chatter. Isabella twisted the ends of her blanket, staring straight ahead at the lamp. A minute later, she shook her head and pulled the blanket over it. The rush she had felt under the tangled moonlit silhouettes had dissolved in the cosy afternoon warmth. But she knew she had to do this.

And then, Isabella had a brainwave. Will was the answer. He was the oldest amongst them. Her mother had put her trust in him. And he seemed quite keen on doing something. So why not this?

CHAPTER 4 – REAL METAPHOR

Emilio sat on the bean bag, his face frozen and eyes on the verge of watering. He had been staring at the screen for three hours, his chubby fingers pounding the life out of the PlayStation 5 controller. But the numbing pain was finally going to pay off. Just then, there was a knock on the door.

"Go away, Bella," he shouted. "I'm busy."

There was another knock.

Emilio's face began to swell up like a berry. "I swear I'll stuff all my dirty socks in your closet if you knock again."

There was another knock. "It's Ben."

Emilio ground his teeth to control the agitation that was boiling in his belly. But alas, it reached his tired fingers. A primal howl escaped his mouth as he threw aside the controller and clobbered the sides of the bean bag. He waded through the mess and pulled open the door. "What is it?" he fumed.

Ben forgot his question when he saw Emilio. "Why is that vein throbbing so much?" he asked, pointing to his forehead.

Emilio thumped his head on the edge of the door. "Because of idiots like you," he hissed. "I was this close… this close… what do you want?"

Ben gaped at the shiny chocolate wrappers scattered all over the carpet. "I see you've been busy. Anyway, I was wondering if you've seen Isabella."

Emilio stepped aside. "Do you see her here? No. Do I care where she is? Still no. Now leave me alone."

He was about to shut the door, but Ben stuck his foot in the gap. "We may have a problem."

"Of course, we do," Emilio shouted, pushing harder. "You're the problem."

"Emilio, I'm not joking. We can't find your sister."

Emilio crossed his arms and glowered at his older cousin. "Humph, so now you want to talk to me? What happened to all the 'I'm in charge' stuff?"

Will fiddled with the remote. "Look Emilio, this isn't about you or me."

"Then why did you call me down here? I don't even want to see your sorry faces."

"Just shut up and listen," Will shouted, suddenly standing up. "We don't know where Isabella is."

Emilio shrugged. "She must be around here somewhere. Is there anything to eat?"

"What's wrong with you?" Will cried, throwing aside the remote.

"I'm hungry."

Ben caught Will's arm before he lost his temper again. A few minutes later, their cousin was holding a microwaved burrito.

"You know," Emilio said, taking a large bite, "this tastes much better than the one I had at that restaurant."

"Emilio," Will sighed. "Are you listening to me? Isabella's missing."

Emilio wiped his mouth against his sleeve. "I don't understand," he mumbled. "What do you mean she's missing?"

Ben shrugged at Will. "This isn't working. It would be better to give him a detailed account of the entire episode."

Emilio's hand stopped midway and slowly descended back into the bowl. "What's going on?" he demanded, staring at both his cousins. "What's happened to Bella?"

Will wiped his palms against the couch. "Isabella came down about an hour ago. She said… she said… "

"What did she say?" Emilio asked, squinting at him.

"That she's found a new place."

"A new place? Like a shop? Or a hiding place?"

Will thumped the coffee table. "Right? That's what I thought as well. That perhaps she's found some new food joint or something."

"So, what was she talking about?"

Will bit his lips. "A new land. A place that's not part of our world."

"A new land?" Emilio said, keeping down the half-eaten burrito. "You guys have gone nuts."

"We're serious," Will replied. "I thought she might be talking about a make-believe place. But she insisted it was really there."

Ben nodded. "I can vouch for that. I was on my way to get some bleaching powder for… never mind. Anyway, Isabella had this book with her… with a black cover… it had some map… and some verse. She claimed it would take us to this land."

Will threw his hands in the air. "I tried explaining it was just a book, a figment of some very creative writer's imagination."

"You don't need to sugarcoat logic, Will," Ben said, raising an eyebrow. "The entire hypothesis is obviously implausible. There is absolutely no scientific basis to support it."

Will punched the cushion. "And you didn't have to be such an ass. She's only nine."

"But she was so adamant about the whole thing. The very notion is preposterous."

Emilio pressed the base of his palms against his temple and shook his head. "I just don't understand anything. But Bella never makes up stories. She's not like that."

Ben leaned forward and slid his spectacles down his nose. "You surely cannot be suggesting such a land actually exists. As a person of science, I cannot even entertain such a ridiculous thought."

"Anyway, where is she now?" Emilio asked, rubbing his eyes. His cousin was right. But his sister would never make up such a fantastic lie.

"After Ben here questioned her intelligence," Will said, glaring at his brother, "Bella stormed upstairs. I thought I'd give her some time to cool off."

"And?"

"About half an hour later, I sent Ben upstairs to apologize."

"Under protest, I might add," Ben said, looking away.

"Not the time," Will said, throwing the cushion at him. "But long story short, she's not in her room and neither is she in yours."

Emilio, who had just begun pacing, stopped. "It's so simple," he said, clicking his tongue. "She must have gone out. I mean, that has to be it."

"There's only one problem with that explanation," Ben said. "We've been down here the whole time. Is there any other way out of the house?"

Emilio gulped and looked upstairs.

After about half an hour, the house had still not spilled any secrets about Isabella's whereabouts. They had checked with the neighbours and her friends as well but had drawn a blank, as expected.

"It's all your fault," Emilio shouted, his eyes glazed with tears. "What if Mom calls? What should I tell her? I wish you guys had never come down here."

"You very well know it's not our fault," Ben said.

"You're not helping," Will whispered, walking past Ben and putting his arm around Emilio's shoulder. "Look, we're not giving up, all right. But it's just not making any sense."

"I don't care," Emilio said, pushing away his cousin. "We have to do something."

Ben removed his spectacles and polished them. "Logically speaking, I see only two courses of action. We either call up Aunt Emily or inform the police."

Emilio's lips twitched. "The… the cops?"

"There is one other option," Will said, rubbing his chin.

"What is it?" Emilio cried, almost grabbing his shirt.

Ben gaped at his brother like a goldfish. "You can't be serious. How can you even think Isabella may have actually gone off to this land?"

"I… I don't know, Ben. What if she has? You're always talking about logic. So, where else could she be?"

Ben sat down and began cracking his knuckles. His brother had posed a very pertinent question. And for once, he didn't have an answer. He closed his eyes. "Fine, I'm willing to explore this option, if only to prove you wrong. I guess we should start with the book."

They all dashed upstairs to Isabella's room. When Emilio flipped the light switch, their eyes fell upon the book, lying on the carpet next to the desk. It stared back innocently, its shimmering design toned by the surrounding shadows.

Will picked it up and handed it to Emilio. "That's the one. But it just looks like any other book to me."

"I think she picked this up at some used book sale," Emilio said, squinting at the title. Now how did one say that word?

Ben walked over to the window and drew the curtains. "She did mention she picked it up at the public library's used book sale."

Emilio tossed the book on the bed. Ben picked it up and flipped through the pages. "Here's that verse she was talking about," he said, scanning it. "Just a lot of nonsense. But here's something that could be interesting."

"What is it?" Will asked, glancing over his shoulder.

Ben ran his bony fingers around the bridge of his nose. "I cannot be certain. The stamp at the end is not very clear, but it appears this book was last borrowed four years ago."

Emilio pulled out a chocolate from his shorts and popped it in his mouth. "So?"

Ben closed the book. "I know it's a long shot, but it may be worth finding out who borrowed this book last."

Emilio went into a coughing fit. "Today's Friday," he croaked, thumping his chest. "The library closes in another forty minutes. I'm off."

"He moves pretty fast for his size," Will said, as their cousin disappeared down the stairs.

"You'll never guess what I found out," Emilio panted, plopping down on the couch and closing his eyes. His cheeks were flushed, and his clothes were soaked. "But I need something to drink first."

Will stared at him with his mouth open. "Seriously? What's wrong with you? We thought you had pulled a disappearing act on us as well. I had half a mind to file a joint missing complaint."

"Sorry," Emilio huffed, running his sleeve across his face.

"Sorry doesn't even cover the half of it," Will cried. "It's almost half past seven. Did you get into some scuffle or something?"

"Puncture," Emilio said, taking the juice box from Ben. He downed it in one go. "Had to walk for almost two miles. One more please."

Ben handed him another one. "Now tell us what happened," he said, blinking his eyes feverishly.

"You see that," Will grinned. "It means he's excited. The last time that happened was two years ago when he thought he'd discovered a new planet."

Emilio stood up. "Can I at least take a quick shower?"

Will pulled him down. "Of course not. Now spill."

"Okay, okay," Emilio grinned. "So, get this. This book's been checked out only once in the last five years, on May 13ᵗʰ four years ago. But it was never returned. It's been listed as missing."

Ben narrowed his eyes. "And yet," he muttered, "Isabella bought it at the very same public library's used book sale. That's very interesting."

"You bet it is," Emilio said. "And I had such a tough time convincing the librarian I hadn't stolen it. But that's not even the best part. What I found out next blew me away completely."

"Must you pause so much?" Ben groaned. "Go on."

"The last person to borrow the book was Blake Prior."

"That doesn't ring a bell," Will said, glancing at Ben, who shrugged back.

"It won't, for you. But he made big news here four years ago. I was eight then, but I still remember it clearly. I'm quite sure everyone in this town does as well. Blake Prior disappeared under mysterious circumstances from his house."

"Wasn't the librarian suspicious?" Ben asked.

"I almost froze when she read out his name. But she didn't show any signs of recognition. Must be from out of town."

"So, what now?" Will asked, a note of impatience creeping into his voice.

Emilio shook his head. "But I'm not done. I did a quick scan of the online newspaper archives and guess what? Blake disappeared on May 18th, exactly five days after borrowing this book."

Ben uncrossed his legs and stood up. "Excellent work, Emilio. But I think we're still missing some details. Let's go online."

"Here's something from a local news site," Emilio said, from his sprawled position on the couch.

"Anything interesting?" Will asked, glancing up from the laptop.

"Let's see," Emilio replied, skimming through the article. "Uh… Blake was sixteen… mother was the last person to see him that afternoon… he wasn't in his room an hour later… she didn't think much about it then as he had done such things earlier… uh… and she filed a complaint with the police three days later."

Ben rested his head back in the armchair. "So, he had done these kinds of things before," he repeated. "Anything else?"

"Not much. The police talked to the neighbours, asked around but nothing came of it. The guy had no friends. There wasn't any ransom note or demand either."

"So, he could have run away. Let's keep searching."

"By the way, this article is dated May 25th, so a week after the incident."

Will sighed with frustration. "I'm done," he said, getting up and heading to the kitchen.

"I've found an interview with the local police chief about the case… looks like it was done a year later," Ben said, sitting up. He clicked the play button as the others gathered around.

"Still nothing new," Emilio said, a few minutes later. He massaged his neck and returned to his screen.

"The only thing it confirms is that Blake was still missing a year later," Will said, popping open a can of soda.

"We still haven't made any real progress," Ben said. "Perhaps we should take a brief… "

"Hold on," Emilio interjected. "This is very interesting. It says here that there was a break-in that very night in the Prior family trailer."

Ben jumped up and pored over his cousin's shoulder. He quickly scanned the short article. "This is intriguing. So, the break-in wasn't reported immediately because the Priors thought that Blake had come back to pick up his stuff or steal money."

"Perhaps he did," Will said. "How could they be sure it wasn't him?"

"Because a neighbour had reported a man with a larger build moving around suspiciously that night."

"The place was filled with shady characters until about a year back," Emilio nodded.

"I think we've done enough research," Will said. "It's time to chalk out a plan."

Just then, Emilio's phone sprang to life.

"Isabella," Emilio cried, staring at the lighted screen. "It has to be her."

Will dashed to the phone. "I'll do the talking," he said. He closed his eyes and took the call. But the next moment, his face muscles went taut.

"What is it?" Emilio asked. "Is she all right?"

"Yes, Aunt Emily," Will said, steadying his hand. "Yes, this is Will."

Emilio's limbs gave way at the mention of his mother's name. He staggered back and looked vacantly at Ben who had also gone ashen.

"No, Aunt Emily… I mean, yes, Aunt Emily, everything's absolutely fine here. You had called on my phone earlier? We must have been in Milo's room. Eh… how's Grandpa doing?"

"But everything's not fine," Emilio sniffed, staring vacantly into the darkness outside.

"Oh, you want to talk to Bella?" Will said, pressing the phone to his cheek and closing his eyes briefly. He pushed it back up. "Eh… Milo says she's gone to bed."

Ben patted Emilio's shoulder. Just stay calm, his eyes said.

A few minutes later, Will closed the call and tossed the phone on the couch. He slowly wiped the beads of perspiration that had appeared on his forehead and turned around. "That was a close call," he said, crumbling into the armchair. "Grandpa's still very ill. They're definitely staying back for at least a week."

Emilio walked up to Will. His eyes were red, and his nostrils flared. "Why are you even in charge?" he yelled. "You've caused nothing but trouble. Bella's been missing for more than four hours now. We should have told Mom."

"Just hear me out, all right," Will said, pushing up his hands. "And if you don't agree, I'll call up Aunt Emily and tell her myself."

Emilio chewed on his nails, his eyes moving slowly from Will to Ben and then back to Will. "Make it quick," he said finally.

Will heaved a sigh of relief. "So, here's the thing. Whatever we've learnt so far tells us that Bella has actually travelled to this land. Do you honestly think our parents or anyone for that matter will believe us? But what if we can go there and bring her back? We have a week to do so."

Ben opened his mouth but stopped at the sight of his distraught cousin. He finally shook his head slowly. "Although it doesn't make sense, I can't find any other way to explain this logically. So, in the interest of my curiosity, I'm in."

"Fine," Emilio said, unwrapping another chocolate. "But if it doesn't work, you'll call my mom."

"It's a deal," Will nodded.

Emilio ran down the stairs, his eyes round as saucers, and almost crashed into Will. "She left a note," he cried, waving a piece of paper in front of his cousin's nose.

Will snatched it from his hand.

If you find this note, I'm already in Sceadu. Please don't follow me as you never believed me anyway.

"She's really gone there," Ben said, almost to himself. He was beginning to feel a little faint. "I need some time to process this."

"Where did you find this?" Will shouted, running his fingers through his hair. "How did we miss this?"

"On the floor, almost hidden under the bed. It must have slipped off the desk."

"There's no time to waste. Emilio, did you get the book? Ben, snap out of it and read that verse."

Ben took the book from his cousin. He flipped to the last page with quivering hands.

The heavenly ring shines through
But the magic lasts for days two
Step upon your best friend's feet
Then face to face, it's time to greet
Chant these words to turn your fate
Bring me in, throw open the gate
Rise, rise from above the floor
Lo behold, you've crossed the door
Beware, your friend will surely change
The cup is full, it means your end.

Will let out a long groan. "Ring… magic… friend," he said. "You were right. It's all nonsense."

"Well, I can't think on an empty stomach," Emilio declared. "Can we have dinner?"

"Sure," Ben replied absent-mindedly, curling and uncurling his fingers. Was this really happening?

"All right, let's do this," Will said, making his way into the kitchen. "I will heat the food. Why don't you try and decipher the verse?"

Ben nodded. "Now let me see. The heavenly ring shines through. Probably refers to the sun or the moon. Perhaps the full moon."

Will popped his head out. "That makes sense. Go on."

"But the magic lasts for days two." Ben dashed to the window and parted the curtains. He could see the outlines of the mockingbirds returning to their nests under a ghostly sky, illuminated brilliantly by a full moon. But its beauty was lost on him. He spun around and glanced at the wall clock. It read half past nine. "Emilio, hand me my phone."

Soon, Ben was staring intently at the screen. "About two hours," he said, tapping the armrest. He closed one eye and thought for a moment. "Yes, that's all we have."

"Are you sure?" Will gulped, handing out the plates.

"Positive. The heavenly ring is the full moon. According to this app, it occurred here at exactly 11.21 pm two nights ago. Since the magic only lasts for two days, we have less than two hours. The next full moon will occur after about a month."

"That's no good," Will said, serving the roast chicken and mashed potatoes.

"Incidentally," Ben added, "the full moon had occurred on May 18th four years ago. We are well aware of what happened on that date."

"Do we have any gravy?" Emilio asked, digging into the roast chicken.

"Moving on," Ben sighed, throwing an exasperated look at his cousin. "Step upon your best friend's feet. I'm not sure how to interpret that."

"Jeremy's my best buddy," Emilio said, looking up slowly. "I'm sure he won't let me step on his feet though. Besides, he's bigger than me."

"Then face to face, it's time to greet. That's the next line."

"But… but he's spending summer in Florida."

Ben poked at the chicken with his fork. "What am I missing? Isabella obviously didn't have her best friend with her."

"Why don't we just move on?" Will said.

"Hasty again," Ben murmured, picking up the book. "Anyway, here we go. Chant these words to turn your fate. Bring me in, throw open the gate."

"That's a no-brainer," Emilio said, taking another helping of the mashed potatoes. "These are really delicious."

"Beware, your friend will surely change. The cup is full, it means your end."

Will poured himself a glass of water. "Sounds like a warning to me. We can worry about it later though."

"Or it could be a betrayal. But we can't be sure until we figure out who this friend is."

Ben sat with an unopened pot of yogurt, slipping it from one hand to the other. Almost an hour had passed, and he hadn't made any headway. "This is so vexing," he said, stretching his long legs under the table. "A nine-year-old got it. Why can't I? Everything is falling apart."

"Bella is very clever," Emilio said. "Can I have that yogurt if you're not having it?"

Ben threw the pot at him, a little harder than he would otherwise have. What did those two lines mean?

"How much longer?" Will asked.

"Stop shaking your legs," Ben replied, rubbing the back of his head. "I can't get my mind to concentrate. Have you found any reference to friends, Emilio?"

Emilio licked the spoon clean and closed the book. "Nope. Just some stuff about creatures."

"I had better check again though," Ben said, glancing at the clock. It was almost eleven.

"By the way," Emilio said, handing it to his cousin, "did you know that Sceadu is the Old English word for shadow? I checked it online."

Ben's hand stopped mid-air. "If I physically could, I would be kicking myself really hard right now," he said, shaking his head. "Don't you see? Your best friend is your shadow. Always by your side."

"Let's move," Will said, pushing himself up.

Ben crossed his arms. "Must you do everything without considering the consequences? Have you thought about what would happen if our parents called?"

Will groaned and lowered himself back into the chair.

"I have an idea," Emilio said, running to the kitchen. "It's done," he said, a few minutes later. "I called up Mrs. Rothschild and told her that we're going to stay at a friend's place. So even if Mom can't reach us, she'll be the next person on her list."

"Good thinking, Emilio," Ben said. "It's the best we can do under the circumstances."

"Are we good to go then?" Will asked.

"We do have one problem." Ben flipped the pages back and forth. "There doesn't seem to be any verse or directions for getting back. The pages at the end have been torn."

"Let's not worry about that now. My first priority is to find Bella. Just take the book along."

"All right," Ben said, cracking his fingers. "I suppose this is it." He stood still for a few moments, wondering if he had lost his mind. Just a few hours ago, he had been vehemently arguing against the very idea. But now, he just couldn't be sure.

"I'm ready," Emilio said, walking into the living room. He had on a figure-hugging black suit. "What? It's my ninja suit. And it's very comfortable."

"Okay then, stand here," Ben said, rubbing the sides of his arms. This was really happening. "We're already stepping on our friend. Now turn so that your shadow is exactly facing you. Hold on."

"What's the matter?" Emilio asked, as Ben ran into the guest room.

"Of course," Will grinned. "His backpack. Ben, time's running out."

But Ben was back within seconds. "Can't leave without this," he said, slinging it across his shoulder. "We all know the words. Here we go then."

They all took a deep breath and clenched their fists. A million doubts had numbed their minds. And an intense fear had seized their bodies. But the time for thinking was long past.

Nothing happened for a few seconds in the unnerving stillness of the night. And then, all of a sudden, everything started getting groggy. They wanted to scream, but their voices were crushed back into their throats. They wanted to run, but their feet remained rooted, like stubborn barnacles on the sides of a shipwreck. Somewhere in their consciousness though, a strange phenomenon was being observed. Their friends were slowly rising out of the floor. And the next instant, they had fallen through their shadows.

CHAPTER 5 – STRANDED ALONE

Isabella stood absolutely still, staring blankly at the choppy silhouettes of towering mountain peaks. The skies were black as ink, bursting with occasional flashes of white lightning. The air was warm, but it was laced with the distinctive stench of evil, like that of burnt milk. A haunting emptiness had started growing within her, until she couldn't take it any longer. She sank to the ground, clutching her head in her hands. Piercing screams followed, the silence repeatedly sliced by her desperation.

The nightmare had ended as it usually did, with Isabella's body thrashing around like a fish out of water. It had been followed by incessant coughing and then a velvety darkness had enveloped her. But when she had finally opened her eyes, there had been no room. Instead, she had found herself lying under giant, grey clouds, hovering above her like torchbearers of doom. She had burrowed her nails in, but they had felt cold, rough gravel, not the warmth of her cosy bed. She had blinked her eyes, again and again, until streams ran down her face.

Isabella stopped screaming. She pulled her sweater closer and shuddered. What had she done? Her mind veered back to that final conversation with her cousins. And then, in a moment of sheer madness, she had changed the very fabric of her existence. She sat down and slumped her head into her knees. What had she proven by travelling to Sceadu? She had left everything behind, everyone behind. Why had she not just dropped the whole thing? But she knew the answer to that. If only there had been some other way. She gnawed at her lips and wondered if the chaos had started back home.

Isabella pushed herself up, trying to rub away the remnants of the headache that had been plaguing her for some time now. She lit the dial of her wristwatch. It had taken her almost two hours to finally accept she was indeed in Sceadu, far away from everything she knew. She suddenly remembered she had left home with a few things. Soon, she was staring at a small compass, a handkerchief, a water bottle and a crumpled piece of paper. But the book hadn't made it.

However, Isabella was thankful for the piece of paper. It was a hand drawn map of Sceadu. She spread it on the dark ground and moved her eyes around. Was there anything that would help her identify her location? But all she could see were dead tree stumps along the slopes of the mountains, standing like an army of lifeless soldiers.

Isabella tilted her watch dial over the map. According to it, Sceadu had three mountainous regions. She immediately ruled out the Hrimgicel Mountains on the western coast. They were the tallest in the land and perennially covered with snow. It was actually a great relief as the Drysmian Desert lay to their east, with thousands of square miles of parched sand. But more than that, to their west lay Atolon, the kingdom of the Ghouls. She had read enough about these loathsome creatures that even the mere thought had sent an icy shiver down her spine.

So that left the Hefig Mountains to the north and the Aglæca Mountains somewhere in the middle. But how could she know which one it was? Isabella prayed it would not turn out to be the Hefig Mountains, home to the very dangerous Gargoyles of Ablendon. The map also showed they had Hatheartia, the kingdom of the little-known Dragons, to the south. There was only one thing to do. She stretched her legs and started trudging up one of the gentler slopes. But she had hardly walked a hundred feet when rapid tapping sounds suddenly echoed through the night.

Isabella almost tripped, but somehow managed to scramble inside a sharp crevice behind the remains of a fallen tree. The darkness had concealed the creatures, but their height gave them away. It was a troop of about fifty Imps, marching in perfect step, with the tips of their spears glistening dangerously under the tepid moonlight. She exhaled softly. It was the Aglæca Mountains.

Isabella waited until the mountains had fallen silent once again. She climbed out of the crack and sat upon the petrified wood. It felt cold and hard. Isabella pulled out the map. Nædredia, the kingdom of the Imps, was probably quite close by. But the place she was looking for was Heafodleas, to the east of the Aglæca Mountains. It was possibly the safest place in Sceadu.

Isabella was soon walking eastwards. Hunger had begun to gnaw at her stomach, but with darkness all around, she decided to make do with sips of water. Suddenly, something grazed her shoulder. Isabella had been so caught up in her thoughts that for a moment she thought it was Emilio. How she wished they had not fought earlier? And what about her parents? Would she ever see them again? She closed her eyes tightly and opened them. And then, she burst into uncontrollable sobs once again.

After the tears had dried up, Isabella continued her lonely journey through the arid landscape. But even after two hours of dragging her tired feet, there was still no sign of Heafodleas. She was about to slump when the corner of her eye noticed a meadow some distance ahead, almost hidden behind some trees. Laced with a mystical serenity, it beckoned her sagging spirit. She somehow goaded her aching limbs to carry her just a little further. Once there, she slowly eased her blistered feet out of her shoes and rubbed her soles against the soft blades of grass.

A cool breeze blew from beyond the mountains and draped itself around Isabella's weary body. Its touch was so soothing that all the angst slowly melted away. Her eyes struggled to remain open. A few moments later, she had gently rolled over and fallen asleep.

"Five more minutes, Mom," Isabella mumbled and turned over. Her cheek grazed a small pebble. She groaned, massaging her jaw slowly. Why was there something sharp on her bed? And where was her pillow? She slowly removed her forearm from under her eyes. "Mom, is that you?"

Isabella opened one eye, trying to reach for the light switch at the same time. But she was instantly smothered by a large shadow. When she looked up, she could see the silhouette of a gigantic bird hovering above. Her mind, still sluggish from its tryst with the sandman, began throwing random bits of information at her. While the term Sceadu was dropped several times, it also surfaced a particularly unpleasant incident from almost four years ago when a mockingbird had chased her across the field opposite her house.

Isabella fell back on her arms and opened her mouth to scream. But it had gone so dry it pinched back, causing her to swallow hard and then burst out coughing. She opened her mouth again but something wet and slobbery moved across her face, causing her to freeze. The creature had licked her, but it could as well have plucked her head off her shoulders.

Isabella slowly wiped the thick saliva. Her heart was still doing cartwheels, but she was quite sure the book had not mentioned this creature even once. She slowly crawled out of its shadow to get a better look. And when she did, all she could do was gape at the astounding sight. The creature shone brilliantly under the starry skies, as if it had been carved out of a flaming golden fire. It had the head and upper body of an eagle, with a gleaming beak that looked like it could shatter boulders into smithereens. Its magnificent wings, with layers and layers of gold feathers, were tucked by the sides of its sinewy lower body that reminded her of a lion's, with a long, bushy tail.

The creature bent over and nuzzled Isabella. She slowly reached out and touched its head, drawing back her hand in the same instant. The creature licked her again and gently drew her towards itself.

"You really have to stop doing that," Isabella laughed, wiping her face with her handkerchief. She rubbed its sides and gazed into its deep, brown eyes. "Are you trying to tell me something?"

The creature lowered its body on the ground and nudged her gently with its beak.

She took a step back. "You… you want me to get on your back? I… I can't. I just can't."

The creature made gurgling noises, as if trying to tell her that everything would be okay.

"I suppose it's the best option," Isabella sighed. If she didn't, it would mean trudging alone through the desolate mountains again. "But I'm still scared. Anyway, here goes nothing." She grasped the thick feathers on its wings and somehow hoisted herself up. Her arms went only a third of the way round, but she clutched the feathers on the sides tightly and buried her face in the soft neck.

What is it waiting for, Isabella thought. The destination, of course. "Heafodleas," she whispered.

The creature raised its head and let out a piercing screech that rang through the mountains like a celestial thunderstorm. The next moment, its golden wings spread wide open, and its massive legs thrust its body into the skies above Sceadu. She bounced on its back like a raggedy doll as the creature tore away through the misty clouds at lightning speed.

By the time they had reached Heafodleas, Isabella looked like a ghost, with her dark brown curls all over the place and her face numbed to a dull white. The creature descended with a gentle flapping and landed with a soft thud on top of a shallow cliff. She scrambled off as quickly as she could. It felt great to be on solid ground again. Before she could say anything, the creature gave her a long lick and took to the skies again.

Isabella wiped her face and threw away the handkerchief. Her watch read quarter to two. They had hardly travelled for half an hour. And yet, she knew they had covered quite a distance.

Now for Heafodleas, she thought. I wonder where it is.

Isabella pressed her neck a few times. She inhaled slowly and pushed out her limbs to loosen the cramps. Just twenty-four hours ago, she had been in bed, yet to read the dreaded words that had got her here. She quickly banished the thought before it led down the familiar road to tears.

A few minutes later, Isabella was standing at the edge of the cliff, staring down at the kingdom of Heafodleas, bathed in silver light. But it wasn't a sight that took her breath away by any means. She looked at it for a few more moments, wondering whether the ruins held a place where she could get some sleep. Moments later, she shook her curls out of her face and turned around.

The road to Heafodleas was a narrow pebbly path that meandered through jagged rock formations right up to the kingdom. The surrounding wall was comprised of uneven blocks of stone piled over each other haphazardly and broken in so many places it no longer served a purpose.

Isabella simply stepped through one of the larger gaps and found herself in an abandoned part of the kingdom. Most of the structures had caved in and strange-looking creepers with curly tentacle-like leaves and tiny pink flowers had coiled their way around the piles of stones. But she wasn't surprised; after all, if her memory served her correctly, Heafodleas was home to the lazy and selfish Pixies. But this was exactly what had drawn here there. They would leave her alone. That and the fact that Heafodleas was largely ignored by the rest of Sceadu.

Isabella walked through all the rubble and stone, carefully avoiding the creepers, until she reached a few houses, rundown but still standing. All of a sudden, she found herself staring at a particularly bony creature with messy hair and slender yet mean features reclining against a broken fence. It was wearing a torn moss green tunic with a dull badge pinned on one side. It was a Pixie obviously, probably a law enforcement officer, she reckoned. Isabella summoned up all her courage and coughed gently.

"Who… what?" the Pixie cried, cowering in the shadows. "Oh, it's only a Child of Leod."

"Can you help me, please? I'm looking for a place to rest."

The Pixie yawned and closed his eyes again. "Why should Sylfid reveal that information?"

"I have nowhere to spend the night. Please."

"Sylfid's shoes have pebbles," he said, opening one eye and pointing at his torn galoshes. "And Sylfid's right toe has an itch under."

Isabella pinched her nose and somehow stuck her fingers inside the Pixie's stinky shoes. "All done," she said.

The Pixie dangled his hands in front of her. "Sylfid's hands are aching."

"That's enough," Isabella said firmly. "Now tell me."

The Pixie made a face. "Follow the lamps till the garden appears."

Isabella could see the first dimly lit lamp a little ahead. She slowly egged her feet on from one lamp to the next until she had finally reached a green patch, lying neglected in the centre of a Heafodlean square. Physical exhaustion had consumed her body. But even as she collapsed in a relatively less overrun corner, her mind refused to give in. It kept flashing images of her brother and cousins. Perhaps they had called their parents. Or worse still, informed the police. How she wished she had never laid her eyes on the book.

Just then, a whispering sound reached her ears. Was it even there? Or was her mind playing some more tricks? Isabella closed her eyes and listened. There it was again. And it was definitely a whisper. Was somebody calling out to her?

CHAPTER 6 – BRUTAL BEGINNINGS

Emilio groaned, pressing the back of his head hard against the ground. It felt like a thousand drums were beating down upon him. He slowly brought his hand up and kneaded his fingers into his forehead. Why wouldn't the throbbing stop? He could hear a muted voice, somewhere in the farthest recesses of his mind. Shadow, it kept repeating, slowly getting louder and louder. And then, in one intense surge, everything came back to him.

Emilio sat up with a start, gasping for air. Was he in Sceadu? Where were the others? His cousins? His sister? What had happened to them? He called out, but his voice choked in his throat.

Emilio's vision was still blurred, but his ears had picked up scraping sounds nearby. He dragged himself slowly with one hand. It turned out to be Will. But his older cousin pushed him away instinctively.

"It's me," Emilio croaked, but only barely, before his cousin could throw any blows at him.

Will turned over and tried to push himself up. His arms gave way immediately. "Eyes burning. Check on Ben."

Emilio crawled to his other cousin who was sprawled a few feet away, his long legs tangled around some roots. "Are you all right?"

Ben made a face. "My tongue tastes really salty," he said, pushing his arms out. "Where's my backpack?"

Emilio held it above his face. "I think you need these as well," he said, dangling his spectacles.

"I still can't really see much."

"That's because it's dark," Emilio said, propping his younger cousin against a tree trunk.

About half an hour later, they had regained control of their senses, and their headaches had subsided as well.

"Unbelievable," Ben said, pulling out his phone and shining the flashlight. They were in a small clearing inside a densely wooded area, completely surrounded by trees with massive trunks that ran a mile high and had gigantic roots twisted all over the forest floor. Above, they could see the outlines of huge palm-shaped leaves dangling from a maze of branches criss-crossing across the top.

"Are... are those two moons?" Emilio asked, pointing to an opening above.

But Ben didn't reply. He was completely mesmerized by the two spheres shimmering down upon them. "How is this even possible?" he gulped, holding up his phone.

"Wait," Will said, holding his hand. "We don't have any way to charge the phones. So use them only if you must."

Emilio clicked his tongue. "We should have charged our phones before travelling here," he sighed, bringing out his device. There was a large crack across the screen. "No, no, no. How could this happen?"

"It must have hit something hard when we landed here," Ben replied, slipping his phone back into his pocket.

"Do you guys at least have a signal?"

"Nope. So no maps. We really are someplace weird."

Will walked up to a trunk and broke off a dark red tendril from a thick bunch growing out of the gashes. A warm, translucent liquid oozed out of the black pores on its surface. He dropped it instantly and wiped his hand on the back of his trousers.

Ben picked it up with a pair of forceps and peered at it closely. "It looks like a parasitic plant. I wonder what its cell structure looks like. I've got my pocket microscope somewhere in the backpack... "

"We're not here to explore," Will said, brushing the twigs off his clothes. "We find Isabella, and we return home. Now hand me the book. Let's see if we can figure out where we are."

"That's strange," Ben said, looking around. "The book's not here."

"How is that even possible?"

"You did have it on you," Emilio said, scratching his head. "Perhaps you dropped it when we fell inside our shadows. I guess Bella dropped it as well. Otherwise, even she would have wanted to carry it with her."

"I should have carried it inside my bag," Ben said, shaking his head. "That was a critical error. I apologize."

Will gave his brother a look and turned to Emilio. "Do you happen to remember anything at all from the book?"

"Are you serious?"

They all looked at each other. So, they were basically stranded in an unfamiliar land with no map and no way to go back.

"So much for auspicious beginnings," Ben muttered.

Will kicked hard at one of the roots, sending splinters flying into the air. "And whose fault is that?" he grumbled, starting to walk. "I can't believe you could be so careless. Let's just take this path. Follow me."

"But why that one?" Emilio asked. He pointed to an opening under a giant root that had grown like an arch between the trunks. "Why not through there? I think this one's better."

"Because I said so," Will shouted, showing his fist. "I'm still in charge here."

Emilio stomped over, his cheeks flushed. "We're in Sceadu now," he barked. "Who made you leader? I should be the leader."

"Get out of my face before I punch you."

Ben walked up and stuck his scrawny hand between their faces. "Are we seriously doing this now?" he asked. "May I remind you we're in an alien land? Our chances of survival are significantly higher if we stick together."

Will forced his fist down and backed off. "I'm sorry," he said, turning away. He shook his head slowly. "I don't know what got into me."

"Same here," Emilio said, backing away as he patted the drops of perspiration that had appeared on his forehead.

"This may help," Ben said, producing candy from his backpack. "I think it was the acidity talking earlier."

Emilio took a large bite and nodded. "This is good. I can feel the sugar kicking in."

"Anyway," Ben continued, using his flashlight, "we should get moving. I don't see any signs of Isabella ever having been here."

Will stuck his hands inside his trouser pockets. "So," he said, "how do we move?"

"Let me put it this way," Ben replied. "It really doesn't matter. So why don't we just take the path suggested by Emilio?"

Emilio puffed his chest and marched through the gap after his younger cousin.

Will sighed and followed a few seconds later. "Now please stay together. Finding Bella is going to be hard enough."

"Yes, I was coming to that," Emilio said, clearing his throat. "Everyone stay together."

The diffused glow of Ben's flashlight guided them through the blanket of darkness, with only the silent tree trunks for company. All around, the red tendrils danced to the tune of a slow wind, humming carelessly through the dark night. Every so often, strange sounds would ring in their ears, breaking the comforting monotony. But other than that, the journey largely proceeded without any untoward incident.

An hour later, they found themselves on the banks of a river, the thick tree cover forming a wall behind them that almost kissed the meandering blue water as far as the eye could see. The gentle waves, streaked with white, moving in complete harmony with the breeze were like balm for their frayed nerves.

"I'm just so pissed off right now," Will said, hurling a flat piece of slate hard upon the placid water. It bounced off the surface a few times before sinking into the water. Slowly, the ripples vanished into the darkness, reverberating with a strange sound.

Ben walked over to his brother and caught his hand. "Please control your impulses," he said tersely. "Things may not work here the same way they do back home. I suggest we at least try and remain as inconspicuous as possible."

Will watched the last of the disappearing ripples. Had he already announced the arrival of three unwelcome strangers to faceless enemies?

Ben dipped the tip of his finger in the water and placed a few drops on his tongue. "It seems fit for consumption," he said, allowing it to flow into his bottle. He sipped at it while the others simply scooped it up with their cupped palms and gulped it down. "I feel a surge in my fortitude. But I suppose its best we get some rest now."

They had soon found a comfortable patch just outside the silent forest cover. The moons had cast a warm glow, lacing the peaks of faraway mountains with an ethereal azure light. The night was absolutely still, with only the occasional whispers from the serene river water.

"I wonder what Bella's doing right now," Will said, twisting a blade of grass in his fingers. He broke it and threw it away. "We do need to find her as soon as possible and get back. This place gives me the creeps."

"This place is so uncomfortable," Emilio grumbled, rubbing his backside. "I really wish Bella had shown a little more sense. Dragging us all here for nothing."

Ben stared at the two moons. "I suggest we enjoy tonight. Who knows what dangers lie ahead?"

The boys were up with the first rays of morning. The mysticism of the night had given way to a more rugged reality. The same mountains which had lent an air of serenity just a few hours earlier were now looking down upon them disdainfully. The deep blue of the skies was hidden behind thick grey clouds slowly rolling over each other, completing the dismal picture.

They washed their faces in the crystal-clear water and had a quick drink as well. The rocky bed was covered with smooth white stones, flickering like diamonds under the gentle splashes of light.

"Why do I get the feeling these waves are trying to tell us something?" Emilio said.

Ben slung his backpack across his shoulder. "That would be your imagination. In any case, I suggest we start our journey again."

"We definitely can't go that way," Will remarked, turning around. The forest behind them appeared even more formidable and uninviting in the morning. "It looks like it's always night inside."

"Then we have to take our chances with the river."

The slopes beyond were steep, but they spotted a beaten path that ran through the thicket of dark green trees that had dropped roots into the river on the other side.

"We might as well," Will said, rolling his trousers up. "I just hope there aren't any creatures in it."

"Do we have anything to eat?" Emilio asked.

Ben pulled out an apple. "Can I interest you in this? But my palate could really do with a pot of strawberry yogurt right now."

The water hardly came up to their waists, but the river was wide, and it took them almost half an hour to reach the shore. Despite the considerable resistance of the flow, they felt surprisingly rejuvenated by the time they had crossed.

The boys climbed over the damp moss covered roots and jumped upon a dry patch. The gloomy shadow of the forest was almost behind them when Emilio suddenly stopped and held up his hand. The next moment, he was flat on his belly, his ear pressed to the ground. "Something's headed this way."

Will glared at him. "If only you had listened to me back then. I knew we shouldn't have taken that path."

"If I remember correctly, it was you who threw the stone," Emilio retorted back, pushing himself up.

"And once again, may I suggest we avoid these petty disputes? For now, how about we pick up our feet and run?"

The argument ceased instantly. The next moment, they were tearing through a choppy tide of thorny branches, leaving a trail of bulbous leaves flying behind them.

"Find a hiding place," Will shouted, as the vibrations started getting louder. "There," he pointed to an opening ahead, barely visible under the dark shadows of the surrounding trees. "In there."

The tiny pebbles around them had started rolling in all directions. But the gap was further away than it had seemed. The boys goaded each other, pushed each other, and finally, a desperate dive later, found themselves sprawled on the floor of what appeared to be a cave. They dragged their weary selves as far away from the entrance as they could. Outside, the ground had begun to tremble.

Ben shone his flashlight and leaned forward, pushing his hand out. But there wasn't any ground, and he toppled. Fortunately, Emilio grabbed his shirt in the nick of time. For the briefest of moments, Ben found himself staring at cold, hard gravel, almost three hundred feet below.

"Ben!" Will shouted, gripping his collar and pulling him back. He could see his brother had gone white. "Talk to me."

Ben fell back, his chest heaving like a rubber pump. His body had gone limp. "I've never felt fear like this before," he said in a shaky voice. He took off his spectacles and wiped his eyes. "I can handle pursuits of the intellectual kind. But I'm not sure about this."

Will put his hand over his brother's shoulder. It had been a very close call. "Thanks, Milo. That was some quick thinking."

Ben licked his dry lips and nodded at his cousin as well.

"Can we just get out of here first?" Emilio said, staring at the entrance. The loose dirt was beginning to slide down the sides.

"I think I've found something." Will pointed ahead with Ben's flashlight. It shone upon a narrow ledge that went around the cave till it reached the bottom. Emilio helped Ben up, and they followed Will with their backs pressed hard against the rough walls of the cave.

"What's this?" Ben said, as his eye caught something illuminated. He took the flashlight from his brother and shone it on the sides. The dark brown walls had been adorned with a few drawings. "If I was to go by the fairy tales from back home, I would classify these creatures as either gnomes or imps," he whispered. "It looks like they're fighting some other clan here. And in this painting, they seem to be worshipping some sort of god."

"Can we please not do this now?" Emilio stammered. He could feel the soil trickling down upon his shoulders.

Will walked up and peered closely. "At least we now have some idea about the creatures here. I bet we could take them on quite comfortably."

"I would rather we not resort to violence of any kind," Ben said, "especially since it's highly likely their numbers would run into the thousands if not more."

"Let's go," Emilio said, tugging at his cousins' sleeves. The noise outside had reached thunderous proportions by now. And then, just as they felt they would have to cover their ears, it suddenly died down and a nervous calm gripped the cave.

Ben stood still, listening. "For some reason, they don't seem inclined to come in. Should we wait?"

"I know they're there… they're waiting outside… what if they suddenly decide to come in?"

"What have we here?" Ben said, shining the beam at a dark portion of the cave directly under the entrance. There were three openings. "These look like underground passages."

"Then let's take them," Emilio said, running into the first one. But he was out in seconds. "Company," he whispered, dragging his cousins into the second passage. He found a tall fracture in the side and pulled them inside. "Let's wait here."

They could hear the sound of footsteps through the wall. Soon, there were chattering sounds outside. The boys squeezed as far inside as they could, not daring to breathe. But a few minutes later, the sounds faded away.

Will slid out noiselessly and crept to the opening of the passage. He pushed his head out just a little and moved his eyes around. "I think the danger has passed. Perhaps… "

A series of deafening roars shook the cave. They were followed by piercing screams, by ruthless snarls, by unsavoury moans, all echoing at the same time. The boys shrunk back inside, pushing their fingers deep into their ears to escape the cacophony of pain.

And then, the pandemonium withered into a familiar shuddering sound. Only this time, it was accompanied by a scraping, as if something was being dragged away. Soon, silence had once again returned to the cave.

Will found his voice first. "That sounded brutal. What do we do now?"

"I think we should continue down this passage," Ben whispered.

"I'm not sure we should be taking any underground routes. Besides, what if we run into those cave creatures?"

"I don't know. Milo, what do you think?"

Emilio pursed his lips and closed his eyes tightly. "I don't want to face whatever it was that was outside there."

"It's been quiet for a while now," Will said, stepping out. "The fight's obviously over. And didn't we hear them leave? Why don't I take a quick look?" Without waiting, he pulled out his phone and bounded up the ledge.

Ben let his backpack slide down. "I would really like to see how his neurons are wired," he sighed.

Will edged his way to the entrance of the cave and tipped his head out cautiously. But before he could even blink, something came flying straight at him. His eyes shut instinctively and his hands jumped in front of his face. But his ears had picked up a gentle whirring sound. It's probably just a bird, his mind offered. Will slowly parted his fingers. But the sight that met his eyes caused his jaw to hit the ground.

"Greetings, Child of Leod," a beautiful creature said in a silvery voice, fluttering all around him in bursts. "Please don't be frightened. I'm a Færy."

"A fairy?" he blabbered, staring at her delicate transparent wings, swaying to the rhythm of her graceful movements.

"Yes, a Færy. How can I be of help?"

But Will was already lost in her jade green eyes, accentuated by the stark paleness of her face. "All that noise," he finally stammered, pointing at the broken spears scattered around.

The Færy hovered in front of his face, her silken locks cascading in beautiful golden layers like a magical waterfall. "Isn't it terrible?" she said, pulling her arms around her dainty body. Her robe, adorned with tiny stones, sparkled under the bright sunshine. "It was the Imps and the Goblins. But please be assured you're safe now."

Will could feel something stirring inside him. He couldn't explain it, but it made him want to follow this creature to the ends of the world.

"Will," Ben's voice echoed through the cave. "Is everything all right?"

Drat, his brother had broken the spell. Will clenched his fists and popped his head back in. "It's okay, guys. You can come out now."

"Greetings, Children of Leod," the Færy said, as Ben and Emilio stepped out. "I'm called Slea. What has brought you to this faraway land?" They were taken aback to see a delicate creature floating in front of them, especially after all the anarchy they had been subjected to.

Will jumped in instantly. "I'm Will," he piped. "And... and I'm the leader. We came here to find our sister, Isabella."

"I think someone's been bitten by the love bug," Emilio said from the side of his mouth.

"I've seen this phenomenon take control of his senses before. Perhaps we should have resolved the leadership issue earlier."

The Færy looked upon them with gentle eyes. "Oh, you poor Children of Leod. But there's no reason to worry. Our generous queen shall do everything to unite you with your sister. I only ask you to wait down by the river so I can fetch wings for each of you."

"Wings?" Ben asked.

"Yes, like mine. They will carry us to the kingdom of the Færies."

"Can they take our weight though? According to the laws of physics… "

"Wings to fly?" Will said, sucking in his breath. "That's so awesome. We'll meet you by the river."

Slea soared into the sky like a shimmering butterfly and soon disappeared from view.

"Come on, guys," Will said, shuffling his feet. "What are we waiting for? I still can't believe we're going to fly."

Emilio raised his eyebrows at Ben. His cousin shrugged and slung his backpack across his shoulders. "I still can't see how those wings could bear our weight."

"Oh, come on, Ben," Will said. "You said Sceadu didn't exist. But here we are. So just stop being sceptical about everything."

They were almost half way to the river when Emilio stopped. "Do you hear that? It seems to be coming from there."

They could hear faint rustling sounds, interspersed with low moans. The boys walked guardedly in the direction of the sound. "Children of Leod, help me," came a rasping voice from beyond one of the trees. "I'm hurt badly. Don't listen to the evil Færy. Help me."

The boys gestured at each other. Was it a trap? But the cries seemed to be laced with genuine pain. They tiptoed around.

"Isn't it from those cave paintings?" Emilio said. They all stared at the bald and bearded creature, not more than fourteen inches tall, with thick bushy eyebrows and a pug nose.

"I'm called Beodan," the creature croaked, his large pale-yellow eyes staring at them from under his protruding forehead. "I'm an Imp. We have to leave now. There were no Goblins. It was the Færies. We walked right into their trap. I barely managed to escape. But if we don't get out of here now, they'll capture you as well and send you to the mines." And then, he fainted.

"No way," Will retorted. "We should head down immediately. Slea may have already reached there with our wings."

"What if he's not lying?" Ben said. "Perhaps it might be prudent to just head back to the cave."

"He has to be," Will said, crossing his hands. "I mean, just look at him. He's so repulsive."

Ben looked down at the Imp. His armour was broken in three places, and his left leg was soaked in blood. "Will, this Imp's blood is real. He doesn't have a reason to lie."

"And why should Slea lie? We have a real chance to find Isabella here. And you're throwing it away."

Beodan's eyes flickered. He stared vacantly for a few seconds and then blinked rapidly. "I'm telling the truth," his thick, bleeding lips pleaded. "Why won't you believe me?"

Will brought his face closer. "Why did Slea ask us to wait by the river then?"

"The Færies live far away. It's easier to drag you there, than to have you walk. And the only reason she asked you to come by the river is so it would be too late to run back into the cave once the truth emerges. Færies hate the dark."

Suddenly, the ground started quaking again. The Imp pulled out tufts of his hair. "Why did you not listen to me? This will be the end for all of us."

"Can we make it to the cave yet?" Ben asked, pulling the others down.

"It would have been possible five minutes ago," Beodan wailed, glowering at Will. "Let's just pray the Fracods don't sniff us out."

Ben parted the branches slowly. They could see five enormous bear-like creatures scuffling restlessly along the riverbanks, with thick white fur bristling out of their silver armour. It was the dreaded Fracods, their black, beady eyes flitting suspiciously and containing not a hint of mercy. Their pointed fangs were dripping with saliva, and their claws, long as knives, gleamed dangerously on their gigantic paws.

"The Færies," Emilio gulped. "They're controlling these beasts."

It was indeed the Færies, with faces as delicate as the gossamer gowns they wore but with expressions so nasty that even Will's insides did a back flip. They cracked their silver whips every so often, the tips flashing violently in the air. And those that had not mounted the Fracods darted back and forth, carrying something rolled up under their arms.

Emilio had gone white. It was only a matter of time before the claws or the whips sliced through them like the sponge cake he had been craving for.

"So where are these Children of Leod, Slea?" the Færy on the largest Fracod screamed.

Slea fluttered around haplessly. "Please forgive me, Unmæta. They must have suspected something. But they couldn't have gone far away."

Will dug his nails into the mud and ground his teeth. How could he have been so stupid?

"I should throw you into the mines with those filthy Imps," Unmæta hissed.

Just then, one of the Fracods gnarled loudly and raised his snout. "It must be them," Slea shrieked.

"Are you sure or is this another false alarm? It turned out to be those tiresome Imps the last time." But another one of the Fracods was on its hind legs, sniffing the air hard.

"We need to make a run for it," Will whispered.

"Towards the cave?" Emilio asked.

"Nope. It's in their line of sight. The only way lies behind us."

"Take me with you," Beodan rasped, clawing at Ben's leg. "You can carry me in your bag. I'm very light. And I can help you."

Ben removed three books and slid the Imp inside. Sacrifices would have to be made.

"Now listen carefully," Beodan said, pushing his head out. "The Fracods are not great with picking up scents. But once they do, they're unstoppable. So, we need to move as far away from here as possible without being heard."

Will nodded, sliding Ben's backpack over his shoulders. "We run as softly as possible for now. But the moment I give the signal, make a dash for it. And do not, I repeat, do not look back after that. Is that clear?"

They all crept away from their hiding place as fast and quietly as they could. The Fracods had begun to push towards the cave, trying to pry the scent out of the air.

They had been running for almost ten minutes when Emilio stopped and turned. "Perhaps they gave up and decided to head back," he said, bending forward.

"No, we must keep going," Beodan urged. "The Fracods will be upon us any moment. You don't know them."

As if on cue, the ground started shaking.

"Move," Will shouted, and all three tore through the trees, with the thorns once again scraping against their bodies mercilessly, "and don't look back."

"There," Ben shouted, pointing about five hundred feet away where the landscape suddenly changed into a labyrinth of tall red rocky formations.

They could hear the Fracods, charging at them through the trees, gaining upon them with every passing second.

The branches came at the boys, fast and strong, battering against their already bruised bodies. It was only their desire for survival that kept them from falling by the side. But their energy had begun to wane. And yet, what had seemed like an eternity had actually been only a few minutes.

"Zigzag," Ben panted, as they finally reached the columns. "May slow them down."

Alas, the Fracods, large as they were, could manoeuvre around obstacles with a snake-like agility. And the rocky outgrowths that did land in their paths were simply wiped out with a swipe of their powerful claws.

"Left, take a left," Beodan hollered.

Without thinking, they turned. A split second later, something flew above them and landed a few feet away. It was followed by sizzling sounds.

"What was that?" Emilio gasped.

"Enchanted net," Beodan shouted back. "It cuts through the skin. That's how I got injured."

Ben motioned to him. "There's a dark brown bottle with an orange label somewhere. Throw it to me." Physically the weakest of the three, he knew his life couldn't depend on his legs any more.

Beodan dived inside and came up almost instantly.

"Throw it, throw it," Ben huffed. With every step, he could feel the whips cracking closer to his ears.

Beodan hurled the bottle. Ben staggered but somehow latched onto it at the very last second. He tore the top off and sprayed the contents upon everyone. The finger didn't come off the nozzle until the bottle was completely empty. But would the plan work?

A few minutes later, the shuddering ceased all of a sudden.

The boys continued to run for some distance until Ben fell upon his back, holding his chest. "Not built for this," he panted. "Can't feel my feet any more."

"Must have water," Emilio cried, clutching his throat and crashing on his knees.

Will leaned against a conical rock formation and closed his eyes, but Beodan grabbed his collar from behind. "We must keep moving. The Fracods will be upon us any moment."

Ben shook his head, breathing heavily through his mouth. "Not possible. Any caves nearby?"

Before Beodan could say anything, the ground started shaking again. Will hauled up his brother and pushed him roughly. The brief stop had given them some time to recover. But it wouldn't be long before they would completely run out of fuel.

"Cannot go on," Ben groaned, clutching his thighs but somehow throwing his feet in front.

"Right, take a right," Beodan suddenly screamed in Will's ears. "There's water nearby. Just jump into it. Don't stop to think."

Will pointed to the right frantically. "Don't stop," he shouted. "There's water ahead. Don't stop. Just jump."

The Fracods were almost upon them, goaded by the sharp whips of the Færies. The boys ran over to the edge and hurled their bodies across. For the briefest of moments, they found themselves floating in the air, like puppets at the end of a string. And then, piercing screams rang out as they plunged into the frothing water below.

The nets flew high in the air and landed with a dull thud on the spots where they had stood only a fraction of a second before. The red dirt caught fire and crackled fiercely.

Down below, the boys surfaced from the icy cold water, taking in large mouthfuls of air. But danger was once again about to rear its ugly head. All of a sudden, a strong current of water caught hold of their exhausted bodies.

"Ahead, ahead," Will spluttered, but his voice was drowned by the waves crashing into each other. He finally pulled his hands out and gestured wildly at his brother and cousin.

A ring of jagged rocks, with sharp spear-like ends, was jutting out of the rapids about a mile away. The boys lashed at the vicious waves with all their strength. But the ruthless pull of the water was drawing them closer and closer to their doom.

Just then, Emilio spotted a dark opening on one side. He caught hold of Ben's arm before the current got hold of him and dragged him along. Will followed with strong strokes. The force of the water diminished suddenly as they approached the mouth of what looked like a cave.

"That branch there," Emilio pointed.

A few seconds later, the three of them had grasped the overhanging branch. They twisted around and shook the water out of their faces. In the distance, they could see the silhouettes of the Fracods under the muffled sunlight, shuffling impatiently at the edge of the cliff, with the Færies cracking their whips furiously.

They had escaped by the skin of their teeth.

Chapter 7 – Stark Betrayal

The mighty river had transformed into a serene body of water by the time the boys reached the inside of the cave. They crawled out and lay on their backs, their minds numbed by their recent experience. But their bodies were feeling surprisingly invigorated.

"I can't believe this," Beodan cried, pushing himself out of the backpack. He had pulled the flaps together tightly just before they had landed in the water. "We actually escaped those vile creatures. And we're in a cave."

Will pushed himself up slowly. "I feel like such an idiot," he said, removing his t-shirt and squeezing it tightly.

"I thought you were really into Rachel," Ben said, glancing at him sideways. "I know I didn't approve of her, but after this, I think any female of the human species will do just fine."

"Will's got a girlfriend, Will's got a girlfriend," Emilio giggled.

Will went red in the face. But soon, they were all laughing loudly.

"So, what is this place?" Will asked, looking around. An Imp warrior battling three hideous looking creatures glowered down upon him from one of the walls.

"We're in Nædredia, the underground kingdom of the Imps. There are thousands of such caves all over. And that is the great Imp king, Listeran, fighting the Nietens, savage beasts that once roamed wildly across Sceadu."

Emilio sat up. "Do you hear that?" he asked, rubbing his belly. "That's my stomach eating its own lining. Do we have anything to eat? And not another apple, please."

"But I thought you were thirsty," Will said, handing Ben his backpack.

"Did you see how much water I swallowed in the river?"

"And that reminds me I owe you a big thanks for saving me again," Ben said, pulling out a few chocolate bars and handing them out. "I'm so relieved my backpack's mostly dry on the inside."

Emilio peeled away the foil and bit into the dark chocolate. He fell back again and chomped away with his eyes closed. "By the way," he mumbled, licking his lips, "what was it that you sprayed us with?"

"It was a masking scent used by hunters to prevent animals from detecting their presence. It wasn't as effective as I'd hoped it would be though."

"But it did give us a breather," Will said, breaking off a piece of chocolate and handing it to Beodan.

"But why did you have a masking scent? I'd have never had you down as a hunter," Emilio said.

"I most certainly am not," Ben said, zipping his backpack. "It was from my wildlife watching phase last year. It didn't work too well then either."

Will flipped on his stomach. "Wait a minute. Didn't that masking spray contain— ?

"Premium grade fox urine," Ben smiled while the others screwed their noses in disgust.

"So, tell us something about these Færies," Will said, changing the topic to a more savoury one.

Beodan's thick lips trembled. "The Færies are as despicable as this brown thing you gave me," he said, spitting the chocolate and tugging at his beard fiercely. "Their kingdom, Gifredia, ruled by the evil Queen Siriana, is in the southeastern part of Sceadu. It is a cold and desolate place, but not colder than their cruel hearts. They only seek Eorcanstans, stones that shine as brightly as Scimitor, the brightest sun over Sceadu."

"How many suns does Sceadu have?" Ben asked, suddenly remembering his phone. He fished it out, but alas, it wasn't switching on after their encounter with the gushing waters.

"Five, of course," Beodan retorted. "Anyway, since the Færies are afraid of the dark, they capture us Imps to work for them in the Mines of Deoria. An ancient spell makes escape impossible."

Emilio chewed on his lips. "We still haven't found Bella," he said in a low voice.

Will struck his fist hard on the ground. Their own ordeal had served as a distraction. But they had to remain focused. "Beodan, we really need to find our sister. Can you please help us?"

"But... but how can I... I really need to report back... "

"We did save your life."

Beodan pushed his hands behind his back and walked over to the edge of the water. "All right," he finally said, turning around. "I do owe you for that. But we shall have to head to Nædredia. The great Imp king, Lytegian, is the only one who can help you."

"We don't have to go outside again, do we?" Emilio asked, rubbing the back of his neck. Even the thought of encountering the Fracods again was a terrifying one.

Beodan's laughter echoed around the cave. "Of course not. Although Imps don't mind the light, we are basically creatures of the dark. See those passages there. The first one will take us to our destination, Forstelan, the capital of Nædredia."

"We saw three passages in the other cave as well," Ben said.

"Actually, there may be two or even four. The first always leads to the three main cities of Nædredia. The others lead to the smaller towns around the cave."

Ben narrowed his eyes. "I don't understand one thing though. If the Imps are creatures of the dark, why do they get captured by the Færies?"

"Nothing grows in Nædredia," Beodan replied, stepping into the first passage. "We have to travel long distances, sometimes for several days, in search of food."

"Speaking of food," Emilio said, "do you think I could get a banana sundae in your kingdom?"

Beodan muttered a few words and clapped his hands twice. Green flames instantly burst out of the old wooden torches mounted along the rough walls as the others watched in astonishment.

"So Ben, what does your science have to say about this?" Will asked.

Ben breathed onto his spectacles gently and polished them with the tails of his shirt. "I'm afraid my science doesn't speak this language," he said. "But that doesn't mean there isn't a science behind it all."

"Still not ready to give in, eh?"

"I cannot deny what my eyes have seen. But I'm unwilling to give up the idea that things in this place work according to some laws, although these laws may not be applicable in our world."

"It's magic," Beodan said, inhaling deeply. "Don't you just love the smell of these tunnels?"

The others crinkled their noses but didn't say anything.

"Ben," Emilio whispered. "Is it my imagination, or is his shadow purple?"

"I did notice this phenomenon earlier. Slea had a purple shadow as well. It must be something peculiar to creatures of Sceadu. As you can see, our shadows are the usual grey." Ben pointed to their own shadows, swaying unevenly on the brown walls.

Soon, a heavy wooden door appeared, with two large torches mounted on either side. Beodan chanted a few more words and tapped the brass ring three times. The door started creaking as mud and rocks began to crumble from the ceiling and the sides. It was quite apparent the route was a seldom used one.

They entered a cavern, dimly lit with fires hanging from the low ceiling and with tracks running down three dark passages. A rusted metal cart stood in front. "Get in," Beodan said, jumping in deftly.

The boys heaved themselves over and squeezed upon some rather uncomfortable planks fixed inside. It felt like they were in a mine.

"This thing looks quite unsteady," Emilio said, stomping his feet. The hollow sounds echoed around. "And what if another cart comes right at us?"

Beodan tapped his head playfully. "You worry too much, Child of Leod. Everything works on magic here. But do hold onto something."

They all clasped the planks and tucked their legs under as tightly as they could.

"Forstelan South," Beodan shouted. The cart instantly sprang to life and rattled down the tracks, sending bright orange sparks flying through the air. It bumped through the sporadically lit tunnels, swerving around sharp corners, squeezing through narrow spaces, and plunging down quick slopes.

"Watch out," Will suddenly shouted, pushing his brother and cousin down. The ceiling had dipped on one side, growing downwards like a spiky jackfruit.

"That would have taken our heads off," Emilio gulped.

He had hardly completed his sentence when the cart came to a screeching halt, almost hurling them off the plank. Another cart with a bunch of singing Imps whizzed across and disappeared into the darkness.

"See, it all works on magic," Beodan explained, but the others were too shaken to say anything.

The journey continued for almost two hours down the stuffy, dusty tunnels until the cart finally rumbled to a halt in another cavern, a much larger one. The boys stumbled out, clutching their backs, their faces and clothes covered in mud.

"I feel dizzy," Emilio groaned, getting down on all fours and shaking his head.

Ben lay down on his back with his eyes closed, while Will staggered over to a pillar and pressed his head hard against it.

Beodan, on the other hand, seemed quite buoyant. "We've almost reached Forstelan, the most magnificent city in Sceadu."

After their heads had cleared, the Imp led them down a large and brightly lit passage that ended at a massive iron door, towering over thirty feet, with intricate carvings set in ornate squares depicting events from Nædredia's history. At the bottom, they spotted the head of an Imp jutting out of the metal. "What are you looking at?" it yelled suddenly.

Will, who had bent down, tumbled backwards. "It's alive," he gulped, holding his chest.

Beodan slapped his thighs. "That's Durugan, the Imp of the door. He's always grouchy. You would be too if you were stuck on a door for all eternity."

"If only I could figure out how things work here," Ben said, throwing stealthy glances at the touchy Imp.

Beodan marched over and whispered something in his ear. Durugan bobbed his head twice, all the while muttering something angrily under his breath. The door opened without a sound.

"Welcome to Forstelan," Beodan said, leading the way.

The boys found themselves staring at a sea of massive rocks rising out of a deep gorge with molten lava inside its belly, meeting the mile high roof through gigantic brown and ochre columns. The rocky islands were connected by hundreds of stone bridges crisscrossing across the dull orange haze like a spider's web. They could see cavities carved inside the mounds, with crudely chiselled paths winding below them at every level and large torches burning alongside to light up the underground city. The entire place was teeming with Imps, pouring in and out of the holes, busy with their daily lives. There were guards on every bridge, riding what appeared to be large rat-like creatures wearing metal armour.

"What is this place?" Emilio whispered, catching hold of Will's arm. "If this is supposed to be magnificent, I really wonder how the rest of Sceadu is."

"Let's just hope we don't have to see the rest of Sceadu. The sooner we get out of this dump, the better."

Emilio nodded back readily.

But Ben was captivated by the sight. "I would like to spend some time observing these Imps. Their social behaviour reminds me of the busy subways in New York or London. I think this may have the makings of a great experiment."

"I thought you wanted to find your sister," Beodan said, a little gruffly.

"And we absolutely do," Will replied, pushing his brother along.

When they reached the first bridge, one of the rat-like creatures suddenly came sniffing up, its long, conical teeth ready to rip into their shoes. Ben and Emilio jumped behind Will, who had also stumbled back a few steps.

"These are the Radati," Beodan said, giving the creature a kick. It instantly shrunk away. "They may not be that fierce, but they're surprisingly effective against the Fracods."

"I'm going to have giant rat nightmares," Will said.

They crossed a few bridges until they spotted an imposing fortress-like structure hewed out of the rock. It had towers with large metal domes rising above in several places, shining dimly under the flickering flames from the surrounding fire pits. A thirty-foot wall covered with iron barbs circled the structure, with tall watchtowers built every hundred feet. The outside was swarming with guards, armed with an assortment of metal weapons that looked like they could cut through bone like a hot knife through butter. They had finally reached the palace of King Lytegian.

Beodan came to a halt near one of the fire pits. "Wait here," he instructed, walking over to the cave-like entrance of the palace that was flanked by two fierce-looking guards.

"I'm not sure I want to go in there," Emilio said.

"Not even if it had a gigantic peach cobbler?" Will asked with a grin.

"Why did you say that? Now I really want one."

Beodan walked back with quick strides. "It's all been arranged. King Lytegian has graciously agreed to meet you even at such short notice."

They soon found themselves standing in the court of King Lytegian, in front of a fountain cast out of iron with the statue of an Imp impaling a Færy at the very top. A gentle spray of water flowed down the different levels into a shallow pool below with a strange buzzing sound.

"We plundered these from the Færies," Beodan said proudly, pointing to the floor which had been paved with a fine cream-coloured marble inlayed with gold streaks. "And those tapestries there are over five hundred years old."

"I think it's time they were laid to rest," Ben whispered. "I'm no expert in matters of interior decoration, but the word that jumps to my mind is garish."

The others couldn't help but agree. The walls had been chipped away roughly and covered with what could only be described as moth-eaten, dust-filled tapestries. The pillars that led down the court were tall but had not been rounded properly and held up a series of domes that gave off a dull glow, akin to the lighting in a horror movie. And although the floor had been laid with marble, the Imps had covered most of it with a carpet that seemed to be made out of animal skin. But the worst part of it all was the smell.

"Did one of those rat creatures die in here?" Will asked, trying hard not to pinch his nose.

"More like a pack," Emilio replied.

At the far end, King Lytegian sat upon a crude throne, an anxious expression clouding his bloated face. But what really caught their eye was the ornate gold sceptre mounted on the wall behind, with a dull brown stone set on top of the carving of an Imp's head. Would this one talk as well, the boys wondered.

They bowed courteously, following Beodan's lead. "My dear Children of Leod," King Lytegian greeted, rising from his throne. "I'm ever so grateful to you all for saving Beodan, my most trusted general, from our sworn enemies. I shall do everything in my power to find your sister. But as the esteemed guests of Nædredia, I must offer you some food first."

At the very mention of food, Emilio's stomach gave a roar of approval. Even Ben and Will suddenly realized how hungry they were.

King Lytegian clapped his hairy hands. Scores of Imps ran out, carrying plates filled with different kinds of food, and placed them on a grand wooden table on one side of the court. The air was soon filled with the thick aroma of aged cheese and spiced meat. But the boys could hardly restrain themselves from ploughing into the food, their hunger barely stemmed by their sense of etiquette.

King Lytegian swept his hands through the air. "What are you waiting for, my dear Children of Leod? All this food is just for you. So please help yourself."

No sooner had the king uttered these words than the boys pounced upon the food. Even Ben's usual demeanour could only get him to the cutlery, but it went all downhill after that when it came to dinner table manners.

The feast ended for Ben with a large burp. He suddenly got conscious and dabbed his mouth with a rather dirty napkin. "I do apologize for my behaviour," he said. "Thank you for this most delicious meal."

Will followed soon after, but Emilio continued his gluttony for some more time. Eventually though, they all fell back upon their chairs with their trousers unbuttoned and their legs stretched under the table.

"I could really use some sleep now," Emilio said, burping, and following it with a loud yawn.

"No, we must find… " Will started, but his eyelids suddenly began drooping. He desperately tried to reach for the table, but his hands fell by his sides.

A few seconds later, they were all snoring away peacefully. Beodan glanced at his king and nodded.

Will winced as something cut into his wrists and ankles. He tried to move his body, but every attempt brought more pain. It finally dawned upon him that his arms and legs had been bound tightly. He slowly pushed open his eyelids. His vision was blurry, but he could soon make out slimy looking grey walls all around. What was happening?

"Ben, Milo," he mumbled, coughing loudly as he choked on some dirt. He could hear muffled sounds nearby. His brother seemed to be mouthing incoherent words which meant the rhythmic snoring belonged to Emilio. Will moistened his lips. At least they were all still together.

He rolled over a few times and somehow reached one of the walls, ignoring the bruises on his knees and elbows as they scraped the cold rough slabs of stone. Bit by bit, he managed to slide his way up using his shoulders and back until he had propped himself against the wall. When his eyes moved up, the outline of a thick metal railing stared back frostily. They were obviously prisoners.

Ben's groggy voice echoed in the small chamber. "I had the strangest dream," he yawned, trying to stretch himself. "Am I still in the dream? Why can't I move?"

Will nudged his brother with his foot. "Wake up, Ben. We're in some sort of a cell. Wake up.

Ben twisted his neck awkwardly. "What's happening, Will? Why are we all tied up?"

"That rat betrayed us," Will fumed. "They must have mixed something with the food. That… that ungrateful wretch."

"My hands have been pulled back tightly," Ben said, trying to loosen them. "Where's Milo?"

"Still sleeping. If I could only get my hands around the scrawny neck of that… "

The chamber was suddenly illuminated with green light from the torches on the outside.

"Ah, my dear gullible Children of Leod," Beodan said, walking up to the metal bars. He was dressed in a shining new armour and headdress. "I trust you've enjoyed your little nap. All thanks to Onslepanus, the one herb that does grow down here. Oh, the chubby one is still asleep. Well, that's what he gets for being greedy, just like those loathsome Færies."

Will could no longer hold himself back. He forgot about the ropes and threw his body at the Imp. But he only managed a few feet and landed hard on his side. He pushed his face up and roared, "You slimy little fiend. Wait till I get my hands on you."

Beodan didn't move an inch. He clapped gently and flashed a sardonic smile. "I'm right here. Why don't you just hop over?"

Ben's jaw had gone taut, but he bit his lip hard and spoke as submissively as he could. "But why, Beodan? Is this how you repay us after we saved your life?"

"Repay you?" the Imp screamed, shaking the metal railing hard. "Repay you for what? I saved your life from those filthy creatures."

"But we're not your enemies. All we want is to find our sister and return home."

"But even we want to find your sister. And very soon, we shall."

"Why you dirty… " Will started, trying to wrench himself free, but Ben interrupted him.

"Will," he sighed, managing to sneak in a wink, "we have to accept the Imps have outsmarted us."

Beodan loosened his grip on the metal bars and smiled. "You walked right into my brilliant trap. I had been racking my brains about how to get you to Forstelan. But your leader here provided me with the perfect opening. I hope you liked my little act back there."

Ben's ears suddenly rang loudly with Unmæta, the chief Færy's words. 'Are you sure or is this another false alarm? It turned out to be those tiresome Imps the last time.' The Færies and the Imps had both been after them.

He could feel goose bumps all over his body. They had never stood a chance. "So you had reached there with the intention of capturing us as well. Unfortunately for you, the Færies also had the same plan."

Beodan flashed a toothy smile, but his eyes remained cold. "Yes, we were always after you. It was our bad fortune those disgusting creatures landed there before us. But here's the best part. The other

Imps are slaving in the mines, and I don't have to share the credit for your capture with anyone else."

"But how did you know about our location?"

"The river told us all."

Ben threw a fleeting glance at Will. "I still don't understand why you captured us in the first place."

Beodan brought his face closer. "You would like to know that, wouldn't you? I wish we had your sister as well. But three out of four still puts the Imps in a very strong position."

Will's face went red. "You lay one finger on her and… "

"And you'll what?" Beodan smirked. A wicked grin lit up his face. "Do you really think you can escape from here? The walls are made of solid stone, and there are five guards with spears outside. Even if you do manage to get past them, we're many miles below the surface. If you get lost in the tunnels underground, I can assure you Nædredia will be your final resting place." The Imp stepped back, and the cell was once again thrown into darkness.

The next few minutes passed in silence.

"I'm sorry about the water," Will said finally. "And the Færies. I've let you all down."

"Let's not worry about it right now," came a voice from the corner. "We need to figure out how to get out of this hellhole." It was Emilio.

"You okay?" Will asked, trying to get a better look at his cousin.

"I've got a very bad itch on my stomach which I can't reach. But other than that, I'm absolutely fine. I've been awake for some time, but there wasn't any point in joining the conversation."

Ben wriggled slowly, trying to get his long legs in a slightly more comfortable position. "I wonder if I could calculate the probability of being betrayed twice within a few hours."

"Can you please calculate the probability of our escape instead?" Emilio asked.

"That's easy. It's zero."

"No, it's not," Will said, glaring at his brother. "Why can't you be a little more positive, Ben?"

Ben shot back. "I can do that. I'm positive you'll get us into trouble again."

"I guess I deserved that," Will said, turning his face away.

"Okay, look Will. I really did not mean that. But you have to understand we're a team. Anything one of us does affects the others as well. So we have to be extremely careful."

"You're right, of course."

"Okay then, the guards seem to be snoring outside. I propose we get out of these ropes first."

Emilio rolled on his other side. "I really wish we had read that book. Even if we escape from this place, we shall probably end up in another trap."

Will ground his teeth. "I don't care even if we die in these tunnels as long as we don't give Beodan the satisfaction of holding us captive here."

And so, they started twisting and turning, slowly at first and then violently as the ropes around their wrists and ankles refused to relent. Within no time, warm blood was oozing out of the cuts, and soon, the stings became quite unbearable as well. A few moments later, their struggle for freedom came to a fruitless end.

The Imps had done a thorough job with binding their limbs.

CHAPTER 8 – NARROW ESCAPE

"I have this sudden urge to get lost in a concrete jungle of tall high-rises," Ben said. "That's how much I find myself despising this place."

Emilio pushed his head to the ground. "Why is this happening to us? I'm… I'm afraid to even think of poor Bella."

"I can assure you she won't be harmed. Beodan said they had three out of four. The logical conclusion then is they need all four of us for whatever plan they have. So we should be okay until the Imps capture Isabella."

"But what if the Færies get to her first?" Emilio gulped.

"That is a scenario which can have a really unpredictable outcome. But I strongly suggest we curb our minds from indulging in theoretical possibilities."

Suddenly, loud thumping sounds reached their ears followed by dull thuds, like bowling pins being knocked down. Moments later, there was a click, and the railing slid open abruptly with a loud clang. They could hear soft steps approaching them. Was this going to be their end?

"Milo," a voice whispered out of the dark. "You there?"

A stunned silence followed. It was Isabella's voice. But how was it even possible? Weren't they in some obscure part of Nædredia, many, many miles under the ground?

"Is that really you?" Will asked, as something sharp cut through his ropes.

"It's me all right. But we must move quickly. The Imps will be here any moment."

The boys could sense the movements of another person outside the cell. But the questions could come later. They rubbed their wrists and ankles and straightened their cramped bodies.

"We must leave now."

They all stepped out slowly. The five Imp guards had been knocked out, gagged and tied to their chairs.

"Ben, your backpack." Will's foot had grazed it.

But before he could hand it over, the sound of hundreds of footsteps came hurtling at them through the passages.

"Follow me," a deep male voice whispered. They all dashed down another passage.

"Do we know the way?" Beodan's words were still ringing in Will's ears.

"Yes," the male voice replied, "although it would have been nice to have some light. It's going to be tough finding our way to the tracks."

"I can help out with that." Emilio brought out his flashlight. It was the only one that was working now. In that brief moment, they saw the man's face. It had a long scar on the left cheek, almost buried under a thick beard.

The next half hour went by ducking in and out of the labyrinth of passages. But the Imp brigade was beginning to close in. Despite their long legs, their progress was being impaired by the numerous halts they kept making to figure out the correct way. The Imps had been shrewd enough to keep the passages in darkness.

"Almost there," the man shouted. "Just jump in the cart and keep to the floor."

They soon reached a cavern similar to the ones they had been in earlier. The man helped Isabella while the others clambered across. They all pushed their bodies to the floor, keeping their heads close to their thighs. The man jumped in last and whispered, "Gehydan."

The cart thundered down the tracks. But the next moment, a spear flew through the air and battered it on the side, shaking it viciously. It was followed by more clanking sounds. The Imps were right behind them in another cart, hurling spears with a vengeance. Isabella screamed as one of the spears crashed into the planks, narrowly missing Emilio's hand.

But all of a sudden, the rattling from the second cart began to ebb away. Will slowly peeped out. He was just in time to see the Imp's cart take a turn down another passage. In that instant, his eyes met Beodan's. One end of Will's mouth curved upwards, mocking his former captor.

"Stay low," the man shouted. "These tunnels have very little light. And there may be places where the ceiling's come down."

The cart moved at a steady pace, but the loud rumbling made it difficult to have any conversation. An hour later, they had reached their destination.

"How do we move past that?" Emilio asked, shining the flashlight upon the door. "Do you know the magic words?"

"There's another way," the man replied, taking the phone from him. They all stretched their bodies and made their way down the passage. "Here it is. Do mind your head though."

"Through that?" Emilio groaned, glancing at the narrow opening in the wall. "I'm not going to fit in."

"Just pull in your stomach and squeeze through," Will grinned. "Otherwise, we're all there to push you."

Emilio contracted his stomach muscles as much as he could and pressed his body in the gap. The others followed quite comfortably although Ben bumped his head a few times on the low roof.

They emerged into a faintly lit cave, similar to the earlier ones although much smaller, and with fewer drawings.

"How could you do something so stupid?" Emilio shouted, spinning around. "This is not how I dreamt of spending my… "

But Isabella ran over to him and buried her face in his chest. "I'm sorry, I'm sorry," she wept.

Emilio pushed her away. But when he saw her cuts and bruises, he couldn't hold back the tears. He pulled her back and hugged her tightly. "You have no idea what we've gone through. But I'm just so relieved to see you're all right."

"I also must apologize for my rude behaviour earlier," Ben said, putting his arm around her.

"I'm sorry as well," Will said, kneeling down and giving her a tight hug. "But you're safe. And that's all that matters."

Isabella shook her head. "Please don't say that. I had no right to do what I did. It must have been terrible for you guys. Do our mothers… ?"

"Nope. But now that we've found you, we'd better get back soon."

Isabella had a lump in her throat. "I can't tell you how happy I am to see you all. I really am."

"By the way, who's your friend?"

"Introductions can happen later," the man's voice floated from the background. "We're still in Nædredia. The only safe place for us is up in the mountains. Let's go."

They approached the mouth of the cave guardedly, wary of an ambush.

"I'm really thirsty," Emilio said. "Is the river nearby?"

Isabella stopped in her tracks. "I'm quite sure you don't know this," she said. "But that river's the reason you were caught. It's called the Mælan or the whispering river. According to the legends, it was enchanted by Fordon the Ieldran, a revered figure in Sceadu. The moment your skin touches the water, the waves carry the news through all the areas through which it flows."

"I knew it," Emilio said, snapping his fingers. "The humming sounds just didn't seem normal."

"You have to listen carefully. The river keeps whispering about all the creatures that touch its waters. But news about three Children of Leod would definitely be out of the ordinary. And for some reason, important enough to bring the Færies and the Imps after you."

"You know about the Færies?" Will asked.

"You'd be surprised at how much I know."

Ben, who had been quiet all this while, trying to come to terms with Isabella's revelation about a river that whispered, walked over to his brother. "In that case, I owe you an apology. We all assumed it was because of that stone you threw in the water."

"That's all right, Ben," Will said, although a huge burden had been lifted off his shoulders. "It was still careless of me. It could very well have been the reason."

"Here, take this," Ben said, throwing the water bottle at Emilio. "I did fill it up earlier."

They stepped out of the cave into the fading evening. But there was just enough light to give them a better look at Isabella's friend. He was tall and in his early forties, with long brown hair and an unruly beard, both speckled with lots of grey. But his most prominent feature was the scar on his cheek that ran all the way from the edge of his left eyebrow and disappeared into his beard. He was clothed in a dull blue tunic made out of rough cloth and had on a pair of worn-out shoes which seemed quite uncomfortable.

The children followed him up the gentle slopes, trudging through the dried leaves and twigs and pushing aside the thin, reed-like plants that infested the place.

Emilio took in a long breath of the fresh mountain air when they reached the first peak. "This feels great. I just couldn't take any more of that stinking underground air. By the way, Bella, you were pretty fast in those tunnels."

"You certainly ran faster than I did," Ben said. "So I still remain the weakest link in this group when it comes to any kind of ambulatory activities."

Isabella grinned. "I did, didn't I? If only Mr. Doherty could have seen me."

"By the way," Ben said, falling in step with Isabella's friend, "whispering the name of the destination in the cart was a brilliant move. So how did you manage to locate us?"

The man winked at him. "I think I'll let Isabella do the honours."

Their ascent up the second peak began with a magnificent view of Sceadu's five suns setting across the horizon. The sky had turned a deep orange, rising and falling into softer shades, filtered by the wisps of lazy clouds floating around.

Isabella's friend led them down a hidden trail until they reached a narrow ledge that ran around one of the mountain peaks. The children found themselves staring down a cliff that disappeared into a black chasm. "Please be careful," he said, turning around. "It's the price I have to pay to remain unnoticed in this place. But I'm used to it by now. A tributary of the Mælan actually flows down there."

After almost half a mile of walking with their backs flat to the curved mountain wall, they reached a cave, craftily hidden behind some rocks and shrubs. When they looked the other way, they got a magnificent view of a valley carved within the Aglæca Mountains. Beyond the valley, the gentle brown peaks continued to roll over one another, crowned by a serene cover of thin white mist.

"You can never be too careful, especially when the world you're in is not your own," the man said, parting the shrubs to reveal a crudely made wooden door. The children knew exactly what he meant.

The door opened into a large cave, dimly illuminated by a fire torch. The floor was covered with thick rugs fashioned out of animal skins. A clumsily made table and a few wobbly chairs sat in one corner. The cave curved into a rectangular section on the right, where a bed made out of logs sat next to a few uneven planks that had been fitted into the wall. On the left was the crudely carved out kitchen area, with a few vessels piled on one side and a small fireplace.

The man lit another torch. "Welcome to my humble abode. My name's Evan Polanski. We have all night to talk, but why don't we take care of those cuts first?"

A few minutes later, the wounds were all cleaned up and bound in mustard-coloured leaves with yellow veins.

"They sting," Emilio said.

"It means the healing has started."

"What's this?" Isabella asked, pointing to a wooden carving on a small table.

"Just something I keep myself busy with."

"It's really good."

"I've had a lot of time to get this good," Evan sighed, pointing to the wall along the bed. "Do you see those scratch marks? That's my calendar. You're the first humans I've seen in four years."

The children gulped. Evan had been in Sceadu for four years. Was there no escape? They looked at each other in dismay.

"You boys must be dying to ask questions. But let's eat first." Evan placed some wooden bowls in front of them with strange looking fruits.

"This is delicious," Emilio mumbled, taking a large bite out of a long purple fruit. He ran his sleeve over his mouth as the juice flowed down the corners.

Ben and Will watched with their mouths wide open. Their cousin seemed to carry no memory of what had happened just hours earlier at the feast hosted by the Imps. But they soon realized their suspicions were ill-founded and dug into the fruits as well.

"This water's from a stream nearby," Evan said, handing them cups.

After the meal, they all settled down upon the thick rugs.

"That was fantastic," Will said, loosening his trousers, "but we really need to figure out a way to get back home."

Emilio bobbed his head vigorously. He was sorely missing the comforts of his own house.

"Why don't we let Isabella tell her story first?" Evan said.

"I was about to suggest the very same thing," Ben said. "It would be interesting to learn how you found us in Nædredia."

Isabella stared at the shadows cast by the placid torch flames and flicked her curls back gently. She was ready to begin her narrative.

Chapter 9 – Isabella's Narrative

"I thought I was losing my mind when I heard that whispering," Isabella said. She had just finished describing her journey to Heafodleas. "But I finally realized it was coming from the broken fountain a few feet away. And imagine my surprise when I heard it say three Children of Leod were in the Pur-Flod."

"I suppose these fountains serve as messenger systems for the kingdoms," Ben said. "Do you remember the fountain in King Lytegian's court? That's how those Imps must have found out about us."

Isabella nodded and pulled her animal skin coat closer. "I knew it had to be the three of you. And I was so happy the book hadn't come through with me. But I still had no idea then what the Pur-Flod was. By the way, it's a small tributary of the Mælan. So I waited, hoping the magical creature would show up again and take me there. It was the longest wait of my life. But just knowing you all were somewhere nearby made me feel so much better."

Emilio patted his sister's hand.

"And then, things started going horribly wrong. I suddenly felt the ground shaking under my feet. A group of Fracods charged through the street a few minutes later. One of the Fracods even slowed down by the garden, but fortunately, the Færy riding it whipped it hard. But her words really freaked me out. 'The Children of Leod are not here, you clod.' They were after you guys. I thought of running after them, but the Fracods were already out of sight by then. That's when I met Evan."

Evan scratched the back of his head. "I was there to steal fruits," he said. "I'm not proud of it, but not much grows around here. And the Pixies are too lazy to wake up before noon."

"I was in shock, but Evan assured me they wouldn't harm you. The ground started trembling again. I remember it was five minutes past seven then. The Fracods came charging back down the street. You have no idea how relieved I was when I saw them dragging a bunch of Imps in their nets. But almost immediately, this Færy came flying furiously and told the leader she'd spotted the Children of Leod. I almost fainted when I saw about five Fracods charging back. But Evan reminded me once again you wouldn't be harmed. He knew where the Pur-Flod was, but we would never have reached there in time. Besides, I don't think it would have been possible for the two of us to take on the Fracods."

"I agree," Will said, giving a little shiver. "I can almost feel them breathing down my neck."

Ben wiped his palms against the animal skin. "I think you mean down my neck. If I recall correctly, I was the one staring at your necks."

"I'm glad someone's slower than me here," Isabella grinned. "Anyway, we started making plans to travel to Gifredia, the kingdom of the Færies. But the river whispered again that three Children of Leod and an Imp were in the Cre-Flod. It was quite easy to guess what had happened."

"What do you mean?" Will asked.

"The Færies were after you but returned with some Imps instead. So it was obvious that both the Imps and the Færies were after you. Unfortunately for the Imps though, they ended up running into the Færies and got captured instead. You then somehow befriended this one Imp who had escaped. But the Færies chased you again until you all jumped into the Cre-Flod. The Færies couldn't pursue since the Fracods hate water. I suppose you asked this Imp for his help in finding me. And the next thing you knew, you were lying in a prison in Nædredia."

"I must confess I'm quite impressed by your powers of deduction," Ben said, albeit a little grudgingly. "I suppose you also know we didn't read the book."

"You wouldn't have touched the waters of the Mælan if you had. But my suspicions were absolutely confirmed because of the Imp. If you had read the book, you would have been wary about him. Imps are extremely cunning creatures."

"By the way, that Imp was Beodan, the general of Nædredia," Will said. "But how in the world did you manage to find us?"

"The Cre-Flod is very close to Nædredia. Forstelan, their capital city, was the obvious destination. But the problem was we didn't have the password to the doors that lead into the caverns. Fortunately, Evan had an enchanted map of Nædredia, probably made by one of the Imp robbers. It shows all the locations where there have been cave-ins."

"I had never imagined I would ever need to use that map," Evan said.

"We started our journey from Aweorpan, which was the closest village with a cave-in. It was almost noon by the time we reached the tracks. The cart took an hour and a half to reach Forstelan. There was no way we could get past the gate here as the Imps are very careful with plugging all the cave-ins near their main cities. And we would have been too conspicuous anyway. But we knew we had reached the right place when we heard a few Imps murmuring something about three Children of Leod."

"Did you guys see Durugan, the Imp of the gate?" Will asked.

"I don't think so," Isabella replied, taking a long sip of water. "The problem was that as long as you were inside, we couldn't come in after you. But then we got lucky. At about two in the afternoon, the gate opened and we saw scores of Imps dragging the three of you out on a large wooden plank with wheels. Lucky because Forstelan has three gates. I couldn't bear to see you all tied up, but I knew we had to wait for the right moment. And that happened when those guards dozed off. The rest you know."

Chapter 10 – Purple Nemesis

"I don't know what to say, Bella," Will sighed. "We came here to rescue you, but you ended up rescuing us instead."

Isabella tucked a few loose curls behind her ear. "You're only here because of me. Do you suppose our mothers have called?"

"I can only hope not." Will explained what they had done. "But let's not worry about that now. Since we're all together, it's time we start thinking of escape."

"Now you're talking," Emilio said, straightening up.

Evan covered his mouth and coughed gently. "I don't know how to break this to you," he said, turning his gaze around. "But the battle has just begun."

The boys sat up with a start. A battle? What was Evan talking about?

"You haven't even scratched the surface yet. And the creatures you've run into so far are nothing compared to some of the others you will have to face in Sceadu."

"But why do we have to face these creatures?" Emilio asked, chewing on his nails. "And this battle you talk about. We don't even have an army."

"Why don't we get to that later?" Evan said.

"Later?" Will cried, running his palms down his face. "When later? You're talking about a battle here. Four children versus creatures you say are even more dangerous than the Imps and the Færies. I can't even make sense of this any more."

Evan looked at Will with calm eyes. "I just want to hear about your time in Sceadu. Once all of us are on the same page, we can tackle this situation better."

"Evan's right," Ben said, removing his spectacles. "I'm quite disturbed with all this talk of violence as well. But if we act in haste, we may lose the battle even before it has begun."

"It's really getting chilly," Evan said, getting up. "Let's get a few blankets. Why don't you two help me?" Emilio and Will followed him.

Ben turned to Isabella. "You said you'd made a map of Sceadu?"

Isabella handed him a crumpled piece of paper.

"Beodan mentioned Færies capture Imps to quarry some stones. Is that true?"

Isabella's eyes glazed over. "Eorcanstans," she sighed. "I wish I could have just one. It's true though. The Færies are afraid of the dark, so much so they can't even sleep in the dark. So they capture the Imps to mine these stones which are used to light up Gifredia."

"But according to this map, Gifredia is quite far away. How then did they manage to travel in the dark of the night?"

"The Fracods wear armour made of Eorcanstans. And the Færies were also decked in those stones. So they had sufficient light throughout the journey. But still, they must have been really desperate to capture you to risk travelling in the night."

"So are we ready then?" Evan asked, handing out the blankets.

"I guess I could do the honours," Will said. He had soon described their experiences in Sceadu, from the time they had awoken in the forest until their capture by the Imps.

Ben fixed his eyes upon Evan. "The first time I saw you, the name Blake Prior crossed my mind."

"Exactly," Emilio said. "But Blake was about sixteen when he disappeared. So he'd be about twenty now. But Evan looks much older."

"It is very puzzling though. Blake disappeared four years ago, and Evan's been here for about the same time."

"Blake Prior is another person who we believe travelled to Sceadu four years ago," Will explained, seeing the confused look on Isabella's face.

"Another human being? In Sceadu? Are you guys serious?"

Evan uncrossed his legs and propped his back against the wall. "I haven't heard that name in four years. I think it's time I tell my story."

"A quick question," Emilio said, his eyes focused on the wall behind Evan. "We've noticed that creatures in Sceadu have purple shadows. But why is your shadow purple as well?"

Ben suddenly pointed to the wall and drew in his breath. "Our shadows are taking on purple hues as well. What is this strange phenomenon?"

Isabella's face had gone white. "I… I thought you knew. The last two lines of the verse… "

And then, it hit them hard.

Beware, your friend will surely change
The cup is full, it means your end.

Their best friend, their shadow, was changing. But what would happen if it turned purple?

Evan had read their minds. "You will never be able to leave Sceadu."

"How long do we have?" Ben asked.

"According to my knowledge, it takes three days for a shadow to turn completely purple." Evan peered at Ben's shadow. "I would say you have two days, perhaps slightly more."

"No," Ben sighed, "we have less than two days. Isabella landed in Sceadu a few hours before we did."

"So… so does it mean we have to battle these creatures in the next couple of days?" Emilio gulped.

"I would rather we avoid any hostilities altogether. Do we have any idea about how to leave this place? Is there another verse or clue perhaps?"

Isabella patted her eyes. "I'm so sorry for getting you all into this mess," she sniffed.

"Don't blame yourself," Evan said. "This was destined. I shall soon explain why. But there may be a way for you to prolong your stay in Sceadu by three more days. By getting your shadow cleansed."

Will gawked at Evan. "Prolong our stay? Out of the question. We leave the first opportunity we get."

Evan dragged his fingers through his beard a few times. "It's not quite that simple. For one, there's no other verse I know of that will take you back. But more importantly, I've heard of an ancient prophecy. There's no doubt the Imps and the Færies came after you because of it. And they'll keep coming after you as long as you're in Sceadu. But things will become clearer once you hear my story."

"So we'll never be safe as long as we're here. And that's exactly why we should try and escape as soon as we can."

"My dear fellow, there's nothing you can do right now. So at least hear me out. Does that sound all right?"

Ben caught his brother's arm. "Will, your argument is logical, but fails at the most critical point. We don't know the way back. So why don't we just hear what Evan has to say?"

"But what if we can't get our shadows cleansed in time?" Emilio asked, beginning to feast upon his nails again.

"That is a valid question. But again, as Evan correctly pointed out, there's nothing we can do right now. So let's hear his story first. We can engage in a discussion after that."

"All right," Emilio said, nudging his younger cousin gently. "I just need to go for a wash because the stench is bothering, even for me."

"I'll join you," Ben replied.

They were soon outside, making their way to the stream around the cave.

"Can we trust Evan?" Emilio whispered.

"I must confess the thought did cross my mind," Ben said, scratching his eyebrow. "But he doesn't have any reason to lie to us. Besides, he also helped Isabella rescue us from the Imps."

"But Beodan did that with the Færies. And we all know how that one turned out."

"I don't think we can really compare the two."

"But what if Evan's working for some of these other creatures? Don't you think he's trying a little too hard to stop us from doing anything? After all, he's permanently stuck here. So why should he help us?"

"I do see your point." Ben gazed into the dark valley for a few moments. "But I have to consider him our best option for now. It's a risk we have to take."

"I suppose," Emilio mumbled.

CHAPTER 11 ~ PSYCHOLOGIST'S TALE

The blackness of the night was accentuated by the thick clouds covering the moons. The only sounds audible were the crackling of the fire amidst the stillness enveloping the mountains.

"My story begins 11 years ago," Evan sighed, prodding the burning wood with a stick before tossing it in the flames. He stared at the sparks that rose up and into the darkness. From the moment he had met Isabella, Evan knew he would have to go back in time, that it would not be too long before he would have to revisit a past he had pushed into the farthest recesses of his memory. After a few moments, he nodded. "But before I get into it, let me first ask you a question. What do you know about shadows?"

"That's easy," Emilio replied. "They're formed when objects block light."

"That's the definition from physics. But let me explain the meaning of the shadow from a psychological perspective. In psychology, we deal with two states of the mind, the conscious and the unconscious. At the core of the conscious lies the ego, which comprises everything about yourself that you're aware of. But when it comes to complete self-knowledge, the unconscious also comes into the picture. It essentially represents everything you're not aware of about yourself, or at a subtler level, want to deny about yourself. And that's where the shadow comes in."

"What do you mean?" Isabella asked, pulling her animal skin coat closer.

"Even if you think of the shadow literally, it is created when an object blocks light. Similarly, in psychology, the shadow represents everything about yourself you want to deny. Most often, these are aspects of your character you find unacceptable, that you perceive to be unwanted, that you prefer to hide. However, these qualities or traits don't vanish into thin air. Instead, they're dumped into your shadow, the dark side of your personality."

"So are you saying that our shadows represent everything that's negative about us?"

"We don't necessarily deny only negative things. There may also be positive traits we tend to repress due to societal pressures or for other reasons. So the answer to your question is no. Now answer this question. Do you think your shadows are the same as mine?"

"How can that be?" Ben asked. "You would tend to suppress different things than us, right?"

Evan smiled. "The answer is not that simplistic. Here's the tricky part. How can we be certain about this especially since it's not in our awareness?"

"That's an interesting point. Go on."

"So far, we've been talking about the personal unconscious, as opposed to the collective unconscious which is something shared by all human beings."

"A collective unconscious? Is this where everyone's negativities are dumped?"

Evan nodded. "Let's get to my story now," he continued. "I got interested in the shadow during my doctoral studies at the University of Cambridge in England. As my fascination grew, I started reading as much about it as I could. Around this time, a friend managed to set me up with a private collector in New York who had an original copy of 'Psychology of the Unconscious' by Carl Jung. It was one of the first published in English in the year 1916. His grandfather had obtained it as part of Lord Chisbury's private collection in the late 1950s. But this is where the story takes a turn."

Evan paused momentarily and took a few sips of water. "On my next visit to New York, I got to look at this original copy of Jung. As I was going through it, a few old handwritten sheets of paper fell out of the book. I put them aside and continued reading. I didn't think of them again until I found them in my briefcase on my way back to London. I must have inadvertently picked them up along with my own notes. And that's when I first heard about Sceadu."

"Just like in the movies," Emilio gulped, biting his nails.

Evan looked at them keenly. "Are you familiar with the myth of Pandora's Box?" he asked.

Apart from Ben, the others had muted reactions.

"Then let me refresh your memory. According to this myth, Zeus instructed two Titan brothers, Prometheus and Epimetheus, to inhabit the earth with living creatures, and bestowed many gifts upon them to distribute amongst their creations. Epimetheus produced many creatures and handed out all the gifts hastily. Prometheus, however, channelled all his efforts into creating man in the likeliness of the Gods, but ended up using all the gifts. When Zeus refused to give him more gifts, Prometheus stole the scared fire from Mount Olympus and handed it to man. Zeus was furious and decided to punish both Prometheus and mankind. Prometheus was chained to a mountain and a vulture was set upon him to eat his liver. Although the immortality of Prometheus meant that his liver grew back in the night, he still had to endure the torture until he was freed by Heracles, son of Zeus, thousands of years later."

"Sounds painful," Will said with a shudder, even as the others nodded.

"I'm sure it was. But Zeus wasn't quite done yet. He next created a woman called Pandora to punish mankind. Now Prometheus had warned his brother about accepting any gifts from the Gods. But Epimetheus immediately fell in love with Pandora and married her. She was gifted a box by Zeus although the original myth probably mentions a jar. Pandora was inquisitive about its contents, but Epimetheus warned her never to open it. They had an argument, and Epimetheus decided to take a walk alone. Pandora, however, couldn't contain her curiosity and ended up opening the jar, exactly as Zeus had planned. The jar contained all the maladies of mankind, which brought untold suffering and misery to human beings. However, the jar also contained one more entity, hope, which was later released by Pandora and served to ease some of the suffering. It is also important to note this myth appears in numerous cultures all over the world."

"All this is very fascinating, but what about those handwritten sheets of paper?"

"I was just coming to that," Evan said, tossing a few more logs into the fire. The flames roared upwards. "The sheets were written by Lord Chisbury, an English aristocrat and amateur archaeologist, probably sometime in the early nineteen hundreds. They documented Lord Chisbury's journey to a remote cave in Macedonia where he discovered an ancient tablet. It not only contained the original myth but also a continuation. After Prometheus was unchained by Heracles from Mount Olympus, he became furious upon learning that mankind, his creation, had been subjected to a cruel fate. Epimetheus, however, refused to accept any blame, holding his brother responsible since he had stolen the fire. An enraged Prometheus destroyed all the creatures of Epimetheus. Zeus, still bitter about Prometheus, sided with Epimetheus, who had vowed to destroy mankind. They summoned all the evil spirits but hope from the jar and infused life into them. The physical manifestations of these spirits began causing havoc on earth, killing humans mercilessly. The humans prayed to Prometheus for help. In the end, an epic battle was fought between the forces of Prometheus and Epimetheus. Epimetheus was defeated, and all the evil creatures were banished into the underworld, Tartarus."

"So we have another myth?" Isabella said.

"Or do we? Anyway, the story doesn't end there. The tablet also mentioned the location of the place where Prometheus had first brought the stolen fire from Mount Olympus. Lord Chisbury immediately put together a team and went in search of this place which was somewhere in the Caucasian mountains that border modern day Turkey and Iran. But the mountains had experienced an unusually heavy amount of snowfall that winter, and all but Lord Chisbury perished in an avalanche. However, the avalanche had also exposed an opening in one of the mountains. When Lord Chisbury crawled inside for warmth, he was surprised to find himself inside an ancient chamber with paintings and inscriptions on the walls and a large black jar, about ten feet tall, at the back. There was also a fire burning in front of it. It had probably been burning for centuries without any human intervention."

"And you think this jar was Pandora's Box and the fire was the one Prometheus had stolen from Mount Olympus?"

"The thought did cross my mind. But wait, there's more. Lord Chisbury tried to read the inscriptions, but they were in a language he couldn't understand. So he copied them all and brought them back to England. As it turned out, the script was ancient Persian and from what he gathered from his archaeologist friends, the cave was probably a Mithraeum, used by the ancient Mithras to conduct rituals. Mithraism was an ancient religious cult that originated in Persia around 700 BC and was practised in the Roman Empire from around the first century BC until about the fifth century AD. Hence, the paintings and inscriptions were most likely before the first century BC. Over the next few weeks, Lord Chisbury learnt ancient Persian and carefully translated the inscriptions. He had initially assumed it would be a Mithran version of the myth of Pandora's Box. But imagine his surprise when he found that not only did it name the land to which Epimetheus' counterpart in Mithraism was banished, but it gave explicit directions to this place as well."

"You mean, to Sceadu?" Emilio asked.

Evan nodded. "In Lord Chisbury's opinion, this place is the basis of Tartarus in Greek mythology. The only difference is that it's real.

And I have every reason to believe the creatures of Sceadu are manifestations of the maladies that plagued humans at one point."

"But that last bit doesn't make sense," Ben said, shaking his head. "If the maladies were dumped in Sceadu, why do we still see them in our world?"

Evan clenched his fists and slowly raised them to his head. "I know, I know. That's been bothering me as well. But I don't have an answer to that."

Chapter 12 – Mithraic Legacy

van pushed his head back and stared into a void. It had been so long since he had allowed himself to dwell on what had transpired that day.

"So… so how did you end up here?" Isabella asked.

"Well, Lord Chisbury's notes were incomplete. They only mentioned a way to Sceadu, not back. But these notes were for a book he was going to write. So I got in touch with my friend the next day, but he didn't have the book. I was so obsessed with Sceadu that I tried everything, including attempting to retrace Lord Chisbury's journey into the Caucasian mountains. However, it was only after six years that I made a breakthrough. I happened to run into my friend once again, and he mentioned he had found the list of books secured from Lord Chisbury's library. Sceadu was on the list. But the reason he hadn't found it was that he had offloaded part of the collection to a local library in his hometown about a year before I had first met him. That's how I ended up in your town. But when I went to the library, Blake Prior had already checked it out. I kept returning to the library every day with the hope it had been returned. I also kept a watch on his trailer. But when I saw his mother searching for him that afternoon, I knew he'd left for Sceadu, especially since the full moon had occurred. I almost thought it was all over until I spotted the book lying on his bed. I nearly got my hands on it, but one of the neighbours saw me and raised an alarm. There wasn't any time to lose as it was the second day of the full moon. But I had lost my courage. So I got a junkie to steal it that very night."

Emilio snapped his fingers. "That explains the burglary at the Prior's trailer."

"And that's how I ended up in Sceadu. But as you can see, impatience was my biggest undoing. Lord Chisbury's notes had already shown the way in and I was so sure the book contained the verse that would help me return, I didn't even bother to open it. Nor did I consider the possibility it would slip out of my hands."

"I don't think any of us did," Ben said.

"And that's why not only am I stuck here, but I've also had to learn everything the hard way." Evan softly massaged his scar as a painful memory resurfaced.

Will stretched his legs. "But what I don't understand is how the book got into the library used book sale? And who tore the last few pages?"

Evan wrenched out a few animal hairs from the rug. "That's something I would give an arm and leg to find out," he cried. "Isabella did mention the missing pages. I wonder whether they were there when I was holding the book for those few minutes."

"I suppose I could put together a logical sequence of events," Ben said, staring intently at the rhythmic movements of the flames. "The book was returned to the library by someone. But it was never lent out again. The record on the inside page of the back cover is testimony to this. So it was obviously removed from circulation. The only reason would be the pages were torn. Hence, it would be reasonable to conclude the pages were already torn before it was returned. So in all likelihood, the pages were either torn by Blake or even before that. There's the possibility the pages were torn after Evan left but that seems quite remote. So I would have to conclude the pages were missing when Evan had the book in his possession."

Evan swallowed hard. The simple act of turning a few pages would have made a world of difference, literally.

"I wonder what happened to Blake," Isabella said.

"There's no chance he could have survived." The children shuddered at the thought.

"What about the prophecy you mentioned earlier?" Will asked.

"Actually, Lord Chisbury mentioned it in his notes. He didn't elaborate much, but said the prophecy would come true no matter what. I only know the wheels begin to turn after the arrival of four Children of Leod in Sceadu. And that's why I said earlier that Isabella shouldn't blame herself for anything. That's also why all these creatures are after you."

"But what could they want with four children?" Isabella asked.

Evan shrugged. "It's hard to say. But whatever it is, they definitely need you all. And that's why it's unlikely you'll be harmed, at least for the time being."

"So how do we get out of this pickle?" Emilio asked.

"Sceadu still means shadow. And we can use what we know about it to our advantage."

Isabella slowly pushed her finger towards the ground. It felt strange when it connected with her shadow, almost like a river meeting the sea. "So we are trapped in this collective shadow? But it all sounds so fantastic."

"If we were to combine the psychological hypothesis and our own personal experience, I would say it makes perfect sense," Ben said. "I do have a faint recollection of falling into my shadow. Since we're all together, it must be what Evan calls the collective shadow."

"Anyway, because of this prophecy, I don't think you can just leave this place. But as I've already pointed out, Sceadu still displays characteristics of the psychological shadow. Or more precisely, of the collective shadow. As Isabella knows very well, the creatures of this land are embodiments of negative characteristics. But here's the important part. If you remember, I had mentioned the shadow can have positive traits hidden as well. And the best proof of this is the creature Isabella ran into earlier. It was a Griffin. It can only be seen by those whose shadows haven't turned completely purple. And there's another group of divine beings in Sceadu, the Eorls, who can be of tremendous help."

"But I'm quite sure I don't remember reading about them," Isabella said, trying to think hard.

"They were probably mentioned in the last few pages. Anyway, the Eorls are found beyond the Forhtian Forest, a place so dangerous not even the creatures of Sceadu ever dare set foot into it. So your next step would be to reach the Eorls and get your shadows cleansed. But you must reach there before your shadows turn completely purple. Just like the Griffins, the Eorls also cannot be seen by those with purple shadows."

Will blew into his hands. "But how can you be so sure these beings exist?"

"Lord Chisbury specifically mentioned them in his notes. In fact, he stayed in Sceadu for five days, something impossible without the help of the Eorls."

"But… but what if we don't make it on time?" Emilio asked. "It will be game over for us."

"That's why you must. It's your only chance. While the thought of escape is appealing, it's not practical. You don't know how to. Besides, I think the Eorls could probably tell you about the prophecy and perhaps even a way out of Sceadu."

Ben scratched his chin slowly. "Did you ever try and make contact with them?"

Evan pulled his lips back. His throat had gone dry. "It was the first thing I thought of when I realized I didn't have the book on me," he said, after a few moments. "I landed somewhere near Heafodleas. But I had no idea where the Eorls were, just that they were somewhere beyond the Forhtian Forest. Unfortunately, I never met a Griffin. Things would have been so different otherwise."

"So what happened?"

"I got as far as the Mor Forest, which I mistook to be the Forhtian Forest," Evan replied. He bit the end of his lip as a painful memory resurfaced. "That was where I ran into a Ghoul. He clawed my face and was about to strike me with his mace when there was a call to battle. It was the Goblins. They saved my life inadvertently."

"Is… is the scar from that?"

Evan nodded. "I can never forget his hideous face staring at me that evening, ready to club my head."

"How did you make it to the Aglæca Mountains then?"

"I somehow dragged myself back to the Mælan. The water healed the wound, but I had to hide myself quickly. The Aglæca Mountains were the closest."

"I suppose it was too late to find the Eorls after that," Will said. He couldn't help but admire the courage of this man who had survived alone for so long. They had hardly been there for a day and a half and despair had already set in. "By the way, who won?"

"I think it was the Ghouls. I've only heard whispers, but I believe the Goblin king was killed in battle."

The children exchanged glances. Finally, Ben stood up wearily. "I suppose we have to find the Eorls," he said, pinching the tip of his nose. "I don't see any other way out. Evan, is there anything else you think we ought to know?"

"I can't say for sure, but just keep in mind the conscious and the unconscious are not separated by a defined boundary. The only way to overcome the negative elements in your shadow is to bring them into your conscious, to accept them."

"So where is this Forhtian Forest?" Will asked. "And how do we get there?"

Emilio's nails had once again found his way to his teeth. "What I'd like to know is what lies within this forest."

"I remember now," Isabella said, pulling out her map. "It lies in the north-eastern part of Sceadu, stretching from the Hefig Mountains all the way across. So Hærlicana must be the kingdom of the Eorls. I kept wondering about it while I was reading."

"The only way for you to reach the forest in time would be on the back of the Griffins. But I have no idea about how to find them. They have a way of finding you, as I'm sure Isabella knows. But I'll come with you as far as I can."

"And how far will that be?" Emilio asked, hoping it would be right up to the forest.

Evan shrugged. "As long as I'm with you, you'll never meet the Griffins. But let's get some rest now. We need an early start tomorrow."

Chapter 13 – Goblin's Gambit

King Egesa, the Ghoul king of Atolon, had called an emergency meeting of his generals to discuss an extraordinary development. The Goblins, sworn enemies of the Ghouls for many millennia, had extended an invitation to the Ghoul king.

"Do you think Mortuus can be trusted, your kingship?" Cempa, head general of Atolon, asked, stroking the horns on his large bald head.

King Egesa watched the glistening white peaks through his narrow eyes, set deep inside large hollow sockets. "I'm not sure, Cempa," he replied, a few moments later. He pounded the table hard, causing his polished iron armour to quiver. "The message didn't state the purpose of the invitation, but it was sent under the seal of Fordon. None would dare commit treachery under the sacred mark."

"But this is the Goblins we're talking about, your kingship," Cempa said with furrowed brow.

"It could be a trap," King Egesa said, after some thought. "But it may have something to do with the prophecy. We do have information the four Children of Leod are in Sceadu."

"That's true, your kingship. It is indeed unfortunate the Mælan doesn't flow through our lands. Otherwise, our soldiers would have been upon them in no time."

King Egesa blew hard through his tiny nostrils. "So what do you propose then?" he asked, looking at all his generals.

"If I may say something, your kingship… " It was Genga, a fierce general from southern Atolon. He continued after the king's nod. "The Goblins wouldn't dare try anything if the generals of Atolon accompanied you."

"It's settled then. Have the Brogas ready within the hour."

The Ghouls raised their spiked wooden maces and sang praises to the king. King Egesa hoisted his large iron sceptre and shouted, "Long live, Atolon." The dull grey carving of the Ghoul's head shone ominously on its top.

Manlice, King Mortuus' personal manservant, ushered the Imp king, Lytegian into the Deogol Chamber, buried deep inside the tallest tower in Awestan, the Goblin king's fortress. "King Mortuus will be with you shortly," he grunted.

The chamber was circular in shape, lined with the finest black marble plundered thousands of years ago from the Ghouls. The golden flakes in the marble shone like yellow sapphires under the volatile flames from the torches mounted on the walls. The torches alternated with exquisite silky black tapestries ending in ornate tassels woven out of gold thread. The ceiling was in the shape of a dome, with a beautiful glass chandelier hanging from the centre, shining down upon a large oval table made out of black granite.

But the first thing King Lytegian noticed was the beautiful Færy at the opposite end of the table, admiring her reflection in the huge Eorcanstan set in her ring. It was none other than his arch nemesis, Queen Siriana of the Færies. "I demand an explanation immediately," he shouted, his bushy face seething with fury. "I shall not be in the presence of this evil witch for a single moment. You have not only insulted me but also my people."

"You smell worse than the Nietens," Queen Siriana screamed, her voice reverberating icily through the chamber. "If I'd known an Imp would be here, I would have ensured my absence for a thousand miles around Fyren."

"Welcome, my esteemed guests," a voice said from behind the door. But it was drowned in a flurry of insults.

"Please take your seats." Queen Siriana and King Lytegian stopped talking instantly. The voice had been laden with so much evil it felt like barbed wire had been wrenched through their skin. "I have an urgent matter to take care of and will join you shortly. Please make yourselves comfortable till then."

The two heads glared at each other but without a word, their differences temporarily suspended at the emergence of a seemingly common threat.

The platoon of Brogas, ridden by the fearsome Ghouls, descended through the murky skies over Atelic, the capital city of Fyren, and landed with massive thuds inside the sprawling courtyard of Awestan.

The Ghouls got off and marched proudly towards the short and stumpy Goblin soldiers standing in attention even as King Mortuus walked towards them with open arms.

"I thank you for gracing my humble abode," he said, embracing King Egesa.

"What is the meaning of this, Mortuus?" King Egesa demanded. "We have been enemies for centuries. Why this sudden change of heart now?"

"Come, come, my dear Egesa," King Mortuus replied. "There's no need for any hostility. We can have peace if the Ghouls agree to work for us."

"The Ghouls working for the Goblins!" King Egesa said, tightening the grip on his mace. "I shall never agree, not in a thousand years. This meeting is over. We shall head back immediately."

"I was afraid of this." King Mortuus raised his arm. "So I decided to take a few precautions in advance." Suddenly, hundreds of Goblin soldiers with swords drawn burst out of the adjacent towers and surrounded the Ghouls. Goblin archers appeared over the tower walls as well.

"It's a trap, your kingship," Cempa cried.

"You dare dishonour the mark of Fordon, you piece of filth," King Egesa growled.

"On the contrary," King Mortuus said, "I have every intention to honour the mark of Fordon. My gesture of friendship was sent to the king of the Ghouls. But you no longer hold that position." He stepped forward and removed the crown off King Egesa's head.

"How dare you!" Cempa fumed.

"We shall never go down without a fight," King Egesa shouted, drawing his mace. "Attack the Goblins, my fellow Ghouls. Let's fight for the honour of Atolon." But only Cempa moved.

King Mortuus gazed right into the eyes of King Egesa. "As I said Egesa, you're no longer king," he sneered. He then marched towards Genga and placed the crown on his head. "Hail Genga, king of the Ghouls, king of Atolon." The other Ghoul generals joined him even as Egesa and Cempa looked on in horror and contempt. They had been betrayed by their own.

"So as you can see, I never intended to betray the Ghouls," King Mortuus said, glancing disdainfully at his fallen foe, now restrained by his own generals. "But my Goblins were screaming for revenge for the fate you inflicted upon my predecessor, the great King Necrotus. The slate has been wiped clean, and there shall be no more enmity between the Ghouls and the Goblins."

"My brothers got killed in the last battle because of you, Egesa," Genga snarled. "And I hold you responsible for their deaths." He gripped King Mortuus's arm. "I extend our hand of friendship to you and pledge my support to Fyren. As the new king of the Ghouls, my first course of action is to condemn these traitors of Atolon to death."

Cempa slowly turned his head and glared at his former compatriot. "Our people will ask questions. You will face a death worse than us."

"You need not worry about that," King Genga said, yanking his neck and pulling his face close. "A message has already been sent that Egesa and Cempa have been killed by the Children of Leod." He slapped Cempa's horns and pushed him down hard.

"Let's not waste any more time with these pathetic creatures." King Mortuus gestured to his soldiers to take away the two Ghouls. "We have urgent matters to confer upon. My people will ensure your generals are well fed and shown a good time."

"The traitors must be executed immediately, my friend," King Genga insisted, following King Mortuus inside the fortress.

"They shall certainly meet their end, but not before they have truly felt the pain."

Queen Siriana and King Lytegian got up the moment the door opened. Their host, covered from head to toe in gold armour, stepped in softly. "Please sit down, my friends," he said. "I take great pleasure in introducing you to King Genga, supreme ruler of the Ghouls and a friend to the Goblins."

King Lytegian somehow found his voice. "But… but… I thought King Egesa… "

"You're mistaken, my dear friend," King Mortuus explained, as a parent would to an errant child. "Egesa's actions not only caused constant misery to my Goblins, but were also a source of suffering for the Ghouls. And so he had to be replaced. With King Genga, I hope to build a new order in Sceadu and spread its glory to worlds beyond our own."

Queen Siriana flicked her long golden tresses past her slender shoulders. "A new order in Sceadu? What's wrong with the existing one?"

"My dear Queen Siriana, I can assure you that you all are integral to my grand plan."

"And what makes you think we shall cooperate?" King Lytegian asked, raising his voice ever so slightly.

"At least hear my proposition first," King Mortuus said, almost amused at the Imp king's manner. "You can then decide whether you'd like to join me or not. Does that sound reasonable?"

"We must listen to King Mortuus," King Genga chipped in. "He wouldn't have imposed upon us if it hadn't been a matter of extreme importance."

The Goblin king nodded his approval and continued, "I've called you here to discuss the prophecy. We all know the Leod filth is in Sceadu. Some of us have even had encounters with them."

Queen Siriana and King Lytegian glowered at each other.

"But let me ask you this," King Mortuus said, moving forward so that his golden mask gleamed under the chandelier light. "Even if you were to capture the Children of Leod, what would you do with them? Do any of you even know the prophecy?"

King Lytegian scratched the warts on his pocked cheek. "I always thought it would be revealed after the Children of Leod were captured."

"You're wrong, my dear friend," King Mortuus said, his mouth straightening into a thin line. He wanted to clip the Imp king on the side of his bulbous head but curled his fingers tightly under the table instead and continued. "I have unearthed the prophecy. It not only requires the four Children of Leod but also four sceptres, of which each of us possesses one. And that is why you all are here. According to the prophecy, we shall be transported to another world, a world much larger than Sceadu and far richer as well. So I propose we all join hands and rule this new world together."

Queen Siriana pursed her dainty lips. "Why would the Færies even want to go to this world? The Mines of Deoria have all the Eorcanstans we need for a thousand years."

"What if I told you this new world has stones that give off light at least a thousand times more than your Eorcanstans do?"

Queen Siriana slowly adjusted her ring and nodded.

King Lytegian was not willing to give in just yet. "The Imps will never agree to work with the Færies, no matter how great the reward."

"Not even if the Færies release all the Imp prisoners." King Mortuus had offered a deal the stunned King Lytegian just could not refuse. Before Queen Siriana could protest, King Mortuus raised his hand. "This world has millions and millions of creatures the good queen can enslave. And they're much more hardworking and efficient than the Imps."

King Lytegian shuffled his stumpy feet under the table. "And what if any of us decides to not join you?"

"Would you like to ask Egesa?" King Mortuus asked wryly. He let his words sink in and gently added. "But I know I can count on my friends, right?"

Nobody said anything more.

The Goblin king stood by his chamber window, staring at the rising tops of the stone towers of Atelic against the ghostly light of the two moons. "So what do you think of my little plan?"

"None can match the guile of your supreme highness," Manlice cackled with delight. "The Goblins shall finally take their rightful place as the masters of all creatures."

"Our poor gullible friends are in for a big surprise," King Mortuus laughed. But his eyes were as hard as the walls of Awestan.

"And what of the Children of Leod, your highness?" Manlice asked, his pale grey eyes fraught with concern.

"Time is on our side," King Mortuus said, turning around. "They, on the other hand, are running out of it. I promise you they shall be captured soon."

CHAPTER 14 – OBSTACLES GALORE

Evan only had to mention shadows and the children scrambled out of their make-shift beds the following morning. The purple appeared even more pronounced during the day.

"We must head to Heafodleas first," Evan said, handing some fruit to everyone. "I think I can manage to get us rides up to the Mælan. Then we cross over into the Mor Forest. This shouldn't take us more than eight hours. We can then decide how to proceed further."

They had soon started their descent towards the kingdom of the Pixies. A mass of gentle brown peaks, smooth and bare, caressed the clear azure skies as far as the eye could see. They wondered what secrets lay concealed within the serene mountains, quiet witnesses to all the strife in Sceadu for centuries.

"The Drysmian Desert lies beyond these mountains, on the other side."

"Evan, did… did you have any family back home?" Isabella asked.

A flicker of despair crossed Evan's face, but he continued down the mountain without missing his step.

"I hope I didn't offend you."

"No, it's… it's just that… I've been alone here for so long now."

"You don't need to answer."

Evan looked away. "I grew up in Rye, a small town in East Sussex. My childhood memories are wonderful. However, everything changed when my parents died in a car crash just before my A levels. It was a difficult time, but I managed to channel all my grief into the field of psychology."

"I'm so sorry, Evan."

"But things got better when Julia came into my life. She was a master's student in the department of sociology. Her personality was so different from mine, but we clicked immediately. I was happy after a long time. But I guess things began to change after I found those sheets. At first, she thought it was a passing phase. She tolerated my obsession for years until I told her I wanted to travel to Sceadu. She broke off things with me on that day."

"But how could she have known that it was actually there?"

Evan pushed his head back and sighed. "The question wasn't about whether Sceadu existed or not. It was about the fact that I was willing to leave her to go there. I realized this much later. And I have regretted it ever since."

"I'm truly sorry," Isabella said, squeezing his hand.

Evan turned his face away and blinked his eyes to hold back the tears. If only he had not become enamoured by shadows. If only… but there were so many to contend with. And here he was, stuck forever in Sceadu.

"We should carry a bottle of that water with us," Emilio said, trying to change the topic as they reached the Mælan. "It could prove useful if any of us gets hurt."

"That we should," Evan said. He massaged his neck and exhaled audibly. "My past has already sealed my future. So let's not waste any more time on that. We should be on our way."

They had soon reached the outskirts of Heafodleas.

"We made good time," Evan said, glancing at the sky.

They all slid quietly behind a few blocks of slate, once proud guardians of the kingdom but now worn down to a crumbling mass by the elements.

The boys could see why the place had long been abandoned by the rest of Sceadu. Heafodleas existed in a completely different paradigm, in a world long forgotten and far removed from the power struggles that plagued the rest of the land. But the lethargy was laced with a certain comfort they had not experienced elsewhere in Sceadu.

"I wish we had a change of clothes," Will said, running his right sleeve against his brow. His eyes circled the place. "How are we going to get these rides anyway?"

"We're going to steal them," Evan replied, without batting an eyelid.

"But… but is that okay?" Isabella asked in a low voice, glancing at her brother.

"We don't have a choice," Emilio said. "Our survival depends upon it."

Evan ruffled Isabella's hair. "Don't worry. We shall release the Gebeorgans once we reach the Mælan. They can find their way back."

"Don't you think it's awfully quiet?" Emilio whispered, beginning to bite his nails.

"That's because all the Pixies are fast asleep. Now follow me."

They all crept towards a large shed made out of logs, barely held in place by the vines growing all over. The door had rotted away and was hanging on its hinges. But the moment Evan pushed it inside, the children froze. The towering shadows wobbling upon the walls behind had given them a jolt.

Evan swept his hand across Isabella's mouth. "They only look like Fracods," he whispered. "I'm sorry I didn't mention it earlier."

"Are you absolutely certain?" Will stammered, trying to loosen his tangled insides.

Evan nodded and stepped into the shed. The children followed cautiously, grim memories of their earlier encounter still clearly etched in their minds. But he was right. The Gebeorgans were smaller versions of the vicious Fracods but without any fangs or claws. They were extremely docile and nuzzled everyone gently.

"They're not as fast as some of the other creatures, but they'll be much faster than if we walked."

Suddenly, a sneeze rang through the shed, throwing up a little dust storm in the corner. Evan's left index finger instantly jumped to his lips while his right hand slowly reached for a stick. He softly parted the herd and tiptoed towards the back.

"Don't hurt Leof," a short, podgy Pixie squeaked, shrinking as far as he could inside the last Gebeorgan's shadow.

Evan caught hold of Leof's ragged tunic and hoisted him up, leaving his stumpy legs dangling in the air. "Why are you awake at this hour?"

The Pixie's light brown eyes flickered and then turned away.

"Answer my question," Evan hissed, tightening his grip and pulling Leof closer so that their noses almost brushed against each other.

Leof turned his eyes at the children and swallowed hard. "The Imps woke us up. They wanted to know if we have any information about... about the Children of Leod."

Evan stared at the Pixie for a few moments and finally let him slide to the floor. He pulled a few dried pieces of vine from the wall and began tying them around his ankles.

"Leof won't tell anyone."

But Evan stuffed the Pixie's mouth with a few pieces of cloth and continued to twist the vine around his body.

"Do... do we have to?" Isabella asked.

"Yes," Evan replied, checking all the knots one last time. "I can guarantee you the Imps will be back. And if they find this guy, it won't be hard for them to pry the information out of him."

Ben glanced at the limp Pixie. "While I can see the rationale behind this, I do wonder if the others have already spotted us."

"The thought did cross my mind," Evan replied, beginning to untie the Gebeorgans. "The Pixies have no reason to go to the Imps. But the Imps will come back. And the farther we are by then, the better."

"Do you think these will help?" Emilio asked, pointing to some dark brown robes hanging on the wall. "For camouflage, I mean."

A few minutes later, they were on their way to the Mor Forest. The thick brown robes clung to their perspiring bodies under the vengeful rays of Sceadu's suns. The hoods, which hung limply over their bobbing heads, did not make things any easier. But other than the heat, the journey across the arid plains was largely uneventful.

"There it is," Evan said, pointing to a bridge a little distance ahead.

Will dismounted and threw back his hood. "Five hours," he said. "My body feels like it's been put through a grinder."

"Let's get out of these robes first," Emilio said. "I could do without the extra weight."

"I concur," Ben said, throwing aside the robes. He walked a little ahead and then turned around with a shake of his head. "I wouldn't call this a bridge. If I were to describe it accurately, I would say it comprises of a set of rotting wooden planks held together by flimsy ropes. And may I point out it is dangling right above a dangerously choppy river."

"Well, it's the only one around," Evan said, setting the Gebeorgans loose.

Ben stared at it for a few moments. "But it will snap like a twig."

All of a sudden, the ground began shaking, throwing up a cloud of dirt that seemed to be charging right at them.

"The Imps," Emilio cried, dashing towards the bridge. The decision had already been made.

"Don't be hasty now," Evan said. "We can't afford to rock this thing too much."

They all gripped the side ropes tightly and pushed their feet forward, one at a time, making sure the planks were firm. Ben, who ventured last, screamed as the edge of one of the planks disintegrated, causing his leg to plunge below. Will swung around and grabbed his arm, but his toes had already touched the water.

"Forget it," Will whispered, glancing up.

The first rung of Imps, riding the vile Radatis, had emerged out of the dust and was almost upon the bridge.

"What are you waiting for?" Emilio cried, after Ben had clambered across the last plank.

"In a minute," Ben replied, intently watching the approaching Imps. When they were about half-way through, he pulled out a knife and slashed hard through the ropes. The Imps tried to scramble back, but it was too late. The bridge swung downwards, and the Radatis and their mounts were swept away in the gushing waters of the Mælan.

The Imps on the other side raised their spears, but Beodan held up his hand. The instructions had been clear. The children were not to be harmed. He glared at them from across the river.

Will walked right up to the edge on the other side. He picked up a large piece of slate and hurled it across. It fell short, but the message was clear. "Good thinking, Ben. Let's keep moving."

A few minutes into the Mor Forest, Evan stopped. "I'm reluctant to let you proceed alone, but you won't meet any Griffins with me around. So I'll let you decide whether you want me to come with you."

"It's your choice, Evan," Will said. "We trust you completely. Just remember there's no bridge across the river, and the Imps may still be around."

Emilio came over. "Perhaps if I walked ahead, I may be able to spot a Griffin."

"That may work," Will replied, throwing quick glances at the others. "But are you sure about this, Milo?"

"I just think it would be better if Evan is with us as long as possible."

"I agree. But what if we lose you?"

Ben pulled up his backpack. "I can minimize that possibility," he said, removing a couple of white chalk sticks. "You can use these to mark your trail. And Isabella, I think it would be prudent if you gave him your compass."

"My stomach could really do with a little something right now," Emilio said, scratching the top of his head. He had spotted a bar of chocolate tucked away in a side pocket.

"I would suggest you ration that for… " Ben started, handing it to him.

"Like that's going to happen," Emilio grinned, tearing it open and taking a large bite. "Wish me luck."

"Be careful," Isabella shouted, as her brother disappeared into the trees.

CHAPTER 15 – SUDDEN DEATH

"That's it," Evan said with a quick nod. He tugged at his beard a few times and nodded again. "I think my journey with you all must end here. It's getting dark as well. And you really need to find the Griffins as soon as possible. Will, please call Emilio."

Will took his brother's flashlight and ran ahead. A little over twenty minutes had passed when the stillness of the forest was broken by frantic shouts.

"That's Will," Ben said, looking at the others. They sprinted in the direction of his voice.

When they reached Will, they found him bent over Emilio's prone body. "He's still breathing," he said with quivering lips. He pushed his ear to his cousin's chest again.

"Milo," Isabella screamed, falling upon her knees. "Get up, Milo. Get up. What's happened to you?"

Will pointed the flashlight ahead with trembling hands. "That… that tree. It was choking him. I somehow pulled him down and dragged him here."

"Oh, my god!" Evan gulped. "A Cwalu tree. But it can't be. I've only heard rumours, but… "

A gigantic tree emerged out of the darkness. It looked like a skinny hunchback, bare down to the last bone, with hundreds of wiry branches lashing out violently through the tepid forest air. At the centre of its striated trunk was a deep gash, heaving up and down, as if the tree were breathing.

"Evan, what can we do?" Isabella cried, vigorously rubbing her brother's hand. "There must be something. The water… yes, the water from the Mælan."

Evan knelt down and gently placed Emilio's head upon his lap. "The water only heals physical injuries. The Cwalu tree has squeezed out all his emotions."

"There must be something we can do," Ben said. His face had gone deathly pale.

Evan pushed his fingers to his head. They could see his veins throbbing. "I think the Hælan Forest has the cure," he finally replied.

"But it's a long distance from here. If we don't get it in the next few minutes… "

Will jumped up. "Just tell me what to look for. Perhaps we can find it here."

"I wish we could. But the Hælan Forest is the only place where these plants grow. They're red in colour and grow in bunches out of the gashes of the Halwende trees."

"That stupid red fern," Will shouted, throwing his head back. "We were there yesterday. Just yesterday. Surrounded by those damn things."

Isabella buried her face on her brother's chest and broke into sobs. "It's my fault," she cried. "I wish I had never laid my eyes on that cursed book."

"The questions can come later," Ben said, holding a red tendril in front of Evan's face.

Most of it had dried up, but Evan squeezed out a few drops on Emilio's lips from one end. He convulsed a few times and opened his eyes slowly. "That's vile," he sputtered. "I'm going to need some chocolate."

"He's going to be okay." Evan wiped his face. "But the leaf… how?"

"I wanted to study it later," Ben said. He stared at the Cwalu tree, which had suddenly gone still. "I had to dig really deep, but I have discovered the silver lining to this experience. I don't think the Fracods will appear in my nightmares any longer."

"Your brother may be different," Emilio whispered, as Will helped him up, "but I wouldn't have it any other way."

"And I wonder how far we would have gotten without that backpack of his."

Just then, something whizzed past them.

"Duck for cover," Will screamed, as an arrow lodged itself in a tree trunk a few feet away. He pushed Ben and Emilio down and dragged Isabella to the ground, covering her with his torso.

Another arrow flew through the air. It was followed by two more. When Will glanced sideways, he felt a numbing pain shoot through his head. He saw Evan, on his knees, staring right back at him, a look of anguish clouding his shocked face. A long, metal arrow had pierced his chest, sending out a stream of blood down his old blue tunic. There were two arrows wedged into his right arm. He raised his other arm, barely, and slowly slid to the ground.

"Evan," Will shouted, scrambling towards him as fast as he could. "Somebody, get the water. Now."

The others pushed their heads up, wondering what had happened. But when they saw Evan lying down, they crawled towards their fallen friend.

Emilio poured the water over the wounds as fast as he could, but the blood continued to gush out. "Ben, do you have some gauze?"

"Too late," Evan said haltingly, slowly shaking his head. He coughed a few times, spraying blood all over. "Arrows… poisoned… water not fast enough. My… time's up."

Evan slowly raised his left hand. Will grasped it immediately. He wanted to let their friend know that everything would be all right. But he couldn't stop the tears as he stared into his glassy eyes.

"It's okay," Evan continued, his bloodied mouth curving into a wry smile. "Mor Forest… finally… got me. Find Eorls. Trust… no one." And his body went limp.

Will sat down with a thump. "He… he's gone," he said. "Why didn't I just tell him to leave earlier?"

Emilio could feel a lump at the back of his throat. "It's my fault," he said, pulling Isabella close. She had not shown any emotion yet.

"Please listen carefully," Ben said, a note of urgency in his voice. "I have no doubt we shall once again be taken prisoners, probably by the Goblins. It won't be easy to extract ourselves from their clutches. I know it's a tall order to ask under the current circumstances, but I would request you all to reign in your sentiments."

"We should fight," Will sputtered, his hands beginning to shake violently.

Ben caught hold of his brother's hand. "I can't fault your reaction," he said, his voice beginning to crack. "But if we have to survive this place, it would be meaningless to resort to force, especially since we're drastically outnumbered. As cold as my logic may seem right now, there's nothing we can do to bring Evan back. So please don't act out of haste."

All of a sudden, the children were surrounded by short, ugly creatures with mops of hair dangling between their pointy ears. They had deep set, pale grey eyes and hooked noses with chins that jutted out like cucumbers. It was the Goblins. But rather than accosting them, they formed a protective circle around. Their leader cut through the ring and removed his headgear.

"Another human," Ben muttered to himself, as the torch flames fell upon the face. "Now this I didn't foresee."

They all found themselves staring at a slim man with a pale face sitting under dirty blond hair that fell boyishly over piercing greyish-green eyes. He had a sharp parrot-like nose and thin, dull lips that ran in a straight line.

"I'm sorry about your friend," he said, in a low voice. "It was the work of the Imps. But the Goblins have chased them away, and you have nothing to worry."

Ben stepped forward with a gentle cough. "Those tiresome Imps have been hounding us ever since we landed here. Please allow me to offer my gratitude for saving our lives."

"I shall ensure your friend here gets a proper burial," the man said. "Who was he anyway?"

"A friend," Ben said, almost to himself. He looked at Evan's body one last time. "By the way, my name's Ben. This is my brother, Will, and these are our cousins, Isabella and Emilio."

"I'm Blake," the man said. "I came here about four years ago. I'd be long dead had it not been for the Goblins. But let's get you to Fyren, the kingdom of the Goblins, first. We can talk at leisure there."

The children followed Blake to a small clearing where strange black creatures stood jostling each other. They looked like large stags but had long wings and striking golden eyes that glowed in the dark like flaming pieces of charcoal. The Goblin soldiers were trying their best to keep them under control.

"Heorots," Blake said, stopping at the periphery. "But don't worry. They're just impatient to return home. It should take us about six hours to Atelic, the capital city. We can expect to be there by midnight."

Ben and Will were helped onto the golden seats of one of the larger Heorots and strapped in securely. Isabella and Emilio found themselves on the back of a smaller but rather restless one. Each Heorot had a Goblin rider perched upon its neck, holding a pair of twisted black leather reins. At Blake's signal, the riders kicked the sides and sharply tugged at the reins. The Heorots spread their thick, coarse wings and soared into the cloudless blue skies.

Will could see the Mor Forest, stretching below them like a vast green sea, deceptively silent on the surface but carrying the burden of a cold-blooded murder within its belly. He started to tap his brother's shoulder, but Ben turned back halfway and shook his head. On his far right, his cousins had succumbed to exhaustion. Will closed his eyes and tried to enjoy the sensation of moving through the fine white mist, condensed by the cool wind blowing rhythmically from the sides. But with a million questions frothing in his mind, sleep wasn't easily forthcoming.

The hours wore on slowly, until all of a sudden, the Heorots dipped their wings and plunged into a thick vortex of clouds. The children had hardly had time to catch their breath when their rides emerged from the swirling mass and began their descent upon a large city, carved within a treacherously jagged mountainous region. It was bathed in scant moonshine that had broken through a few crevices in the thick cloud cover.

As the Heorots closed in, the diffused grey cityscape began getting clearer, with tall towers carved out of cold, hard stone piercing the skies out of every possible corner. A wide stone wall, almost two hundred feet in height, encircled the place, giving it the feel of an impregnable fortress.

The Goblin riders manoeuvred the Heorots through the maze of Gothic edifices until they approached a complex of ten circular towers that disappeared into a grey haze, connected by a vast network of bridges at different levels. Within minutes, the Heorots landed in the courtyard in perfect formation.

Blake jumped off deftly and walked over. "I hope the journey was comfortable."

The children caught hold of the sides and stumbled out of the seats.

"It was an experience I will never forget," Ben gushed, trying to steady himself.

Blake led them to the closest tower and up a round corridor of steps. Every level opened into a large dimly lit stone-walled area lined with massive wooden doors and wide passages going in different directions.

"I will never take an elevator for granted again," Emilio whispered, stopping for a few moments to rub his knees.

"That's seven so far… probably around two hundred feet," Ben muttered to himself. "Eh… did you say something?"

Emilio rolled his eyes with a shake of his head.

Almost fifteen minutes later, they finally stopped. "Here we are," he said, turning a thick metal key and pushing the door in. "You are the official guests of King Mortuus. Please make yourselves comfortable while I have some refreshments sent up."

The cold and desolate exterior had raised some doubts about the comfort of their imminent accommodation. However, the children were pleasantly surprised to find themselves in a richly furnished and beautifully decorated chamber, with an inviting four poster bed covered with golden sheets in the centre.

"So how did you happen to end up in Sceadu?" Ben asked, before their host could leave.

"I found this book in the local library. It had a verse which brought me here."

"So why didn't you return home?" Isabella suddenly interjected, startling the others. It was the first time she had spoken after the incident in the forest. "Surely the book told you how to."

Blake forced a weak smile. "The last few pages were torn."

"But then, why did you come here in the first place?"

"I never thought it would work."

"How did you end up with the Goblins?"

"The Goblins saved me from the Ghouls. I'm sure King Mortuus will help you as well."

Emilio's ears cocked up. "Help… you mean as in helping us get back home?"

"Absolutely."

"Can he help us find the Eorls?" Will asked. "Our friend said they were our only chance at leaving this place."

"I… I'm not sure if we can really trust his words," Ben said, but his throat had gone dry.

"Fairy tales," Blake laughed. "The Goblin king is your best bet. Anyway, I would suggest you get some rest now." He stepped out of the room and shut the door softly.

The children collapsed on the bed and watched the gold pattern adorning the high ceiling. The events of the past few hours had caused a radical shift in their already difficult paradigm. But rather than their own circumstances, it was the shocking loss of their friend that had numbed their spirits.

Ben exhaled slowly and sat up. He stared at his shadow, now even darker than ever. "Will," he said, shrugging his shoulders, "are you deliberately trying to sabotage our chances of ever leaving this place? Why did you have to go and mention the Eorls?"

Will jerked his head up, surprised at this outburst from his brother. But before he could find words, Isabella lashed out. "How could you be so casual about Evan? He saved you all. He helped us so much. He even gave his life for us."

"Exactly," Will shouted. "How dare you question my motives when your own actions are so shameful? And the only reason I mentioned the Eorls was because I thought Blake could help us. He's treated us well so far."

Ben crossed his arms. "Will, trying to confuse two completely different issues doesn't get you off the hook. And as far as our younger cousin is concerned, I suggest she evaluate her own motives which are undeniably the reason we're here today."

Will's face turned a blistering red. "You'd better watch your tongue before I…"

"Stop it, all of you." Emilio jumped in before the situation could deteriorate any further, "Frankly, I'm still confused about what's happening here. All I know is we have to work together."

Isabella, however, was in no mood to forgive. "How could he question Evan's intentions?" she demanded, angry tears flowing down her flushed cheeks.

"That's enough," Emilio said in a firm tone. "I trust Ben completely. If it hadn't been for him, we wouldn't even have made it this far. So why don't we at least hear him out first?"

Will glared at his brother. "Fine," he nodded, after a long breath. "Go on then."

"I'm not going to mince my words here," Ben said, "but we're in big trouble. However, I want to first dispel any misconceptions about my loyalty to Evan. I have no hesitation in saying his help has been invaluable to us."

"So… so you didn't mean any of those things?" Isabella sniffed.

"Evan was a true friend." Ben paused, but couldn't prevent his eyes from welling up. "But I had to keep my emotions aside to ensure our survival. We obviously panicked when the arrows came flying at us. But it soon dawned upon me they had always been meant for Evan. If you recall, these creatures need all of us alive if the prophecy has to come true."

"That is so true," Emilio said with a low whistle.

"Since Fyren was close, I expected the Goblins to show up. And that is exactly what happened. But I have to admit two very perplexing developments took place after this. The first was when the Goblins formed a protective wall around us. The second was the completely unanticipated appearance of Blake Prior. It really got me thinking, but the breakthrough only came towards the end of our journey to Atelic."

Ben lowered his voice. "Now tell me this. How could the Goblins have known our location? They were too well prepared for this to be some lucky coincidence. Could my foot plunging into the Mælan have given us away? I think not since the Goblins were upon us within an hour. If the water had told them, it would have taken at least two hours from Fyren's border. So my conclusion is the Imps are in cahoots with them."

Will frowned. "But didn't Blake say the Goblins had chased them away?"

"It was nothing more than a ploy to gain our trust. The tallest of the tall Imps are not more than eighteen inches in height. But did you see the size of the arrows? I refuse to believe those puny creatures shot them."

"Does… does that mean the Goblins killed Evan?" Isabella gulped.

"I'm afraid it means exactly that."

Emilio tumbled out of the bed. "Why aren't we panicking? Don't you guys realize we're right in the middle of Goblin land?"

"It had to be this way," Ben said. "But I can tell you this. Although I figured out the conspiracy later, I never lost track of what the Goblins stand for."

"Then this had better be part of some brilliant plan."

"I don't think you remember the state we were in after Evan died. If we had displayed any hostility, the Goblins would have dragged us here in chains anyway. But here's the thing. According to the map, the Forhtian Forest is quite close to Fyren. So we're already near our destination."

"So that's why you were being so nice to Blake," Isabella said.

"Evan's last words were to not trust anyone. And I certainly don't trust Blake. But here's the bad news."

"There's more bad news?" Emilio moaned. He stuck his fingers up in the air. "Do you see this? No nails left to bite upon."

Ben tucked his hands under his thighs with a wry smile. "Anyway, the bad news is it's not going to be easy to escape from this place. And even if we did, the Goblins are now aware about our plans to reach the Forhtian Forest."

"Oh no," Isabella said, burying her face in her hands. "That's why you said what you did about Evan. I'm so sorry for not trusting you earlier."

Ben nodded. "When Will mentioned the Eorls, I didn't have sufficient time to formulate a proper response. In retrospect, I think my attempt to throw off Blake was quite juvenile. I'm quite certain the Goblins will have started blocking all routes to the Forhtian Forest by now."

Will fell back on the bed. "I just wish I'd kept my big mouth shut. But I honestly had no idea how complicated all this was. There's one thing I don't understand though. What's Blake doing with the Goblins?"

"It's been bothering me as well, but I propose we take this a step at a time. We first need to remove ourselves from this place, which, if I'm not mistaken, is some sort of a prison."

Emilio tiptoed to the door and tried the handle gently. He shook his head.

"Well, here we go again," Will groaned, pulling a pillow over his head. "If given a choice, I wouldn't mind being a prisoner of the Færies. At least they were easy on the eye."

Isabella winced. "The Færies remind me of the Fracods."

"Really?" Emilio interjected, gaping at them. "Is this even the time? I have lost my appetite. That's how scared I am. So does anyone have a plan?"

Ben scratched the tip of his chin. "I may just have one."

CHAPTER 16 – UNEXPECTED ALLY

milio picked at the loose threads of the bed sheet. "I feel like we're trapped in some warped game of musical chairs where these creatures of Sceadu are passing us around. I wonder who gets to have us next."

"We're ten levels up in this tower," Ben said. "That's about three hundred feet according to my calculations. But we… "

"So that's what you were mumbling about back on the stairs."

Ben stretched his long legs. "I've been trying to take in as many details about this place as possible. But we still need a better handle on our location. Will, why don't you take a look out of the window?"

Will parted the curtains. "This is a prison all right," he said. "I don't have a great view from here, but this complex seems to be built right on the edge of a mountain. And it has a huge wall circling it. But there don't seem to be any guards around."

"The Goblins are too smart to take any chances," Isabella said, walking up to him. "I'm quite sure this place will be teeming with them."

"I'd be very surprised if it wasn't," Ben said. He crept to the door and slowly pressed his cheek to the floor.

"Can we just get to the plan already?" Emilio sighed, glancing away.

Ben brushed his cheek. "It's really very simple," he said. "There's only one guard outside. We take him out and escape on the Goblin's mounts."

"It's a big risk," Will said, peering out of the window again, "especially if we don't succeed in overpowering the guard."

"What if he's armed?" Isabella asked. Her face clearly betrayed her fear.

Ben removed his spectacles and rubbed his eyes. "You all are quite aware about my thoughts on violence. But I have logically eliminated any other possible means of escape. This is also one of those rare occasions when we outnumber the enemy, at least initially. We do know for sure that regardless of what happens, the guards will have received instructions to not kill us under any circumstances. In a worst-case scenario then, we end up with a few cuts."

Emilio leaned on his thighs. "So how do we do this?"

"I shall supply the distraction by lighting a fire near the door, which will be followed by an all-round coughing fit. Isabella will exercise her vocal cords to entice the guard in. Since you guys are better physical specimens than I am, you get to batter him on the head. The drama will end with the guard gagged and bound after which we make good our escape. I hope the plan is sufficiently clear."

Without a word, Will picked up the large candlestick holder beside him, while Emilio grabbed the flower vase on a corner table.

"I don't see any ropes," Isabella said, moving around the chamber. "How do we tie him up?"

Ben whipped off the bed sheet. "We improvise. Will, please separate one of the curtains from its apparatus. Isabella, kindly thrust those napkins along the bottom edge of the door. I'm now looking at options to gag our unsuspecting Goblin."

"I have the perfect thing," Emilio grinned, handing over his soiled handkerchief.

But poor Isabella's teeth had begun to chatter. "What if he calls the other guards?"

"It's best we don't speculate," Ben said, picking up a candle from one of the holders. "So are we ready to commence the first phase of this operation?"

Emilio moved behind the door. He gripped his weapon as tightly as his sweaty palms would allow and nodded.

"Yup," Will said, taking his position along the wall on the other side.

Ben lit the tablecloth and pulled out Emilio's handkerchief, ready to shove it down the Goblin guard's throat. The flames rose instantly, sending out black swirls of smoke. Isabella fanned them with trembling fingers, channelling them outside through the gap between the ground and the door. She then closed her eyes tightly and screamed for help while the others started coughing loudly.

"Here we go," Will whispered, tensing his muscles, as the patter of feet reached their ears. It was followed by the sound of someone fumbling with the keys. The moment the door opened, Will hit the Goblin guard fiercely on the top of his head with the candlestick holder. Emilio crashed the vase on his back the very next instant. The guard doubled over and slid to the floor.

The next few steps were executed with clinical precision. Will dragged the guard inside and kicked the door shut. He then stretched his hands behind and tied them with a tablecloth while Ben pushed the handkerchief down his mouth. Emilio stripped him off his weapons and wrapped him in the bed sheet, twisting its ends tightly to prevent any movement. Finally, Will bound him again in the curtain for good measure and rolled him under the bed.

"That went surprisingly well," Emilio said, trying to still his trembling hands.

But Ben had already slung his backpack across his shoulders. "There isn't a minute to waste. Will, take his sword. Emilio, you get the shield. It's time to move to the second phase."

The children slowly crept out of the tower and sidled along its wall until they found themselves concealed inside a dark shadowy patch.

"Where are those flying stag things?" Emilio asked, straining his neck out as far as he could.

"I distinctly recall a large stone building on my right when we flew into the complex," Ben said. "It would be their logical holding place."

"But… but that would mean we have to move to the front of the complex," Isabella said.

Emilio pointed to the thick, white fog that had descended upon the chasm beyond the mountain edge. "I don't think going in that direction is even an option. But I have this sudden craving for vanilla icing."

Ben stared at the fog and then at Emilio. "My brain is trying to caution me about something, but I can't seem to access the information. I suppose we should just keep moving."

They stole along the blackest parts of the ground until they found themselves smothered by the shadow cast by the bridges overhead, just behind the first tower.

"Do you hear that?" Isabella asked suddenly. "It's coming from that shed over there."

"It must be those creatures," Will whispered excitedly.

Ben caught hold of his brother before he made a predictable dash. "The building I was referring to is the one over there," he said, pointing to a large stone structure with a huge mouth about a thousand feet away that seemed to have been carved into the mountain peak behind. "I'm not quite sure if this is the right time to take a detour from our plan."

"It would be easier to check the shed first," Isabella pointed out. "We should be able to manage with only one creature. That place looks like it may have guards."

Ben peered at the hollow black opening ahead and nodded slowly. "I suppose it does make sense. Speaking of guards though, isn't it strange we still haven't spotted a single one yet?"

Emilio groaned under his breath. "Did you have to say that out loud? I'm sure you've jinxed everything now."

Will put a finger to his lips and crawled out. Less than a minute later, they were standing at the wooden gate. "I think I see something," he said, pushing his eye to a crack. And then, he tumbled backwards, almost stomping on Ben's foot. "It's a… monster… like… "

But before he could utter another word, the entire place erupted with loud sirens. Their absence had been discovered. The children were about to make a tear towards the stone structure when out poured hundreds of Goblins. It had never held the Heorots.

The children almost froze in their tracks, but Will swung to action and pushed everyone towards the nearest tower on their right. "Don't fall behind," he said, as they tore up the steps.

But after ten minutes, Isabella tugged at her older cousin's sleeve and shook her head. He skidded to a halt and leaned upon the sword. "Only for a few minutes."

Isabella slid down and clutched her aching legs. "How did they discover our absence?" she gasped, like a fish pulled out of water.

"Blake must have sent food to our chamber," Ben replied quietly. He turned and wiped his sticky palms on the cold stone slabs. "I can't believe I overlooked something so obvious."

Emilio watched his reflection in the shield. "I suppose it wouldn't have hurt to try a few Goblin delicacies. So what do we do now?"

"Okay," Ben said, scratching his eyebrow. "This complex holds ten towers in all with every tower having at least thirty levels connected by bridges. So in my opinion, the probability of our pursuers finding us is minuscule unless they're favoured by a healthy dose of luck."

"But the Goblins have numbers," Isabella reminded him, as Emilio helped her up. "So it's only a matter of time before we land in their clutches again."

"I really have nothing to counter that with," Ben said, exhaling slowly. "I assume complete responsibility for this gaffe."

Isabella slid her hand through his. "It's all right, Ben. We're all in this together."

"And it's time we move again," Will said. "Let's take this bridge."

"I'm not sure if that's the best choice. It will lead us back to the first tower in the complex nearest to the Goblin quarters while the one on our right will lead to one of the peripheral towers. The first and last towers have two bridges, while the other towers on the sides have three bridges at each level. Only the two towers in the centre have four bridges, which present us with more options. If you guys still dare place your faith in me, I propose we take the bridge in the middle which leads to the first tower in the centre."

Emilio looped his arm around Ben's neck and squeezed playfully. "Don't be so dramatic. You know you'll always be our go-to man."

Unfortunately though, the moment they reached the end of the bridge, they spotted a Goblin squad running right at them.

"Back, back, back," Will shouted, as the others almost toppled over each other.

Their longer legs allowed them to quickly build the lead, and soon, they were up a few more levels.

"Which one now?" Emilio shouted, halting momentarily in front of another fork.

Will pushed him into the one in front and cried, "Don't stop for any reason."

The children goaded their feet through the labyrinth of bridges until Isabella collapsed in the stone-walled area of the first central tower on the twenty fifth level. "I just can't keep doing this any more," she croaked.

"I don't think we shall need to," Emilio said, moving to the centre. "Do you hear that?"

It was a low humming sound, coming right at them from every possible direction. The Goblins had flooded the towers, and they had finally been driven into a corner. The children backed up slowly, their hearts pounding like African drums as the footsteps started sounding closer and closer. It was only a matter of time before the guards would appear.

Just then, something hard poked Emilio in the back. It was a key. Without thinking, he turned it and hauled the others inside. They found themselves plunged into darkness mixed with the pungent odour of stale air. The patter of Goblin feet approached. A few tense minutes later, it faded away.

Ben brought out his flashlight and shone the beam along the damp grey walls until it landed on a lifeless body slumped in chains, with blood splattered all around. He almost dropped the flashlight, while Will tried to shield Isabella from the gory sight.

"It's a Ghoul," she said in a low voice.

"It's my general, Cempa," came a coarse voice from a corner of the chamber. "The Goblins tortured and killed him."

Ben's hand wobbled in the direction of the voice. It was another Ghoul, bent over and breathing heavily, his skinny body hanging limply, fettered in thick iron chains.

"Who are you?" Will asked, after taking firm note of the clamps restraining his limbs.

"I'm called Egesa," the Ghoul replied. "King, or I should now say, former king of the Ghouls."

Isabella let out a little gasp. "The Ghoul king in a Goblin prison? How is such a thing possible? Have the Ghouls and the Goblins been to war again?"

"I'm no longer king of the Ghouls. My own general betrayed me after forging a pact with the Goblins. It's because of him my faithful Cempa lies dead, and I find myself in chains."

"But how did the Goblins take the leader of the Ghouls alive?"

Egesa's head slumped. "Don't remind me of this indignity. I should have fought and died by the sword rather than have to suffer this miserable death, tied up like an animal inside the prison of my worst enemy. And I would have, had the betrayal not caught me by surprise. Treachery was to be expected of the Goblins, but never from my own."

"Can you help us escape?" Isabella asked. The question was so unexpected the others were left staring open-mouthed.

Egesa's mirthless laughter echoed around the chamber. "I've been humiliated by the Goblins, betrayed by my own, and my only faithful servant is dead. Why would I even care about escaping?"

Isabella chose her words carefully. "To avenge your humiliation. To redeem your pride. To fight like the true warrior you are. And even if it leads to your end, you will have died with honour, with valour, and not a muted death at the hands of the Goblins."

Egesa's narrow eyes burned brightly, vengeance written all over them. "What do you have in mind?"

"We must get to the Forhtian Forest," Isabella said. "Can you help us get there?"

"Atelic's quite near the Byrgen, and the easiest way to reach the Forhtian Forest would be to fly directly over it. However, the Nicors would make that route impossible to navigate."

"The Nicors?" Will asked.

Isabella shuddered. "They're dangerous creatures that infest the Byrgen, a large swampy area northeast of Fyren. What other options do we have?"

"The only other option is to cross over into the forest from Mundbyrd's Rock," Egesa replied, after a minute's thought. "You have to first travel across the Gamol Forest to the north of Fyren, and then move eastwards through the Hefig Mountains till you reach the rock. It lies at the confluence of the Modsefa and the Heofon, two rivers that join together to form the Freod, which flows in the northern regions of Sceadu."

"Can you help us then? We don't have much time."

"You do realize we're still in a Goblin prison," Egesa replied, staring at his fallen general. "If only I had my Broga. But I don't know if he's here or has been taken back to Atolon."

"What does this Broga look like?" Emilio asked.

"It has four blunt horns on its head and red eyes which… "

"Glow in the dark," Will completed, with an abrupt shake of his shoulders. "It's the creature I saw in the shed."

"Do we have a deal then?" Isabella asked. "We shall free you, and you will help us escape."

Egesa pulled at the chains fiercely. "Upon the name of Fordon the Ieldran, I solemnly swear to keep you unharmed from the Goblins until I hold the last breath in my body."

"I must interrupt this for just a moment," Ben said, glancing at Egesa's long claws and then facing Isabella. "We have already suffered betrayal on more than one occasion in Sceadu. I would urge you to reconsider this plan."

"I cannot fault your thinking," Egesa said. "But vicious as my kind is, we are warriors first, and our word is our honour."

"I find that difficult to believe given you were betrayed by your own. A scenario where you use us to negotiate with the Goblins is definitely conceivable."

Egesa spat with contempt. "I would sooner die than deal with that filth," he replied, staring right into Ben's eyes. "I have sworn to help you on the name of Fordon the Ieldran. I cannot break my word even if my life depended upon it."

Isabella strode over to Egesa. "We can trust him," she said. "I have read Ghouls are honourable creatures. Moreover, an oath in the name of Fordon the Ieldran is considered sacred in Sceadu."

Ben dipped into his bag without a word. "The chains have a fairly standard locking mechanism," he said, bringing out a piece of wire. "I should be able to work my way through."

"How did you end up in Fyren?" Isabella asked, as Ben began to work on the chains.

"Mortuus sent me an invite, which I mistakenly assumed would lead to a peace treaty between the Ghouls and the Goblins. However, he wanted the Ghouls to work for the Goblins, a proposal I obviously rejected. My disloyal general had other plans though."

Ben popped open the lock around Egesa's right ankle. "And why did they kill your general Cempa but keep you alive?" he asked, moving to the other side.

Egesa couldn't answer for a few moments. But when he spoke, his entire body quaked with an untold fury. "The Goblin cowards tormented my loyal Cempa and murdered him in front of my eyes, knowing I was helpless. They were about to start with me when news came in about the capture of the four Children of Leod. So they decided to finish the job tomorrow."

"Do you have any idea about the prophecy?" Will asked.

There was a soft clanking sound as the chains rolled off the Ghoul's arms and waist. Egesa kneaded his bloodied wrists. "Only that it requires four Children of Leod for fulfilment. But I have a feeling Mortuus knows more."

"You mentioned Mortuus wanted the Ghouls to work for him," Isabella said with a frown. "We also think the Imps are working for them. It has obviously got something to do with this prophecy. But can it cause such major changes in Sceadu?"

Egesa shrugged. "All I know is my betrayal was orchestrated by the Goblins as vengeance for killing Necrotus, their previous king, four years ago in the fifth Battle of Sægan."

"So what is this Mortuus like?"

"I can't tell you much about him other than he wears an enchanted golden mask and gold armour. But the strangest thing was I couldn't smell him."

"I didn't quite understand what you meant by that last sentence," Ben said, removing the last shackle from around his neck.

"When you entered this chamber, I could smell Leods," Egesa said, twisting his sore neck. "Similarly, Goblins also give off a typical odour. But for some reason, I couldn't get any scent from Mortuus."

"But how could you have known we were Leods?"

"Because I almost killed one four years ago. Once a Ghoul picks up a scent, he never forgets it."

The children could feel their hair stand on end. It was Egesa who had inflicted the scar on Evan's face.

"You have kept your end of the deal," Egesa said, stepping forward. "I shall now honour my word and help you escape this place or die trying. The first thing we need to do is find Gæstlic."

They slowly opened the door and began running down the steps, taking random passages on different levels, and basically crisscrossing through the towers until they somehow reached the first level.

"According to my calculations, we need to go down that passage to reach the tower closest to the shed," Ben said.

But a troop of Goblin soldiers suddenly emerged out of nowhere. The children froze in horror, but Egesa seized the sword from Will's hand and charged at the stunned Goblins like a raging bull. Egesa's wrath and skill were unmatched, and the Goblins went down like a pack of cards.

Within minutes, they had reached the shed. The children waited in the shadows, watching the mighty Ghoul approach the Broga. It gave a shriek of delight and then followed it with low growling noises, sensing strangers in its midst. But Egesa rubbed its sides vigorously to calm it down.

"I was hoping we could hasten our departure," Ben said, glancing around nervously. "The Goblins will be aware about our alliance with Egesa. It won't be hard for them to deduce our next destination."

Egesa mounted the Broga and held its neck firmly. "The might of the Brogas is only exceeded by that of the Nicors and the Dragons. Now climb on and hold as firmly as you can to Gæstlic's feathers."

The children clambered across the thick, large wings onto its back and grasped its feathers tightly. They were rough and hard but without any sharp edges.

Just then, the wooden door burst open and in poured a horde of Goblins. But Egesa had already yanked the reins. The Broga beat its mighty wings, knocking down a few of the Goblin guards like bowling pins, and flew straight into the stone wall, seemingly unmindful of its existence. The children barely managed to duck when the massive creature made contact with the stone, hurtling sharp pieces into the approaching Goblins. It trampled through about a dozen more before soaring into the dark, foggy skies over Atelic.

The enemy of their enemy had come through.

CHAPTER 17 – MUNDBYRD'S ROCK

The children glanced over their shoulders to catch a glimpse of the aftermath. But the sight that met their eyes sent a cold shiver down their spine. Amidst all the rubble and ruins, a golden mask was looking right back at them, an expression of manic fury plastered upon it. It was Mortuus, just as Egesa had described physically, but with an aura so evil it singed their being even hundreds of feet away in the air. Somehow, they knew this would not be their last encounter.

"What's the time?" Emilio asked, trying to shake away the remnants of the sinister feeling.

"Almost four in the morning," Isabella said, sliding her head against his back with a loud yawn.

But Will was thrilled beyond words. "I just can't believe we outsmarted the Goblins. This has been our most amazing escape yet."

"I think your celebration may be a tad premature," Ben said, pointing to the tower tops. They could see Heorots taking off, one after another, through the mist. "Another colossal mistake I shall have to live with. At least the Goblins will dare not use their weapons against us."

Soon, there were a hundred Heorots in pursuit of the escaped prisoners.

"We may still have a chance," Egesa said, patting Gæstlic's side. "The Brogas are quicker than the Heorots. But they tire out faster as well. We can only hope Gæstlic keeps his strength till we reach Mundbyrd's Rock."

"I was curious about something," Isabella said, poking her head out from the side. "If Gæstlic is so strong, how did the Goblins manage to hold him inside the shed?"

Egesa guided the Broga through a series of tears in the choppy mountains. "It was because they plugged his ears" he replied, a few minutes later. "Brogas have very acute hearing and become disoriented without it."

Ben stared in wonder at the Heorots and their mounts. "It was quite evident from the way you demolished the Goblins earlier that your strength and fighting skills are unmatched. There's also no doubt the Brogas are far more powerful than the Heorots. I fail to understand why the Goblins are still even around."

"There's a ring of truth to your words. But they outnumber us, and grudgingly as it may be, even I have to admit their guile is unmatched. I think it's quite apparent from the way Mortuus dethroned me."

The Heorots soon became specks in the sky and disappeared altogether by the time they had reached Fyren's border with the Gamol Forest.

"At long last," Will exhaled. "They will never catch up with us now."

Ben moved his hands through the mist with a sigh. "I must caution you against underestimating this particular enemy. They're well aware of our superior speed, and even if they were to keep up, it would lead to no benefit. I surmise they've split up into two or three groups and are approaching the Gamol Forest from different directions while also judiciously conserving their energy. They're simply awaiting a predictable situation where the Broga tires out and we continue our journey on foot. Besides, they probably have already marked out an ample number of points to intercept us knowing our final destination."

Will cursed the inauspicious moment when he had let slip the word on the Eorls. Things were beginning to look quite distressing again.

"How much longer to Mundbyrd's Rock?" Isabella asked.

"If the journey occurs upon Gæstlic's back, I would say about six more hours. Our route becomes longer since the Byrgen extends almost up to the Hefig Mountains."

Emilio's shoulders slumped. "That's that, I guess. I'm hungry. Do we have anything?"

Ben somehow fished out the fruits Evan had given him before their fateful journey into the Mor Forest. Everyone munched away silently, staring at the Gamol Forest below, stretching across many miles and finally disappearing into a brown line beyond which lay the Byrgen, home to the fierce Nicors. All of a sudden, the cool green of the forest below transformed into a soft purple with the early morning rays casting their glow. A few minutes later, the five suns of Sceadu glided smoothly across the horizon in perfect harmony.

"Our shadows!" The daylight had awoken Will to the reality they had conveniently chosen to neglect in the face of greater perils. But it wasn't possible to make out anything against the black body of the Broga.

Isabella pressed her cheek to Emilio's back. "We only have twelve hours before we get trapped here permanently."

Egesa tugged at the reins and swerved the Broga past some thick ominous-looking clouds. "You should get some rest now."

The children were rudely woken from their slumber by a sudden jolt. The next moment, they found their faces squashed like pillows, with the wind playing around with their noses and cheeks like putty. Their vision was blurred, but the direction in which they were moving, and all the knots in their stomachs, could mean only one thing. They were plunging through the skies, approaching the ground at lightning speed. A fraction of a second later, their vocal cords decided to join the ride.

"Hold on," Egesa hollered, leaning back and pulling the reins tightly, his rib cage almost breaking out of his body. "Gæstlic's tiring out. We're in for a rough landing."

The children dug their fingers into Gæstlic's back and closed their eyes tightly. The Broga continued to dive downwards, until Egesa drew the reins back sharply at the very last moment. Gæstlic hit the forest floor hard, leaving a small crater and then skidded for almost a hundred feet before coming to a grinding halt, resting upon his right wing.

Egesa was left hanging by the reins but seemed to be fine otherwise. Isabella, Ben and Will lay tangled amongst each other but had escaped with only minor bruises and scrapes. Poor Emilio, however, had been thrown off, landing heavily on his left ankle. A deep gash also ran down his left arm. The others rushed over to him as he lay all twisted, clutching his arm in pain. Isabella quickly poured the water from the Mælan on his arm, and the pain had soon subsided. But alas, there was none left for the ankle.

"I'll be fine." Emilio got up slowly with help from his cousins.

"Are you sure?" Isabella asked anxiously.

"Quite sure," Emilio replied, with a quick nod. The ankle was stinging, but they were so close to the Forhtian Forest now. "Where do we go from here?"

Egesa drew the sword and pointed north. "We should be about four to five hours away from the Modsefa, provided there are no interruptions. But let's move quickly as the Goblins won't be far behind."

Ben threw a thoughtful glance at the Broga, who was munching away at one of the bushes. "Is there even a remote possibility we can be air borne again?"

"Brogas can usually fly comfortably for about eighteen hours at a stretch, but Gæstlic's already flown all the way from Atolon. So it looks quite unlikely he will take to the skies for at least another four hours."

Egesa picked up Gæstlic's reins, and they all started trudging through the Gamol Forest, cursing their stars at the frustrating turn of events. The Forhtian Forest seemed a lot further away now, and their focus had suddenly shifted from imagining the terrors that lay within to the more pressing matter of evading the Goblins for the next few hours.

An hour later, the Goblin threat appeared to have largely diminished, at least in the minds of the children. Unfortunately though, they had barely relaxed when the soft rustling of leaves interspersed with the sound of footsteps reached their ears. It was time to run once again.

"I'll stay back and fight," Egesa roared, his eyes on fire and the sword held high.

"You must come with us," Isabella pleaded. "There are just too many of them."

"I cannot thank you enough for helping me escape, not from the Goblins but from a cowardly death," Egesa said, looking at her with grave eyes. "I must now fight like a warrior and die like one. Leave now for I can hold them back for only so long." Saying this, he drew the sword and waited, intent on only one thing: his retribution.

The children took one last look at the towering figure of Egesa, grateful for his mere presence, an almost impenetrable wall between them and the Goblins. And then, they ran like the wind.

The children knew it wasn't about the Goblins any more. It was a race against time. In another seven hours, they would be trapped forever in Sceadu.

"Do you hear those sounds?" Emilio asked, straightening up. They had all stopped for a quick break. "It's as if something is scraping the bark off the trees. Or perhaps digging in the mud."

"Whatever it is," Will said, looking around, "we seem to be completely surrounded. Could it be the… ?"

But he gulped down the rest at the sudden appearance of about twenty cobalt blue, wolf-like creatures from the dark of the forest. Their lustrous flowing manes swished around like violent waves, but it was their gleaming claws, protruding out from the ends of their sinewy limbs, that the children couldn't take their eyes away from.

"How do we get out of this one?" Emilio stammered from the corner of his mouth, trying hard to avoid their rabid ivory eyes.

The creatures bared their sabre-like fangs, making low growling noises as they closed in from all sides. It was the one time the children would have given anything to be taken to a prison. Unfortunately, the creatures did not even remotely seem to have the prophecy on their minds.

"There," Will cried, grabbing Isabella's hand and scrambling towards a bunch of gigantic trees, towering to over three hundred feet, with their thick branches spread all over like a net. Ben and Emilio were only a fraction of a second behind.

The creatures arched their strong hind legs and leapt, crashing their deadly claws into the tree trunks, instead of the children who had stood there just moments earlier. They dug their claws out and pounced upwards, almost piercing Ben's shoes. But he somehow jerked up his lanky frame at the very last instant. The massive adrenalin rush had temporarily endowed the children with a surprising agility, and they soon found themselves staring down at a mass of bristling blue fur.

"My body proportions are simply not equipped to handle such quick bursts of activity," Ben said, rubbing his chest vigorously. He took a few deep breaths and continued, "But I must say their blue colouring is inspiring. The Imps did not do any justice to these magnificent creatures in their wall paintings."

Will almost lunged at his brother. "Do you think we're on a safari here? I swear I will feed you to… "

"Watch out," Emilio cried, yanking Ben's dangling leg upwards. One of the Nietens had soared into the air and come within inches of snapping his toes. "We need to get higher."

Ben moved his toes a few times, just to feel reassured that all ten were in place. He threw a particularly stern look at the offending Nieten. "I see we're in a classic stalemate situation here," he said, slowly pulling himself upon a higher branch.

"Will you stop stating the obvious and think of a way out instead?" Will cried. "Our shadows don't give us time-outs during such interruptions."

Ben raised a stern eyebrow. "If I must, then I shall. But I need to consult the map first."

But before he could reach for the map, a stroke of luck tilted the situation in their favour. A troop of Goblin soldiers wandered into the vicinity, distracting the irate group of ravenous Nietens towards a more accessible prey. The Goblins took to their feet in the opposite direction, but their stumpy legs couldn't match the sheer power of their adversaries. The last thing the children saw was the Nietens tearing into their enemy, hauling them up in their fangs and ripping them apart mercilessly.

"This is our chance," Will said, beginning to climb down. "We must get as far away from here while the Nietens are busy."

But Ben crossed his arms. "Descending a staircase is where I draw the line."

Isabella spoke up before Will could offer a snide remark. "I think these branches lock with the branches of those trees ahead. Why don't we continue our journey from up here until we find a convenient point from where to climb down? We can also avoid running into the Nietens this way."

"A completely acceptable solution," Ben said, before any objections could be raised.

The children walked for almost a mile upon the enormous branches until they found a stray one that crossed over a large ditch and descended gently to the forest floor.

"We should split up and meet at Mundbyrd's Rock," Emilio said, stopping all of a sudden. "Our enemies need all four of us. This way, we can at least put a brake on their evil plans."

Will started to say something but stopped. He finally nodded. "I don't like this at all, but I suppose it does make sense. If all of us get captured, it's going to be game over. But if two of us fall into the enemy's hands, at least the other two still have a shot at returning home."

"I'm not quite convinced by this train of thought," Ben said, a little more forcefully than the others were used to. "If I may remind you, we started out with the notion of uniting with Isabella. I fail to see the sense in splitting up once more, given the possibility of never meeting again remains exceptionally high."

"It's just a gut feeling," Emilio shrugged.

"I would be wary of those."

Isabella bit the end of her lip. "While I agree with Ben, there's just one thing which is bothering me," she said. "The situation has changed ever since this prophecy came to light. So I would have to say a reluctant yes as well."

"I suppose the decision has to be dictated by the opinion of the majority. So how do we conduct this split?"

"Bella comes with me," Will said. "Emilio goes with you. Whoever reaches the rock first waits until the shadows permit and then proceeds into the forest. Please put some mark on the rock to indicate so."

"And do you have the routes thought out?"

Will spread the map on the ground. "We shall cross the Modsefa and proceed north and then eastwards towards the rock. You two move along the banks till you reach the rock."

"Take the map," Isabella said. "I have it memorized."

"And you should take my phone since you'll be going into the mountains," Ben added. "So I suppose… "

The children embraced each other, well aware it could be the last time. Isabella's eyes had welled up, but Will pulled her away.

Isabella steadied her hand for a few seconds, trying to keep pace with Will through the Gamol Forest. Her watch showed they had less than six hours left, or more accurately, she had less than six hours left. For some reason, her mind wandered back to her report card. She almost laughed out aloud. How trivial her physical education grade seemed now. But as irrelevant as the grade was under the current circumstances, it still remained to be seen whether it was an accurate representation of her abilities. Unfortunately, even she had to admit her record in Sceadu so far had been quite dismal.

They had soon landed in the northern parts. The broad forest cover gradually transformed into a scrubby landscape, dotted with thin dry trees with spidery tops and peeling bark. Suddenly, a glare hit the side of Isabella's eyes. It was something shining brightly from under all the fallen debris. Could it be an Eorcanstan, her mind instantly offered. She had always wanted one ever since she had laid her eyes on the Færies. Isabella scrunched her face, trying to keep herself from succumbing to the temptation. But her feet came to a grinding halt.

"What's the matter?" Will cried, continuing to jog ahead. "Come on."

"Only a moment." Isabella was already on her knees, scraping through the dried bark and leaves. But they weren't concealing Eorcanstans. Instead, she found herself staring at four perfectly chiselled stones, crimson red in colour and each slightly smaller than a dime. For a few seconds, she found herself lost in the strange glow.

Will ran back to her side. "Are you tired?"

Isabella quickly closed her fist and slipped the stones into her pocket. "Nope," she said, although her hamstrings had begun to feel sore.

They had soon left the Modsefa behind and arrived at the foothills of the Hefig Mountains. But unlike the Aglæca Mountains which had gentle slopes and a sparse vegetation cover, they found themselves at the bottom of a black mountain wall, almost as steep as a cliff and completely covered with bright green plants with large dangling roots.

Isabella and Will decided to rest their legs for a few minutes before proceeding eastwards towards Mundbyrd's Rock. The sharp topography made it impossible to scale the mountains. Moving along the periphery was their only option.

Will broke off a root tickling his neck. "How are we doing on time?"

"It's half past one," Isabella replied, wrinkling her nose. "So we still have about four and a half hours. I think we should be able to make it well before that."

"At least we haven't had any Goblin trouble so far."

Isabella was about to reach for her fallen handkerchief when her hand froze. "I know why," she whispered, noticing a few specks in the distant skies.

"Flying stags?" Will said, turning his face upwards. "How do we…?"

But Isabella almost tackled him with her shoulder and pushed his head down. "Don't look up," she gasped, almost grinding his face into the ground.

"Bella, what is it?" Will spluttered.

"It's the Gargoyles, not the Goblins. Anyone who looks into their eyes instantly turns to stone. How could I have forgotten about Ablendon? It lies within these mountains."

Isabella and Will crawled a few feet until they were safely lodged behind the gigantic roots that had crawled over the ground. They silently counted five shadows approaching the edge of the mountain. But thankfully, the Gargoyles floated away serenely. Isabella peeped out a few minutes later, just in time to see the scaly black creatures flying into the mountains with their bat-like wings flapping hard and their tails swaying viciously behind like snakes.

Isabella rubbed off the tiny pebbles sticking to her face. "One look into their eyes, and it would have been the end for us."

"Here's a question. Why aren't these Gargoyles ruling Sceadu? I mean, how can you fight an enemy you can't even look at?"

"Because they're cursed," Isabella replied, patting her dress clean. "They can't leave this area. They can't travel over water either as they turn to stone the moment they see their own reflections."

"What if two Gargoyles are in love? Can they look into each other's eyes?"

Isabella giggled. "I somehow don't think so. But I can tell you with certainty they were the reason the Goblins did not follow us."

"Anyway, thanks for the warning."

They started running towards Mundbyrd's Rock once again, wary about any moving shadows. Will was about to turn a sharp corner when his toe stubbed into something. When he looked down, he realized it was a broken statue of a Goblin.

"It's not the only one," Isabella gulped, pointing ahead. They could see more statues scattered around. Some were still standing, many with looks of horror plastered on their faces, others with blank looks as if they had no idea what hit them. The rest had tipped over and broken into pieces.

Isabella raised a finger and touched the arm of what had once been a Pixie. It felt cold and dead. She wondered if there was still some part of it that could feel anything. Perhaps its heart was still beating inside the stone exterior. But the stone rubble around her was testimony to the harsh truth. Everything, down to the very core, had been turned to stone. Did the creatures turn to stone immediately or could they feel their insides hardening slowly? Was it painless or did they scream until their vocal cords cracked like twigs? Isabella buried her face in her hands.

But they had seen nothing yet. The moment they turned the next corner, they found themselves in a sea of lifeless forms. The entire place was engulfed by an eerie silence, with literally thousands and thousands of white statues all over. It was a stone graveyard.

"More Gargoyles," Isabella cried, pointing to the purple silhouettes sliding over the white stumps towards them. "Now what?"

"Only one thing to do." Will caught Isabella's hand and tore down a path between the statues. He kept looking back, trying to judge the distance between them from the size of the approaching shadows, which unfortunately were getting larger.

Will could feel the sweat pouring down his back. "What if we don't look into their eyes?" he screamed.

"They will seize us with their claws and take us to Ablendon to adorn their streets."

"Any weaknesses?"

"No."

"Then we need to get out of their way."

Will searched frantically, trying to find anything that would shield them from these deadly creatures. But they both stood out like sore thumbs against the gloomy canvas of white. And the Gargoyles continued to glide closer and closer.

Suddenly, the predators swooped down. But Will dived at the very last moment, pushing down Isabella in the very same instant. However, one of the Gargoyle's claws tore through his sleeves, scratching his arm.

Will clutched it tightly but somehow struggled to his feet and pulled his tiring cousin along.

The Gargoyles had risen high once again, preparing to dive upon their trapped prey. Will knew they would never be able to lose their pursuers, especially with all the obstacles around. Their only hope was to find a place where the Gargoyles couldn't reach them. At that very moment, his eyes caught the slightest crack in the black mountain wall, almost hidden behind the statue of a Ghoul with his mace raised.

"Can't go on," Isabella panted, beginning to drag her feet.

Will pushed her ahead and continued to run. The opening was still about two hundred feet away, and the Gargoyles were almost down their throats. Without thinking, he hurled his right shoulder hard against one of the statues. It slowly tilted over and smashed into the next statue. Within seconds, the domino effect led to a series of thunderous crashes all around. It was the distraction they needed. The Gargoyles lost their focus for just an instant, but long enough to see the children sprint inside the opening. They fell upon the floor, panting hard.

Will rolled over and held his chest. "Perhaps I should take a quick look..."

"Don't," Isabella screamed, almost pinning him down. "The Gargoyles would be staring inside." Her trembling finger led to a statue in a corner of the cave. A Ghoul had managed to escape only to fall prey to the Gargoyle's prying eyes.

"My shoulder's hurt," Will grimaced, scraping his way further down the cave.

Isabella gently rolled up his sleeve. He cringed when she touched the large bruise that had formed around the shoulder blade. There was also a deep gash on his left bicep from where the Gargoyle had clawed him earlier. They could still hear them shuffling outside, scraping impatiently around the edges of the opening.

"Listen carefully," Will said, haltingly. The pain in his shoulder had become unbearable. "I don't think I can run any more. Wait till the Gargoyle's leave and then head for the rock. If I come, I'll only slow you down."

Isabella gritted her teeth. "Not a chance," she said with a firm shake of her head, "even if it means being stuck in this place forever."

Will gently pushed her away. "Bella, you have a real chance of reaching the rock. This is the only way. You must understand that."

Isabella squinted at the Ghoul statue in the corner. "I... I think there's a tunnel behind," she cried. "I'm sure we can make it now. Please don't give up."

Ben and Emilio ran eastwards along the Modsefa, but kept away from its banks to avoid getting spotted.

"I think we're being followed," Emilio said, turning back.

"Are you positive about this?" Ben asked.

"Just a feeling."

"As reluctant as I am to operate on instincts, your past record is quite stellar with such things." Ben opened his backpack and brought out a bunch of firecrackers.

"Where did you get those?"

Ben struck a match and selected a firecracker that looked like it would make a loud noise. "These are from your garage," he replied, lighting the tip and hurling it far away. "I like to be prepared so threw a few things together just in case."

Moments later, there was a loud explosion.

"I don't want to miss out on the fun," Emilio grinned, picking up a rocket. He launched it in another direction. The rocket sped away, leaving behind a trail of sparks.

"Go for it," Ben smiled. "But we need to keep moving while we try and throw them off our scent."

Ben and Emilio continued their journey, stopping every few minutes to hurl a firecracker in a random direction. While their ruse worked, they were soon out of ammunition.

"We're not quite done yet," Ben said, pulling out a roll of garden wire and running ahead. "This is from your garage as well. I suppose we could have used it to tie up the Goblin guard. It's just as well we didn't."

"What's the plan?"

"Observe." Ben cut a length of wire and tied it across two saplings, about an inch above the ground. "I understand we're losing time in doing this, but it will hopefully persuade the Goblins to desist in their pursuit."

Emilio watched his cousin. "You're really enjoying this, aren't you?"

"An individual blessed with my superior acumen doesn't get to indulge in these kinds of opportunities often. Come on, help me out."

They had soon tied the wire across saplings, crisscrossing a major part of what they predicted would be the path taken by the Goblins, even as they raced ahead.

"Do you think it's all right to take a break for a few minutes?" Ben asked, a few miles later. The fertile riverbank had disappeared, and the cousins found themselves on rough land covered with scorched vegetation. The mighty river, however, continued to flow on their left, a few feet below the rocky terrain.

Emilio turned around and stared. "Sure," he said, collapsing against a tree. "I hope they fell flat on their faces."

"I'm glad to have your acute senses on our side. And I must say I found the experience quite exhilarating as well."

Emilio grinned. "It was, wasn't it? And to think I was afraid of getting bored this summer vacation. I bet none of my friends are going through anything even close to this."

"I can say without doubt we are part of an extraordinary adventure, although I think I would be able to truly relish the experience only if we manage to survive it."

"I wonder what our mothers are doing right now."

"Now that would be near impossible to predict. However, if they were aware of our situation, I can say with near certainty they would be on their knees praying for our wellbeing."

"I just hope they haven't called," Emilio said, looking around with a keen eye. "We have to cross the Modsefa at the earliest. If we keep going eastwards, we might reach the Byrgen."

"A very astute observation indeed. However, it would only be possible at a point where the flow and depth favourably match my abilities. A best-case scenario would be locating a bridge."

They started running northwards, keeping a close eye on the river. Emilio, however, was beginning to experience searing pain in his injured ankle. He kept closing his eyes and grinding his teeth, limping only when Ben was ahead of him. But the pain suddenly became so blinding, his foot simply caved in, causing his already fragile ankle to twist further.

Ben spun around upon hearing his cousin's cry. Emilio lay on the rocky floor, clutching his ankle tightly. He rushed over and undid the handkerchief slowly. Emilio grimaced, barely able to hold back the tears. His ankle had swollen to the size of a melon.

"You're in no position to run," Ben said, looking directly into his cousin's eyes. "Why didn't you tell me earlier?"

But Emilio simply turned away and shook his head. "I'm feeling better," he said, wiping the tears. "Let's just go."

"I confess to my lack of medical training, but I do hope you're not trying to undermine my common sense. It is visibly apparent you should not be exerting any pressure upon that ankle right now."

"But our shadows don't care."

"It's true, they don't. But our shadows do have a five-hour

window longer than Isabella's. And under such extenuating circumstances, we can certainly afford some rest."

Emilio suddenly gripped his arm. "The Goblins are nearby. Probably another group."

"Then I suggest we take evasive action immediately," Ben replied. "This topography is well suited to concealing ourselves. In fact, I do believe I see something right ahead."

"We should split up again," Emilio said, staring at his ankle. "Otherwise, both of us will be caught."

Ben pushed Emilio's arm around his shoulder and hoisted him up. "This is not the time," he said firmly. "Now hop on your good leg."

They had almost reached the entrance when Emilio suddenly pushed him inside. "This is something I have to do. Take care of Isabella."

Emilio started hobbling towards the Modsefa, dragging his feet noisily through the rubble. A few hours of rest weren't going to heal his ankle. In his mind, it had already sealed his fate. But he wasn't going to let it affect his cousin's shot at freedom.

The Goblins went right after him. Emilio stood for a few moments along the edge of the jagged rocks, staring at the sharp current of the Modsefa about thirty feet below. "Now," he shouted, pushing a large rock below, just before the Goblins appeared. Satisfied they had heard the splash, he closed his eyes and jumped in next.

Isabella and Will emerged from the mountains almost an hour later. The compass had been handy, but it was Emilio's flashlight that had really guided them through the dark maze of leaky tunnels. But wet sneakers and damp clothes apart, their journey had progressed without any unpleasant incident. When they eventually walked out, they were relieved to see a massive rock about a mile ahead. It was smooth, without any sharp edges, and rose to almost three thousand feet against a clear blue sky. A tiny figure sat under its shadow.

All but one had made it.

CHAPTER 18 – FORDON'S ASHES

King Mortuus stared at the retreating back of Manlice. He continued to do so for a few moments after the door had clicked shut. All of a sudden, he picked up his gold goblet and flung it hard at the wall of the Deogol Chamber.

King Lytegian, who was sitting closest, almost fell out of his seat. "What's wrong, my friend?" he stammered.

"The Leod filth has reached the northern border of Modsefa." King Mortuus spat.

"How did they reach so far?" King Genga asked, unable to hide his surprise.

"While two of them jumped into the Modsefa, the other two are probably planning on crossing into the Forhtian Forest from Mundbyrd's Rock," the Goblin king continued, without bothering to answer the question. There wasn't any need to create unnecessary unpleasantness by bringing up the role Egesa had played in orchestrating the escape.

"Forhtian Forest," Queen Siriana shrieked. "Why would anyone venture there?"

"To get to the Eorls, of course. But we should be able to get them before the day is over."

"Don't we need all four of them?" King Lytegian asked.

King Mortuus didn't answer immediately. But when he spoke, it was through his teeth. "They're not going anywhere. Even if they manage to find the Eorls, it won't make any difference. The prophecy will come true, and we shall emerge triumphant."

"I'm not so optimistic," Queen Siriana muttered. "Although we haven't captured the children, we know of their existence. But what of Fordon's Ashes or the Temple of Fordon?"

King Lytegian slumped in his seat. "Even if the ashes exist, I've heard they're buried deep inside the Byrgen. And my sources tell me the temple was destroyed many millennia ago."

King Mortuus held his hand up before the newly crowned Ghoul king could offer his pearls of wisdom. "I have already found both. Or rather, more accurately, I have found their location."

His co-conspirators were stunned at this piece of news.

"How did you get past the Nicors?" King Lytegian asked.

"I never said the ashes were in the Byrgen. They're in a southern part of the Drysmian Desert inside the Temple of Fordon. So as you can see, I've already accomplished the two most difficult tasks."

"You actually found the Temple of Fordon," King Genga exclaimed. "But how?"

"That is not important," King Mortuus replied acidly. "I haven't called this meeting to entertain you with stories. It's sufficient for you to know I had to use some extremely ancient and powerful magic. Anyway, I need two things from you. First, each of you will immediately dispatch a thousand of your kind to the Drysmian Desert to help with the excavation. I already have a large number of Goblins working round the clock, but things need to move faster. Second, I will need your sceptres to raise Fordon's Ashes."

Before King Lytegian could protest, King Mortuus continued, "Siriana, release a thousand Imps right away. I don't want to hear another word from anybody. As it is, these blasted Children of Leod are making my life miserable. This meeting is over."

CHAPTER 19 – FORHTIAN FOREST

Ben sat with his knees pulled in and head buried in his arms. "Where's Milo?" Will asked, running over.

Ben looked up with reddened eyes. He tried to find words but could only point in the direction of the Modsefa.

"Ben, you're not making any sense. Where is Emilio?"

Ben hugged his brother tightly and narrated everything. "I just can't understand why he would resort to this extreme step. And anyway, it was something completely out of character for him."

Isabella's knees gave way, and she collapsed on the ground. "I can't go any further," she whispered, shaking her head slowly. "I just can't. It doesn't matter any more."

Will glanced at the tip of Mundbyrd's Rock, almost shaped like the beak of a hawk, shining under the withdrawing rays of Sceadu's suns. "Are you both telling me Emilio can't cross that river?" he said. "I saw him when we jumped into the Mælan. And I can tell you that guy can swim. The Modsefa is nothing."

"Do… do you really think he's fine?" Isabella sniffed.

"I could take the Modsefa. And Milo's a far better swimmer than I am. We cannot give up on him this way. I won't allow it."

Ben walked up to Isabella. "I'm really sorry about all this," he said, wiping his eyes and placing his spectacles back on his nose. "Anyway, I just thought it may be interesting to note the Modsefa becomes the Freod and flows through Hærlicana. So it is only logical to believe he may already be on his way to the Eorls."

Isabella sat up and leaned forward, rocking her body, trying to make sense of everything. Despite her cousins' reassuring words, her mind was still clouded with doubt. "I suppose it's just better we find the Eorls," she finally said, shaking her curls out of her face. "Let's cross the Forhtian Forest."

"That's the spirit," Will said, helping her to her feet.

But when the children walked around the giant boulder, they were just in time to see ten Heorots hovering between them and the forest. While they had been engrossed on the other side, a platoon had stealthily circled around them over the Modsefa, just before the Byrgen.

Ben watched the approaching Heorots. "The numbers finally did us in. Although I must say I'm overwhelmed by an extreme feeling of bitterness at this moment."

"At least Emilio's idea of splitting up made sense," Will said. "We could still try and make it to the mountain tunnel."

But Isabella fell upon the rock, tears flowing down her sunken cheeks. Her last ray of hope had been snatched away. The Forhtian Forest was right there, right in front of her. And yet, they would soon be dragged away to Atelic. She would never see Emilio again.

"I must be getting delirious," Ben said, blinking his eyes a few times.

"No, you're not," Will shouted, as the Heorots and their mounts suddenly turned to stone midair and sunk to the ground, shattering into a thousand pieces upon impact. He grabbed Isabella's and Ben's hands and charged at the forest. "It's the Gargoyles. Don't look behind."

"I can't run any more," Isabella sobbed, stumbling through the rubble.

"But you will," Will shouted, tightening his grip and jerking their hands forward. His injured shoulder flared up, but he ground his teeth and kept going. Staying alive was always going to be the priority.

They could feel the Gargoyles lunging towards them from either side of Mundbyrd's Rock. But they could also see the forest approaching closer and closer. A silent darkness prevailed beyond the boundary, as if day and night existed side by side.

"I'm not sure it looks inviting," Ben screamed.

"You really don't want to test the alternative," Will shouted back.

The faint outlines of trees soon came into view, but their attention remained fixed upon the frightening sounds of the Gargoyle's wings beating through the air.

"I'm done," Isabella panted, her legs finally giving way.

"Not if I can help it," Will said, hoisting her with all his might and launching her into the forest.

"Will… " Ben started, almost too stunned to react.

But Will leapt inside, pulling him along forcibly. They felt a cold draft of air down their back just before the forest swallowed them. It was the Gargoyle's claws, taking a final swipe at their prey.

Isabella broke her fall with her hands. But the moment she raised her head, she found herself staring at the red athletic track in her school. On either side, she could see her schoolmates taking their positions at the start line. A loud cheer went up in the air. It was from the stands. What was happening? Hadn't Will just pushed her into the Forhtian Forest? Or had Sceadu just been a dream?

"I hope you're all warmed up." It was Mr. Doherty, her physical education teacher. "We're about to start the race."

Isabella stopped dusting the mud off her hands. What race was he talking about?

"Take your place between Amanda and Rachel," he continued, removing a big red whistle.

She licked her lips, trying to think of something to say.

"Come, come, Isabella. We don't have all day."

She slowly jogged over to the beginning of the track. Everything felt so real. Perhaps it was. It had to be. Isabella felt an intense surge of relief. There was no book. There was no Sceadu. And Emilio would be at home when she returned from school. All she had to do was finish this race.

The shrill sound of Mr. Doherty's whistle suddenly pierced the air. The stands erupted once again. The girls picked up their legs and started down the track. Isabella somehow goaded her feet to life as well. But the other girls had already nudged past her in a few seconds.

"Faster, Isabella," Mr. Doherty shouted.

"I'm trying my best," she panted.

"That's not good enough. Faster."

"Please, Mr. Doherty, I can't."

"Perhaps you need a little more motivation. How about a taste of leather?"

Before Isabella could make sense of his words, the girls in front faded into a mist and wafted away. Suddenly, the track was filled with cracking sounds. When she glanced back, her legs almost twisted into pretzels. There were five nasty-looking Færies chasing her, striking their deadly whips viciously through the air.

Isabella could feel a nauseating fear gripping her insides. It was accompanied by the realization she had never left Sceadu. In fact, she was still languishing inside the Forhtian Forest. Somehow, it was playing on her biggest weakness. But what could she do? And then, she thought of Emilio. No, she wouldn't give up. Isabella imagined her brother waiting for her on the other side of the forest. She would do anything to reach him.

Isabella begged her feet to move faster, but they continued to plod on. And that was the moment Evan's words hit her. The only way to overcome the negative elements was to accept them. But hadn't she already accepted her weakness?

With every step, Isabella could feel the whips closing in on her. But she had to think. What was she doing wrong? And in one enlightening instant, she had the answer. What if her entire premise, that she couldn't run, was fundamentally flawed? Had Evan also not said the shadow held positive elements as well? Perhaps she could run. Had she not survived in Sceadu so far? Had the real Mr. Doherty not said she had potential?

Isabella tightened her jaw and took to the track with a vengeance. And when her mind commanded, her legs obeyed. She had soon left the Færies behind. When Isabella finally collapsed over the finish line, she had a wide smile across her face.

Will found himself in a small white room with a table and two chairs. But the moment his eyes fell upon the large mirror on the wall, he knew exactly where he was. It was an interrogation room, similar to the one he had been taken to at the airport the night they had travelled to Aunt Sarah's house. Had he travelled back in time somehow?

The door burst open, and a Customs and Border Protection Officer carrying a chocolate donut and cup of coffee stepped inside. "Officer O'Toole here," he said, taking a large bite. "You know why you're here. Take a seat."

Will wiped his sweaty palms down his shirt. It was the same officer who had questioned him earlier. "There's been a misunderstanding, officer."

The officer kicked the chair in front of him. "I said, take a seat."

Will scrambled into the chair. "That knife is from my camping trip," he stammered. "There was an emergency, you see. I forgot to remove it while packing. Can I please go now?"

"Only I ask the questions," Officer O'Toole shouted. He slammed the cup on the table, spilling its contents, and stared right into Will's eyes. "Understood?"

"Yes, sir," Will gulped.

Office O'Toole took another bite of the donut and flicked the crumbs off his uniform. "Now here's how dis'll work. I shall ask you just one question. You answer it correctly, and I let you go. You don't and it's straight in da slammer for you. Got it?"

"Yes, sir." But Will's mouth had gone dry. He thought about all the questions he had been asked that night.

The officer leaned forward and narrowed his eyes. "How many Goblins does it take to catch a Griffin?"

Will arched his brow. There was something very wrong here. Why was Officer O'Toole asking him about Sceadu? Wasn't he in an interrogation room at the airport?

The officer brought his fist down hard upon the table. "Why you starin' at me that way?"

Will realized he had never left the Forhtian Forest. He quickly shook his head, throwing a quick glance at the officer and then looking down at his feet. Everything felt so real.

"Answer da question," Officer O'Toole barked, the vein along his forehead throbbing like a dying mackerel.

Will opened his mouth and almost blurted a number. It was only at the very last instant he managed to catch his tongue. He clasped the sides of the chair and took a few calming breaths. He knew he didn't have a clue about the answer. And yet, he had almost sealed his own fate through his haste. The very same haste had also landed him in a quandary at the airport. In that moment, the truth dawned upon him. This was not only about answering the question correctly. It was also a test of patience.

"Well?" Officer O'Toole said.

"I'm thinking, officer" Will replied, using a firm yet polite tone.

The officer muttered something and crossed his arms.

Will leaned back and closed his eyes. How many Goblins would it take to catch a Griffin? Isabella had said the Griffins were very fast. So it would certainly be more than one. But how many more? Or were the Griffins just too fast to get caught?

A few beads of sweat appeared on his brow. The question was a tough one. But the officer was almost done with the donut. Will did a few calculations and decided the answer was five. But he clamped his lips just before they blabbed it as Evan's words rang in his ears.

Will could feel his heart in his mouth. It had been too close. "The Goblins can't see the Griffins," he answered, "and therefore, they can't catch them."

"That's correct," Officer O'Toole said. "You're through."

The room suddenly started spinning. Moments later, Will had slumped in his chair.

Ben ran right into a pitch-black space. He stood still, hoping his eyes would adjust to the darkness in time. But even after a few minutes, the black cover refused to yield even the slightest bit. All of a sudden, an inexplicable fear began rising within him.

Okay, Ben thought, what I'm experiencing right now is because I'm surrounded by complete darkness. The way ahead then would be to dispel this darkness. Use the phone flashlight, his mind offered. It was the most logical explanation, he nodded. Alas, Will had the phone. You can try the matches, was the next suggestion. Ben quickly unzipped his backpack and brought out the box. But try as he might, they wouldn't spark. He bit his lip, trying to come up with a different idea. But here was a situation like no other. His mind had gone utterly blank.

Ben turned his head in different directions, but he only saw blackness. He again felt a perplexing dread growing inside his stomach. There has to be a logical explanation for this fear, he decided, removing his spectacles, more out of habit than anything else. There is, his mind, instantly offered. What if you remain trapped in this black hole forever? What if there are dangerous creatures around? What if you trip and fall down an endless chasm? And so it went on. "I get it, I get it," he finally screamed, clutching his head.

Ben curled and uncurled his fingers. There had never been a time before when his mind had failed him. And yet, he knew he had to somehow disengage it immediately to retain his sanity. The only way is to move from the domain of thought to the domain of action, he decided. He slowly dipped his body and got down on all fours. He put one hand forward cautiously. Then one foot. It was followed by the other hand. And then the other foot. And then one more step. And one more. It worked beautifully, but only lasted until the monotony set in, prompting his mind to take over once again. So how long do you propose to do this, it asked. What is the point anyway, it taunted. Do you know what colour your shadow is right now, it probed.

Ben buried his face in his hands, trying hard to squeeze the thoughts out of his head. How could this be happening? His mind, his faithful companion, seemed to have deserted him. There had to be a rational explanation. There always was. Or was there? And that's when he remembered Evan's words about bringing the negative elements of the shadow into the conscious. But he, the great thinker, had become so inextricably tangled in his own logical paradigm that he had failed to see the light.

Ben set his backpack aside and sat down with his eyes closed. He allowed his muscles to relax, keeping his breathing slow and rhythmic. It was important to allow his mind to recognize its own limitations, to open itself to possibilities beyond the rational, a phenomenon he had repeatedly experienced in Sceadu yet adamantly refused to accept.

Gradually, Ben began to perceive the forest around him. His eyes remained closed, and yet things had never been clearer. For the first time, he realized how confined his existence had been, trapped in a prison of his own making. How could he have been so blind? There was so much more to life than operating within a set of artificial rules. Ben's spirit exulted in its new-found wisdom, trying to break free. But his body could only take so much, and he slowly slid to the ground.

Chapter 20 – Secrets Unveiled

sabella drew in her breath and sat up with a start, trembling all over. Her vision was blurred, but her hands thrashed about, trying to shield her from her tormentors with whips.

But strong arms gripped her and held her close. "It's all right, Bella. You made it."

She stopped struggling. The voice was distinctly familiar. It belonged to Emilio. But she pushed him away. "Are you real? Or am I still in the Forhtian Forest?"

"We're in Hærlicana."

She blinked at him. It really was her brother. She threw her arms around him. "You're alive," she sobbed. "I'm just so happy."

"That makes two of us," he laughed. "But let's get your shadow cleansed first. You only have five minutes left."

"Did Ben and Will… ?"

"Of course, they did. The Eorls are bringing them to the Fælsian Lake as well."

Emilio led Isabella down a white marble path immersed in light diffused through the crystalline rock that made the arched passageway. A gentle breeze infused with a fragrance which reminded her of lavender drifted through the air. The lake appeared soon, surrounded by brilliantly pallid mountains with steep slopes that cut into each other. The faint outlines of the two moons were visible beyond the farthest peaks, their spotless rays bathing the azure waterfalls cascading down the sides. But amidst all the splendour, it was the exquisite fountain in the centre of the lake which had Isabella completely mesmerized. It was made out of a smooth white stone and towered fifty levels above the soft rippling surface, each level adorned with magnificent carvings of human beings. Water poured down from one level to the next without a single whisper, as if it had been tuned to the sound of silence. At the very top sat a large white spherical stone, its surface shining with a subdued elegance.

Isabella spotted Ben and Will at the periphery of the lake, in the company of tall beings dressed in pure white flowing robes with intricate silver threads around their waists. They had long, white beards and soft, mellow faces but not a single wrinkle on their radiant skin. But their eyes bore an aura of wisdom that belied their true age. It was the Eorls.

"My dear Children of Leod," the Eorl with the longest beard said. "You have braved terrible dangers to reach Hærlicana. You must now bathe in the Fælsian Lake to restore the purity of your shadows. Let go all your troubles, all your fears, as you step inside the lake. It will take care of you."

The children could feel his voice weaving a cocoon of warmth around them. They waded into the water without any hesitation, instinctively knowing they could trust these divine beings. A delicious tingling sensation spread all over, extracting all the weariness from the very core of their beings. They felt safe, truly protected, a feeling which had been long forgotten. It was as if they were being reborn.

When the children emerged, they were radiating with vitality and goodness but were dry as toast. The feeling of uncertainty that had plagued them so far had been replaced by one of supreme confidence. And most importantly, their shadows had returned to the usual grey.

"Your shadows are now free from all negativities," the Eorl said. "But they will start turning purple again. According to the rules of Hærlicana, we can only do the cleansing process once. You now have three more days to leave Sceadu."

The children bowed reverently.

"I'm Halig, chief of the Eorls," he continued. "These are Eadmod, Gloædmod and Mildheort, all senior Eorls who help me with the administrative affairs of Hærlicana. I'm sure you have a lot of questions for us. But first, we have some gifts for you. You shall find them in your right pockets."

"Mine has a pair of white shoes," Isabella said. "Are they for my doll?"

"I have a small silver shield," Emilio said, holding it up.

"This appears to be a crystal marble," Ben said, rolling it in his fingers.

"I have a golden telescope," Will said. "But it's a miniature one as well."

"Your gifts will grow to their regular sizes when you will them to," Gloædmod said. "Use them wisely for you will need them to defeat your enemies."

"I'm still unable to grasp the significance of a marble," Ben said.

Halig ran his slender fingers through the long white strands of his beard. "You all overcame that which has been holding you back to reach here. Isabella found out that self-belief can overcome the biggest of obstacles. Will understood that while action has its virtues, it is equally important to be patient. Ben realized that while logic has its place in the world, it is also necessary to keep an open mind. And finally, Emilio, by sacrificing himself, gave ample evidence of his selflessness. But while you all have gained awareness, mastery is still far away. We are therefore bestowing these gifts to provide you with a fair chance against a very powerful adversary. Isabella will be able to run like the wind. None will be able to catch her. Emilio's shield will protect you from all enemies. There will be no force powerful enough to get past it. Ben's crystal ball will tap into his intuition. It will complement his keen intellect while making decisions. And Will's telescope will provide him sight beyond sight. It will show him anything he wants to see in Sceadu, but it has to be something specific. There's just one thing. The gifts will not work in Hærlicana."

"Of behalf of everyone, I'd like to thank you all for these wonderful gifts," Will said.

"But always remember this," Halig continued. "These gifts will help, but can never replace the power within you. So just believe in yourself."

"Are those statues of us?" Isabella asked, pointing to the fountain in the middle of the Fælsian Lake. And sure enough, there were four new statues in the likeness of the children right at the top, looking upwards and balancing the white sphere in their raised hands.

"They are," Eadmod replied. "The statues are of all the Leods who have visited Hærlicana over thousands and thousands of years."

"Which one's Lord Chisbury?"

Eadmod showed them the statue of an imposing man on the level lower than theirs, attired in clothes characteristic of a century ago. "Now before you ask any more questions, I think we should first take care of those noises I hear from your stomachs."

The children sat upon a white marble terrace extending from the mountain bordering the Fælsian Lake on the other side. A silent mist hung above the still indigo water, almost shielding the fountain, but for their statues shimmering under the bright rays of Sceadu's two moons. The skies above were a vast black canvas, strewn with glittering stars that shone like diamonds.

"The food was amazing," Will said, leaning back and allowing the wind to play with his hair. "And I could have never thought of a better setting. So where are we exactly?"

"We're at the northernmost tip of Hærlicana, surrounded by the Hluttor Mountains," Halig replied. "I sense you all are eager to ask questions. But before you do, would you first like to hear about the origins of Sceadu?"

The children nodded excitedly.

"Until about a hundred thousand years ago, only one world existed. Your world. It was ruled by three brothers, the Ieldrans or the Elders, who lived high in the mountains of the Caucasus. There was Mithras the Wise, Fordon the Strong, and Mundbyrd the Protector. The world then was inhabited by the Firas, the first race of the humans. However, unlike now, they were not the dominant creatures. But while the other creatures wished to exist in peace, the Firas wanted to extend their dominion over the entire world. They killed the others mercilessly, until Fordon, extremely angered by their callous actions, descended from his seat and destroyed them all. However, one of the Firas, Beorn, prayed for forgiveness to Mithras. Mithras calmed Fordon and suggested they remove all the negative qualities out of Beorn and banish them into his shadow. Mundbyrd, the third Ieldran, was called on to aid with this task. For seven days and seven nights, the Ieldrans toiled hard. This was the first glimpse of Sceadu. Beorn became the first of the second race of humans called the Gumas. The Gumas were peaceful, and this heralded the golden age of the human race. Since Beorn was the first of the Gumas, they inherited a part of his shadow, which finally led to their downfall. The negativities were still in spirit form, and they started leaking out from the shadows until the Gumas also became corrupted.

"Ultimately, the Ieldrans had to wipe out the Gumas as well. They caused a devastating flood to sweep them all away with the exception of one Mann, who had been least affected. He was the first of the third race of humans called the Leods. Your race. Hence, while your race is not as terrible as the Firas, it can never be as righteous as the Gumas were at the beginning. As for the spirits, Fordon decided to seal them away in a jar. However, they begged him to create a new land and promised to never escape into your world again. This is how Sceadu was born. But Fordon did a clever thing. He gave physical form to the spirits so they could never cross into your world again. The human shadow became the gateway to Sceadu, where all negativities were now trapped forever. Since they first settled to the north of the Hefig Mountains, they came to be known as the Hefigans. The creation of Sceadu was accompanied by a fierce storm, which lasted for thirty days and thirty nights. At the end of the storm, a divine voice spoke from the skies. It was a prophecy which sought to merge the destiny of the humans and the beasts in their shadows."

The children huddled close together. The prophecy was finally going to be revealed.

"You shall hear it for yourself, exactly as it was first heard all those years ago." Halig faced the lake and raised his arms slowly, chanting strange words that resonated like a stringed instrument through the tepid air. The spherical stone atop the fountain began glowing, casting an ethereal blue light across the swirling mist. Moments later, a deep voice echoed through the night:

> *"That which is separated will seek to unite*
> *There will come a day when the time is right*
> *Three sons of Leod and a daughter more*
> *Combined with the powers of the sceptres four*
> *The Temple of Fordon will show the way*
> *The Chamber of Losian will have its say*
> *But without Fordon's Ashes that lie in the urn*
> *The fortunes of Sceadu can never turn*
> *The day of reckoning comes at a time*
> *When the suns of Sceadu fall in a line*
> *Once the wheels in motion are set*
> *The spoils of the war only one will get*
> *Who will win, that cannot be said*
> *But 'tis clear, one will be dead."*

"But why?" Emilio asked.

"The prophecy originated from the order of the universe. The creation of Sceadu required a large amount of energy from the universe, an act that created a strain on the natural order. The prophecy was meant to be realized at a time when this strain could no longer be sustained. That time is now. Regardless of the outcome, the balance will be restored once again."

Will gazed at the dying glow of the sphere. "Couldn't the Ieldrans have done anything?"

"Every action has a consequence, even an action by the Ieldrans. But while they could not influence the outcome of the prophecy, they knew the Leods would need help. It was for this reason Mundbyrd descended into Sceadu and created Hærlicana. To protect it, he shielded it with the Forhtian Forest."

"But why is this forest so feared? Crossing it was definitely easier than some of our run-ins with the creatures in this place."

"Your weaknesses are trivial. But the Hefigans are physical manifestations of pure negativities. Their very nature is the direct outcome of their weakness. How can they overcome something so integral to their existence? To do so would be to destroy their own essence. The forest was in fact set up in such a way that Leods would be the only ones able to cross it."

"But Egesa, a Ghoul, helped us," Isabella said.

"The Hefigans reflect their respective negativities strongly. However, they still retain their own individualistic traits, the same way Leods do."

"I'm probably going off on a complete tangent here," Ben said, "but I just have to know this. Why is English the language of communication in Sceadu? I keep wondering how we would have survived this place if we had been French. But there's another perplexing thing. I distinctly recall Evan mentioning that the inscriptions found by Lord Chisbury were in ancient Persian."

Halig smiled. "What makes you think we're speaking the same language? In Sceadu, we speak Scegan. But what you hear is in the language you're most comfortable with."

"I would really like to get my hands on whatever translation software this place is using."

"What about the verse that brought us here?" Isabella asked. "Did that also originate from the order of the universe?" It was hard to believe they had been caught in the midst of something so profound.

"It would appear so. Unfortunately, my knowledge is limited to Sceadu."

"Can you please tell us how to get home?" Emilio had only one thing on his mind. But it was more out of habit than anything else, given the conversation they had had so far.

"You are part of a prophecy which has to be fulfilled. It is how things have to be."

"But a way back home does exist," Will said. "Otherwise, how could Lord Chisbury have returned?"

"I'm sure it does. But that knowledge had not been disclosed to us. When the Ieldrans created us, they could not go against the order of the universe. Our existence has a purpose, and it is to guide you towards fulfilling the prophecy."

Emilio slumped in his seat. "But what can four children do against such powerful creatures? We shall be crushed like flies."

"Please do not underestimate yourself. With the gifts from us, you are quite evenly matched against your enemies."

"But can't we just stay here till we figure out a way back home?"

"The Leods cannot remain in Hærlicana for more than a day after their shadows are cleansed."

"It's just not fair on the part of the universe."

The chief of the Eorls looked at the children with gentle eyes. "It will be easier if you accept the prophecy will come true. Given it is past midnight, the five suns of Sceadu will fall in line exactly at noon on the day after tomorrow. That gives you two days and a few hours to thwart their plans."

Isabella twisted the end of her dress around her finger. "What if we hide until after that happens?" she asked, looking up.

"Your shadow will turn purple by six that evening, trapping you all in Sceadu forever. The only chance you have of returning to your world is if you emerge victorious."

"At least our world will be safe."

"The prophecy cannot be avoided. The five suns will fall in line again after a year. The only advantage you have now is a possibility where you may be able to save your world and return home."

"But why don't the Hefigans eliminate it by simply waiting until our shadows turn purple completely?" Ben asked.

"By now, they will be aware your shadows have been cleansed. So until your shadows turn purple completely, there is still a possibility of your escape or so they think. The Hefigans do not understand the ways of the universe, but that makes them even more dangerous."

"I still don't understand one thing though," Isabella said. "You mentioned we have a little over two days to foil their plans. But the Hefigans have specific directions in the prophecy. We don't even know where to start."

Emilio made a face. "It just isn't fair," he said. "Don't you think the universe is playing favourites here?"

Halig smoothed his robes. "The universe works in mysterious ways. You just need to have faith."

"So where do we go from here?" Will asked in a perplexed voice. The prophecy had complicated things beyond his comprehension.

"You have been deprived of sleep for far too long. We shall continue this discussion in the morning."

CHAPTER 21 – LOSIAN CHAMBER

"Why are these imbeciles taking so long?" King Mortuus thundered.

"The Færies and the Imps keep getting into fights, your highness," Manlice grunted. "We don't have enough Goblins to keep them under control."

The king plunged his sword into the coarse sand below. "Those despicable Children of Leod," he spat. "I had to send more Goblins after them since our soldiers got turned to stone at Mundbyrd's Rock. It was obviously those accursed Gargoyles."

"But couldn't your highness have put some of the other creatures after them?"

The king drew away the flap of the tent. "And risk weakening our position? No, it's better they dig here under our watch."

A Goblin soldier came running up. "The Ghouls have unearthed the chamber, your highness."

The king stepped out and cast a smouldering gaze at the necklace of torches throwing tall flames about a mile away. "Nothing can stop us now."

King Mortuus stood about two hundred feet below the level of the parched soil in the southern part of the Drysmian Desert. The Hefigans had been digging ceaselessly for the past two days at the site of the Temple of Fordon. And finally, the chamber had been found.

"This is it," he whispered, looking around the dimly lit cavity, circular in shape. "This is where our fortunes will turn."

The Chamber of Losian was carved out of a smooth grey stone and had four imposing pillars located at equal distances from each other along the periphery. Each pillar had a cavity in the shape of the human form and a hole in front.

The king strode over to the centre of the chamber, where a large sarcophagus, ornately carved out of black granite, sat silently upon a large slab of stone. "Fordon's Ashes," he said, moving around the sides. "They must be inside."

"It carries an inscription here," Manlice said, running the torch flames along its base. He read it out aloud:

"Part of it, but doesn't fit
Not one but more, shapes four
When you turn, turn them all
If you don't, the top will fall
Either leave with head held high
Or buried under forever lie."

The king bent down and peered at the sides of the sarcophagus. The black granite had been adorned with intricate carvings of geometric shapes interspersed with inlay work using Eorcanstans. "Here," he said, running his fingers gently over a protruding spherical shape that had the seal of Fordon carved on it. "This one has a groove that goes around it. We need to find three more. Call two of our most trusted guards down here immediately."

About half an hour later, the four of them were standing in front of the four spherical shapes, each on one side of the sarcophagus. They held them gently while gripping the left edge of each side for support. "Turn them to your right precisely on the count of three," the Goblin king whispered. "Any mistake and we shall all be buried alive."

The sweat poured down their necks, but none dared twitch a muscle. One false move and the Chamber of Losian would become their final resting place.

"One… two… three."

They all turned the shapes and stepped back.

Nothing happened for a few seconds. And then, the entire chamber started shaking, with loose pieces of rock and dirt falling from the ceiling. They gawked at each other, wild panic in their eyes, expecting the ceiling to cave in and flatten them to pulp.

But the rumbling stopped just as suddenly as it had started. And then, a deafening sound quaked through the underground chamber, cracking the sarcophagus into two halves. Each half slid outwards and crashed on the floor. When the dust had settled, they could see a plain metal urn sitting inside.

King Mortuus lifted it out. "All mine. The Goblins shall finally reign supreme."

"What about Blake, your highness?" Manlice asked.

"I think he has outlived his usefulness," he replied, an evil glint lighting up his eyes. "It's time we do away with him forever."

Their laughter echoed ominously through the chamber.

Chapter 22 – Startling Realization

The early morning rays had cast a warm spell over the quiet valley.

"I wish there was some way to counter the prophecy," Isabella said, turning over and facing the lake from their mountain quarters. "It's like playing a game where only one side is aware of the rules."

"Unfortunately, our shadows are not taking cognizance of the unfair conduct of the universe," Ben said, pushing his hand against the wall. The grey shape had once again started taking on purplish hues.

"I know." She clicked her tongue and let her head rest on her forearms.

"Is anything the matter?"

"Something's just not right. But I don't know what it is."

Emilio stood up and yawned. "Why don't we just forget these Hefigans for a bit?" he said, falling back on the bed again. "This place is like a great resort. I could really do with a few more hours of sleep."

"That does sound more tempting than breakfast," Will grinned.

"Did you have to say the magic word now?" Emilio groaned. He stretched his hands and yawned again. "I wonder what happened to Egesa. We were really lucky to run into him."

Ben nodded. "It was indeed an extremely fortuitous coincidence. While I don't mean to condone my error, I do keep wondering how we could have controlled the Goblin mounts even if we had been successful in reaching them."

"They were quite a restless bunch, weren't they?" Will said. He rested his head against the wall with a sigh. "But I do keep thinking about those Færy wings. I wonder how it would have felt to fly like a bird."

Ben reached for his bag. "It's nothing more than fiction, Will."

"You don't know that for sure," Will replied, scowling at his brother. "Anyway, let's just head out. It's almost time for breakfast."

Emilio raised an eyebrow at his younger cousin.

"Our father was a pilot," Ben said, staring at the retreating figure of his brother. "He died in a skiing accident six years ago. Ever since, Will's been obsessed with filling the void and that includes becoming a pilot. At some level, I can assure you he's aware of the truth. But I suppose it's just his way of staying connected with dad."

Isabella came over and gave him a hug. "I'm sure your dad would be very proud of both of you."

The children were soon enjoying a sumptuous breakfast with the Eorls upon the terrace.

"What will happen if the Hefigans succeed?" Isabella asked.

"The Hefigans, if they succeed, will enter your world through a portal in the form of spirits," Halig replied. "Although they were once part of humans, they have acquired a deadly potency over thousands of years. The moment they come into contact with the physical body, they will obliterate it completely. All the Leods will be wiped out in a matter of days if not hours."

The children could feel their skins crawl at the chief Eorl's words.

Isabella pushed back a few curls blowing in her face. "Was Lord Chisbury aware of this?"

"He heard exactly the same words you did yesterday."

"And… and yet, he wrote the book," she cried bitterly. "All this is happening because of that book."

"While there is a possibility Lord Chisbury was aware the book would play a role in fulfilling the prophecy, I think his intentions were to create a repository of information about Sceadu to prepare those journeying into this place. I can assure you of one thing. You would still be here regardless of the book."

"But why didn't he include the verse to return back?" Emilio asked, between mouthfuls.

Ben had the answer to that. "You forget the torn pages at the end."

"That's very interesting," Halig remarked. "The universe made use of the book, but ensured it could not be a tool for escape from Sceadu before the confrontation with the Hefigans."

Will, who hadn't said a word so far, suddenly squared his jaw. "I don't want to escape this place any more," he said, looking down and shaking his head. He straightened up and took a deep breath. "Yes, you heard me right. Why did Evan have to die? Why should our kind suffer? I will not leave this place until we bring the Hefigans to their knees. It's time we went head on against them."

The others were a little surprised but couldn't find fault with his little outburst. This wasn't just about them any more.

"We're with you, Will," Emilio said, as the others nodded in agreement.

A bolt of lightning struck the spherical stone atop the fountain, illuminating the lake with a shower of blue sparks. A deep voice echoed through the Hluttor mountains.

> *The Children of Lead, in united voice*
> *To oppose the Hefigans, they made a choice*
> *Acquire first the Sceptre of Attor*
> *Then journey off to Helofor*
> *Pierce the sceptre through Fordon's Eage*
> *Do it in time to release the rage*
> *The only way to win the war*
> *Evil beats evil, back in the jar."*

Halig was the first to speak. "This is a continuation of the prophecy to guide you towards defeating the Hefigans. It is the way of the universe. There has to be a balance."

"But why are we hearing it only now?" Isabella asked.

"The universe works on cause and consequence, as I have already explained. The creation of Sceadu was the cause of the original prophecy. But you only showed clear intent to battle the Hefigans a few minutes ago. It was thus the right time."

"I don't see any balance," Emilio said, pushing his hands on his hips. "These Hefigans have thousands of years to prepare. But we only get two days."

Halig had a twinkle in his eyes. "The original prophecy has been ingrained in the subconscious of the Hefigans ever since their manifestation. However, they have only known of a prophecy, but not the words. But I always knew they would find out. The universe would ensure that. And I was right. We have received word the Hefigans have uncovered the Temple of Fordon. It is where the portal to your world is located."

Isabella thought for a moment. "I do recall Egesa saying he had no idea what the actual prophecy was."

"I still don't get it," Will said. "How could the Hefigans have not known something so important?"

"The original prophecy was made at the exact instant ned spirits assumed physical form, seven days after the formation of Sceadu. It was stored in the white spherical stone here and in a grey spherical stone in an ancient temple near Hatheartia. However, the temple and the stone were both destroyed during the last war between the Dragons and the Nicors. The prophecy also lost significance in the petty battles that have plagued Sceadu, until four Children of Leod suddenly showed up."

Ben crossed one lanky leg over the other and arched his back forward. "So if the grey stone has been destroyed, would it be accurate to say we're the only ones with knowledge of this part of the prophecy?"

"Yes."

"So we essentially have information which can be used against the enemy but which they're unaware of. That, I would say, provides us with a distinct strategic advantage."

"Only if we know what it all means," Will said, turning to the Eorls.

"An important matter has come up," Halig said, beginning to float away. "Mildheort shall explain the new prophecy."

Mildheort bowed. "Pay close attention for great dangers lie ahead. If you recall, the original prophecy mentions four sceptres. The Imps, the Færies, the Goblins, and the Ghouls, each have one of these sceptres."

"So that's why they're all working together," Isabella said to herself. "It all makes sense now."

"However, there exist not four but five sceptres in Sceadu. The fifth sceptre, which none of the Hefigans are aware of, is called the Sceptre of Attor. It belongs to Draca, the king of the Dragons, and is part of his crown. But he doesn't know that. Your first task then is to get this sceptre."

"I have this sudden urge to puke," Emilio said.

It was exactly what the others were feeling as well. Meddling with the Dragons was the last thing they wanted to do.

"Once you have the Sceptre of Attor," Mildheort continued, "you will proceed to Helofor, the capital city of the ancient kingdom of Grymetiana. It was the first kingdom established by Fordon the Ieldran himself for the Hefigans. However, it now lies in ruins and has been part of Atolon, the kingdom of the Ghouls, for thousands of years. Helofor lies at the northernmost tip of Atolon. There, you must find the Shrine of Fordon and insert the sceptre in Fordon's Eage or eye. According to an ancient legend, Fordon had a third eye on his forehead which gave him incredible strength. I am aware of your encounter with the Gargoyles yesterday. The same legend also says that Byldu, the first king of the Gargoyles, thought he could turn Fordon to stone.

However, the moment he stood in front of Fordon, Byldu saw his own reflection in Fordon's third eye and turned to stone himself. Since then, the Gargoyles have been cursed to remain confined to their kingdom between the rivers."

"But if I remember correctly," Isabella said, pulling out the map, "Ablendon isn't completely surrounded by rivers."

"It is true. But the trees in the Gamol Forest give off a purple haze during the day. If they were to try and cross, they would see their reflection and turn to stone. And the Gargoyles cannot travel in the night as they turn blind."

"So what will happen after the sceptre pierces Fordon's eye?" Will asked.

"As you are already aware, the creatures in Sceadu represent negativities. The Dragons are manifestations of anger. The moment you pierce Fordon's eye, it will magnify the anger to many thousand times, which will annihilate the power of the other sceptres. Hence, evil will destroy evil, and all the Hefigans will be returned in the spirit form to the jar originally intended for them inside the Shrine of Fordon. This must be completed before noon, the day after tomorrow if you have to have any chance of escape."

"Why couldn't it have been the Pixies instead of the Dragons?" Emilio lamented. He stuffed his mouth and got up. "I suppose we should be on our way then. There's hardly any time left."

Halig came by. "The Hefigans will be after you the moment you leave Hærlicana. So take the time to reflect for you may not get the opportunity again."

"We've been so blind," Isabella muttered, pushing her head against the wall.

"You got a headache there, Bella?" Emilio asked.

"You will too when you hear what I have to say."

"It's too soon," Emilio groaned. "Can't you at least wait until the food gets digested?"

Will threw a mock punch at his cousin's stomach. "So what's the bad news?" he asked, turning to his other cousin.

"Mortuus and Blake are one and the same."

"That puny thing," Will laughed. "I could take him down with a few roundhouse kicks."

"Yeah, Bella," Emilio said. "I mean, Blake's human, just like us. How can he be the king of the Goblins? Any comments, Ben?"

Ben removed his spectacles and polished them for a bit. "It's a plausible hypothesis. I would certainly like to hear Isabella's reasoning before leaning either way."

"Just give me a minute to get my thoughts in order." Isabella paced the room a few times, drawing squiggly shapes in the air with her fingers. She finally nodded and continued. "Okay, here's the evidence. About four years ago, Blake travels to Sceadu. At the same time, Necrotus, then king of the Goblins, is killed by the Ghouls. Mortuus emerges as the king immediately after. We can definitely say Blake reached Sceadu before Necrotus was killed since Evan was already here before the battle began. Remember what Egesa told us about clawing a Leod's face. But we also know Blake travelled to Sceadu before Evan. So the timing's correct."

"I can't find any flaw with that," Ben said. "Proceed."

"Now think of this. Why would the Goblins take to Blake but have no hesitation in killing Evan? It doesn't make sense unless Blake is Mortuus."

Will tapped his feet on the ground. "I still don't buy it," he said with a quick shrug. "Perhaps Blake cut some deal with the Goblins. Or they could have killed Evan because he was with us. I mean, how could a human manage to remove Egesa from the throne of Atolon?"

"He could, because the Hefigans have no idea Mortuus is human. What other reason could he have to wear that scary mask? Do you remember Egesa telling us how he couldn't smell Mortuus? Blake must be using masking spray, something similar to what Ben used against the Fracods, just much more powerful."

"But what about the Goblin guards who surrounded us? They would know Mortuus is Blake."

Isabella sat down with a sigh. "No, they wouldn't. They would only know King Mortuus' orders to take Blake to the Mor Forest. And they would never dare question their king's orders."

"I have to confess you make a very strong case for your argument," Ben said. "There's one thing though that continues to elude my understanding. Why would he appear as Blake to us?"

"To gain our trust. They need all four of us in one piece. What if we had decided to run? He couldn't afford to have anything happen to us. And killing Evan wasn't just a random act. It was a calculated move to shock us. But here's the other thing. The Goblins were always prepared to drag us to Atelic in case we had resisted."

Emilio buried his head under a pillow. "What is wrong with this guy?"

"Your reasoning has been nothing short of brilliant," Ben nodded. "I would hope this knowledge enhances our position against the Hefigans."

Isabella drew in her breath. "It does, I suppose," she said, "but here's the scary part. The Hefigans are not working together. They're working for Mortuus. Do you remember what Halig told us earlier? The Hefigans did not know the original prophecy until a few days ago. I would assume they still don't."

"Wheels within wheels," Ben said in a quiet tone. "We're in quite the quagmire, aren't we?"

"Regular English, please," Emilio said, and received an instant nod of approval from Will.

"Blake is probably the only one who knows the original prophecy," Isabella replied. "And he has somehow convinced the Hefigans he is very powerful. The act of replacing Egesa would be part of this charade. Otherwise, why would staunch enemies be working as allies?"

"But how could he have known the prophecy?" Emilio asked.

"The book, Milo, the book."

"Drat, I keep forgetting that stupid book."

"In fact, I'm quite certain Blake was the one who tore the pages as well."

Will threw his hands in the air. "But why?"

"Something must have compelled him, just like it did me with all those nightmares."

Emilio sat up. "Do you suppose he's still kept the pages?"

"I know you're thinking about the way back. But what I'm more worried about right now is what other information is contained in those pages. For instance, does he know we can stay in Hærlicana for only a day after getting our shadows cleansed?"

"So essentially, we have to come up with a plan after factoring all the possible bits of information those torn pages could have fed him," Ben sighed. "That, unfortunately, is going to be a Herculean task."

"But... but if he knew the way back, why didn't he just return home?" Will asked. It seemed to be the most natural thing to do.

Isabella gave a mirthless laugh. "Somehow, I don't think he ever intended to. The Eorls were right about the order of the universe. We just can't escape the prophecy."

"But that doesn't mean we shouldn't try," Emilio said. "I have an idea. Why don't we use Will's telescope to locate those torn pages? If we could get to them... "

"And what if we don't?" Will asked. "What if we get caught again? It would mean the end of everything. No, we must go after the Sceptre of Attor."

Isabella stood up and faced them. "There's no point in trying to find a way around the original prophecy. It will only hamper our progress. But Milo's idea makes complete sense. If we do defeat the Hefigans, we would still need to know how to return home. So we must pursue the torn pages. At the same time, the only way to crush our enemies would be to fulfil the continuation of the prophecy. And I have the perfect plan to achieve this."

"But what of the information Blake may have gained through those torn pages?" Ben asked.

"My plan nullifies that to a certain extent as well. So would you all like to hear it?"

"You know we do," Will said, throwing a pillow at her.

"Okay then," Isabella grinned, skilfully dodging the pillow. "So here's the thing. I shall proceed to Hatheartia in pursuit of the Sceptre of Attor while the three of... "

But she was instantly drowned in a chorus of protests from Emilio and Will.

"If I'm not mistaken, a decision hasn't been taken yet," Ben said with furrowed brow. "Can we at least extend Isabella the courtesy of hearing her out without any interruptions?"

"We're talking about the Dragons here, Ben," Will shouted. "How can she even think of going to Hatheartia alone?"

Isabella shrugged. "Hatheartia is on the other side of Sceadu. And I'm the only one with the shoes."

"I still won't allow it," Emilio said. "I just won't. And... and Will's the leader. Even he agrees with me."

"Milo, I can understand your concern, but just hear me out. If we split up this way, not only do we significantly improve our chances against the Hefigans but we also severely damage theirs. They do need all four of us."

"It sounds great in theory, but there's no question of letting you go on your own. What... what if we try and negotiate with the Goblins?"

"The only thing they want is us."

"Then what if we come up with another plan? Ben, back me up on this."

Ben glanced at Will and then at Isabella. "While I can't find any fault in your thought process, I do wonder about the actual execution. The very first step requires getting past the Dragons."

Isabella turned away. "If I don't make it out alive, it still saves our world. And that's my silver lining. This is not just about the four of us any more."

Emilio punched and kicked at the wall. "It shouldn't have to be this way," he said, his eyes burning red with tears. "It's just not fair. Damn this universe."

CHAPTER 23 – HEFIGAN CONSPIRACY

"Why would anyone want to destroy their own world?" Will lamented.

Halig stroked his long white beard. "The Leods do have elements of the Firas. But this particular Leod seems to have received an inordinately high proportion of the negativities."

"If I recall correctly, you mentioned the Hefigans would assume their spirit forms when the portal opens," Ben said. "But how will this entire phenomenon affect Blake? Since he belongs to our species, won't he pay with his life?"

"The one who wields Fordon's Ashes cannot perish. His body will fall, but his spirit will be released, just like the Hefigans, if they succeed."

"And what about us?" Emilio asked.

"It would be best if you don't fail," Halig said, after a moment's pause.

"So what do you think of our plan?" Will interjected, before any unsavoury thoughts could take root in their minds.

"Once a decision is firmed, it is best not debated," Halig smiled, joining his palms together. "You are now ready to leave Hærlicana and fulfil your destiny."

"What about the Forhtian Forest? I hope we don't have to cross it again."

"I'm afraid you must. But this time, you shall fly over it." He chanted a few words and swept his hand towards the Fælsian Lake.

At first, nothing happened. And then, the placid water started bubbling, slowly at first and then with a tempestuous vigour until the entire lake was frothing at the surface. The waves parted and four beautiful horse-like creatures appeared from the lake, with thick white manes and lustrous tails swaying majestically. They had horns on their foreheads that glowed brilliantly in the waning sunshine. But their most striking feature was their wings, which opened up like beautiful hand fans and swayed gracefully to the rhythm of the wind.

The creatures descended upon the terrace in perfect harmony. "These are the Unicorns, the purest beings in the entire universe. Their aura will protect you from the forest. But they must return immediately since they die in the presence of evil."

The children mounted the Unicorns, almost in a daze, unable to shake off the spell cast by the magical creatures.

"On behalf of all of Hærlicana, I bid you goodbye. May you emerge triumphant against the forces of evil."

"Thanks for everything," Will said.

The children waved to the Eorls as the Unicorns spread their wings and took off into the skies.

The children were taken in by the sight of the stately white peaks surrounding the kingdom of the Eorls.

"Emilio, I have been meaning to tell you this for some time now," Ben said to his cousin, who was flying on his right. "As illogical as I still believe your behaviour was, I do appreciate your gesture back in the Gamol Forest."

Emilio grinned. "I believe my journey through the Modsefa wasn't as painful as your experience in the Forhtian Forest. There's your logic."

"I did miss out on that part, didn't I?" Ben smiled back. The wind suddenly changed direction and he had to shout. "I was curious to know about your experience in the river."

"Most of it's just a blur. The force of the current was so powerful, it just swept me away. But I do remember wondering if my blood would freeze since the water was icy cold. When I regained consciousness, I was lying next to the Fælsian Lake with Mildheort tending to me."

Ben adjusted the straps of his backpack. "I suppose you wouldn't have any inkling about how the three of us reached the northernmost tip of Hærlicana from the Forhtian Forest."

"About half an hour after I made it, the lake started frothing and the three of you floated to the surface. I almost went nuts until the Eorls told me everything was fine. I guess there's some magical link between the forest and the lake."

All of a sudden, the children found themselves staring at a dark fog hovering above the Forhtian Forest, with black vapours coiling through the air like venomous serpents. But the moment the Unicorns reached the fumes, they instantly drew away, like ants threatened by fire.

"There's Mundbyrd's Rock," Isabella said, pointing through the fading mist a few minutes later. The familiarity of the vast expanse brought back a deluge of memories, all painful ones.

The Unicorns soon began their descent. The children were, however, still clutching to the hope that Sceadu would somehow turn out to be just a bad dream. But the sight of the fragments that were once Goblins, lying undisturbed in the shadow of the rock, brought them back to reality. The Unicorns dropped them at the very edge of the Forhtian Forest and soared back into the skies.

For a few minutes, the children simply stood under the fading rays of the sun. The air around was crisp, but it also carried the unmistakable stench of death. A lethargic nausea overcame them at the thought of what lay ahead.

Isabella shuffled her feet. "I had better be on my way."

"There's still time to change your mind," Emilio pleaded.

"Don't worry, Milo. Anyway, I'm just dying to try out my gift." Isabella brought out the tiny white shoes. Only a few days ago, she had been ruing her inability to run. She closed her eyes and thought hard. Moments later, the shoes had grown to her size. She slipped them on and gave them all a quick round of tight hugs.

"Go kick some Dragon ass," Emilio said, beginning to wave, but Isabella had already disappeared from view.

Ben waved the dust away. "That was unreal."

"If we make it back, Bella should definitely try out for the Olympics," Will said. He rubbed his eyes and faced them. "Anyway, it's time we started on our own plans. Any ideas about how we proceed?"

Ben eased out of his backpack and slowly massaged his shoulders. "Isn't it ironic? We now willingly seek a way back into Atelic, the place from where we literally escaped by a whisker only a day ago."

"So it's going to be back through the Gamol Forest, I suppose."

Emilio kicked at a broken Goblin head, staring listlessly at him. "But Blake knows about our plans. He'll have sent hordes of Hefigan soldiers after us."

"I've got an idea. Why don't you use the marble, Ben?"

Ben felt a surge of anticipation coursing through him. He held the marble in his palm and closed his eyes. Soon, it started glowing. "That was surreal," he replied, moments later. "There was no internal discussion, just a download, as if a revelation from the universe."

"So what route do we take?"

"The answer is simple," Ben said, scanning the Hefig Mountains ahead. "We should avoid crossing into the Gamol Forest across the Modsefa. It is something the Hefigans will be expecting. Instead, we should walk as much towards the Mælan as possible and then cross over. The Hefigans cannot deploy their troops along the entire forest border. While this is the safest strategy, there will be a delay, since Fyren lies to the south and east."

"That makes sense," Will nodded.

"And the Gargoyles?" Emilio asked, unable to take his eyes off the stone graveyard.

Will peered at the sky. "It doesn't look like they're going to be stepping out this late. Let's move."

The evening wore on, and Sceadu's five suns began their descent.

"The tunnel would have been a great option," Emilio said, avoiding a sharp piece broken from the statue of a Ghoul warrior.

"It would have ensured safe passage for some time," Ben agreed. "However, since Isabella has taken the compass, we can't risk our sense of direction inside that labyrinth."

Will stopped. The corner of his eye had caught a shadow slinking alongside. "Blast those Gargoyles," he cursed silently, pushing down the heads of his brother and cousin and shoving them ahead. "Whatever happens, don't look into their eyes."

The boys dashed through the maze of statues, avoiding the rubble in their paths as best as they could. The Gargoyle hunting ground, unfortunately, was spread over miles and miles. And with no obstructions, the predators could simply swoop down upon their kill. Five minutes later, the boys had already started cramping. But the Gargoyles were in no hurry. They knew their prey would soon tire, well before the cloak of darkness fell upon the land.

"Gargoyles can't look at their own reflections, right?" Emilio shouted.

Will jumped over the fallen statue of a Nieten. "Yes," he hollered back. "But I don't see any water around here."

"When I say stop, just fall on your stomachs and shut your eyes." Emilio slipped his hand inside his pocket. "Just trust me on this one."

"Anything you say," Ben coughed. A few more minutes and he would collapse anyway.

"Stop," Emilio's voice boomed.

Ben and Will dived to the ground and buried their faces in the grass. Seconds later, a series of deafening crashes echoed through the stillness. When they opened their eyes, they saw their cousin kneeling over them, a huge shield covering them all completely. The Gargoyles had seen their reflections in the shield.

Will rested his head on his forearms, taking short breaths. "That was some really quick thinking," he said, glancing back at the broken pieces. "But it was high time these guys got a dose of their own medicine."

"I felt like Fordon turning that evil Byldu to stone," Emilio said, flushed with excitement. He rolled over and lay next to them.

They continued to remain under the shield until the very last of the suns' rays had withdrawn from the area.

"Isabella would have taken the same route," Emilio said, going a little pale.

Will pulled out his telescope and put it to his eye. "There's no need for panic. I see her by the banks of a river."

"Our plan, sound as it is on paper, has a fundamental flaw," Ben said, sitting down upon the standing half of a Goblin's statue. "We haven't yet confirmed the existence of the torn pages, something which should have happened prior to Isabella's departure. And even if they do exist, we have assumed they're in Atelic, something which may not be true at all."

Will tightened his grip on the telescope. What if Blake had already destroyed the pages? He slowly raised it to his eye once again. "They're there," he nodded. "I can see them inside a golden box, high up in a stone fortress in Atelic. It has to be Mortuus' palace."

"It would also be prudent to know the exact whereabouts of Blake."

"Our friend's not in Atelic. I can see a lot of sand around."

"It's to be expected. He's obviously busy making preparations in the Drysmian Desert at the site of the Temple of Fordon."

"Then we must reach Atelic as soon as possible,"

Emilio stomped upon what seemed to be the petrified armour of an Imp. "I just thought of something. It took us long enough to reach this place from Atelic on a Broga's back. How long do you suppose it will take on foot?"

Will swept his hand and started walking towards the Mælan. "There's no point in standing here and wasting time in useless calculations."

"And what if we run into those Nietens again?"

"If the universe wants us for the prophecy, it had better take care of that."

An hour later, the boys were plodding through the Hefig Mountains. Finally, Emilio plopped upon the grass. "I could swear I saw that very same peak half an hour ago. We have to be moving in circles. And did I mention I am famished?"

Ben pried out a few fruits and tossed them to him. But the spark of enthusiasm that had laced his spirit after their unexpected victory over the Gargoyles had also greatly diminished by now. "I could do with a break as well," he said, easing out of his backpack and stretching his limbs.

Will stared at the never-ending rows of formidable peaks, shining like a bright crescent under the strong moonshine. Part of him still wanted to keep going, but it all seemed so futile. They would never reach Atelic before their shadows turned. He wondered what shade of purple had set in since their departure from Hærlicana. But it was too dark to make out under the gloom of the mountains.

"By the way," Emilio said, "I was wondering why we encountered those Gargoyles since the route was suggested by the marble."

Ben slid to the ground next to him. "The thought did occur to me as well," he sighed. "But I think it's got to do with how you frame the question. The answer I received seems to be specific to my query about the Goblins. I will need to use it more to understand the workings."

"That does make sense."

Soon, all three were lying upon the soft grass, lost in the sight of Sceadu's two moons. They remained absolutely still, with the cool wind caressing their fatigued bodies. Their eyelids began to descend, until dark silhouettes suddenly sprang upon them, jolting them out of their slumber.

The Griffins dropped the boys near a crevice in the city wall, almost hidden behind a crop of unruly weeds.

"That was a massive stroke of luck," Will said.

Ben peeped into the crack, trying to figure out the best way to get through. "While I basically agree with your words, anything that brings us to this place can't be seen as a fortuitous occurrence."

"Then let's get the pages and get out of here."

Ben contorted his body and squeezed through into the narrow space. "If only it would be that simple," he mumbled.

After a little struggle, they were standing within the city walls, not far from the towering edifices that formed the stone jungle that was Atelic. A thin fog circled the city, but the touch of evil was palpable. And somewhere in the midst of all the gloom was their former prison.

"This place really gives me the creeps," Emilio whispered, giving his arms a vigorous rub.

His cousins nodded. There was no more thought. It was a raw fear, crawling under their skins.

"What's the time?" Will asked.

"Close to midnight," Emilio replied.

Ben clenched his stomach muscles, trying to strangle the growing fear. "Do you recognize any of these structures?"

"I don't think so," Will said, straining his eyes hard. "They just seem to merge into one another. What the telescope showed me was a massive fortress."

"I do apologize," Ben said. "I find my concentration greatly diminished in this place. As imposing as these structures are, the seat of Goblin power would certainly stand out. I propose we walk along the periphery of the city and try to identify the fortress."

An hour later, they had spotted the fortress, unmistakable in its grandeur and unmatched in its brutality. They could see tall towers rising in the middle, covered with sinister carvings. The skies were suddenly illuminated by a thunderous bolt of lightning, casting an interrupted blue glow upon the structure.

"There," Will cried, pointing at the tallest tower that rose like a needle right through the centre and disappeared into the thick clouds. "I'm absolutely sure it's that one."

"So what are we waiting for?" Emilio asked.

"In case you haven't noticed," Ben pointed out, "a solid wall that looks quite impenetrable stands between us."

Will crept towards the wall, beckoning the others to follow. "Perfect," he said, tugging at the vines that ran over. "These will easily take our weight."

"This wall must rise to about eighty feet in height. And can I also bring to your attention those unsavoury spikes on top?"

Will ran his damp palms down the wall. "I'm as scared as you are. But the only reason we're here is to get those torn pages."

"I… I can't do it, Will. I just can't."

"I'm not leaving you behind."

Emilio looked his cousin squarely in the eye. "Ben, listen to me. Isabella may well be on her way to Helofor as we speak. If we don't get those pages, we remain stuck here forever. Besides, what can be a better time than now? Blake's away, and the Goblins will never expect us to return to Atelic, let alone raid their king's palace."

Ben pushed his head back and took a good look at the wall. It wasn't as if Emilio's words had enlightened him. He had always been aware of the facts. Yet, no amount of rationalization was going to quell the fear that had taken over. He finally ground his teeth hard and clasped one of the vines.

"Don't worry, Ben," Will said. "It's like climbing a ladder. Just make sure you don't look down."

Ben was about to heave himself up when he stopped. "One has to wonder whether it can really be this straightforward to get inside the Goblin king's fortress. It has all the makings of an elaborate trap."

"I would have agreed with you had it not been for one thing," Emilio replied. "The Hefigans are preparing to invade our world. Their focus lies on the Temple of Fordon where the portal to our world is located. So the Goblins will either be digging in the Drysmian Desert or searching for us in the Gamol Forest. Why would they even think we would return to Atelic?"

Ben found a footing and hoisted himself reluctantly after his brother and cousin. But amidst the obvious fear, he could also identify a growing uneasiness about the entire situation.

The climb was painfully slow, hampered by the rough, itchy creepers. The boys, however, somehow inched their way to the top. Despite Will's warning, Ben had made the mistake of looking down half way through. The sight had almost sent him spiralling towards the ground.

"Careful," Emilio said. The fog had descended, and the boys found themselves barely able to spot the tips of the spikes that ran along the top.

"I urge you both once again to reconsider this," Ben pleaded.

"I have an idea," Emilio said. "Why don't you check the crystal marble?"

Ben pulled it out of his pocket once again. "We should descend," he replied.

"Perfect," Will said, his voice betraying his relief. "Let's get those pages."

Ben arched forward. The entire site appeared abandoned, punctuated with a barren silence. And yet, he couldn't help but feel there were eyes on them, that everything was being orchestrated to lure them into a trap. But the marble had said otherwise. "Here goes nothing," he said, crawling to the edge and grabbing the creeper his cousin had pulled and thrown across the other side.

"Don't worry," Will grinned. "We'll be in and out before the Goblins know it."

They were soon standing in the shadows of the ominous edifice that held the key to their escape. But they had hardly brushed off the leaves when a wave of Goblins poured out and surrounded them.

Ben turned skywards. "We kept looking at only one side of the equation," he groaned. "It was ultimately the pages that did us in, not what they contained. Blake always knew we would pursue them. We sorely underestimated our foe."

CHAPTER 24 – OVERCOMING ANGER

Isabella reached the banks of the Mælan at about the same time the boys had taken refuge under Emilio's shield. The clear water shimmered under the dying rays of the sun. She sat among the long grasses, lost in their gentle waves rolling along to the rhythm of the blithe wind, a stark contrast to the turmoil brewing within Sceadu. Isabella slowly shook her head. What if all this had been a mistake? What if she couldn't get the sceptre? She suddenly didn't feel so brave. If only Emilio or Will had been by her side.

"Draca," she said out aloud, the name Mildheort had mentioned. It had a nasty ring to it. Isabella turned her gaze to the stretch of the sharp brown slopes she had left behind. Would the Dragons be as large as the peaks, she wondered. She fell back and pulled the curls out of her face. So what did she know about these creatures? They were personifications of anger. But that seemed to be about it. And that was why it also made so much sense to just stay away from them.

Isabella bit her lip hard. It wasn't as if she had had a choice. The fate of her world rested upon her shoulders. But what could she do? There was no question of any kind of physical engagement with the Dragons. She could use her wit, of course. But would that even work against an irrational creature, probably inclined to responding with explosive bursts of fire? And although speed was on her side, it only meant her exit strategy was in place.

After coaxing her brain for another hour, Isabella's mental faculties finally succumbed to a splitting headache. She dug her fingers into her temple and rolled over. Unfortunately though, sleep wasn't easily forthcoming either. She kept tossing and turning, trying to shut out all the chatter about prophecies and battles and Dragons. But gradually, her mind gave way to physical exhaustion, and she settled into a state of reluctant slumber.

Isabella's eyes twitched and snapped open at the blurred vision of the overhead silhouettes, coming together like the Dragon she had just dreamt about. She turned over onto her forearms, trying hard to breathe. Only a nightmare, she told herself repeatedly, her face awash with perspiration. The stinging sensation in her chest dulled after a while, but the burden of her mission returned to plague her mind. It was still night, but she knew there would be no more sleep. She finally decided to embark upon the second leg of her journey.

Isabella drilled her way through the parched sand across the northern part of the Drysmian Desert. The first signs of Hatheartia appeared almost two hours later, when the skies, a dark blue until then, abruptly rolled into shades of deep orange. It wasn't long after she found herself dwarfed by large rock formations, at attention like sentries around a gigantic brown mound speckled with yellow which rose many miles above the treacherous terrain. She had finally reached the kingdom of the Dragons.

Isabella stood behind a tall rock column, looking intently at the faint outlines inside one of the cavities, rising and falling rhythmically. There were hundreds of such cavities covering the mound, humming with low growling sounds. Hatheartia was asleep, smug in its aura of invincibility. But could it really be this simple, she wondered. There was only one way to find out. She closed her eyes tightly and said a quick prayer.

Isabella crept up to the mouth of the closest cavity. She clutched the sides and pressed her back against the wall. The inside was teeming with Dragons. But these were nothing like the one she had dreamt of. They were at least twenty times the size of the Fracods, with mighty wings that had sharp spines running on the insides. Long, pointed spikes rose from their heads, going all the way down their serpentine bodies and ending with vicious barbs on their tails.

Isabella held her breath and stepped into the shadows, squeezing past all the claws and fangs and spines protruding along the periphery. She had almost reached the opening inside when a stray tail came swishing right at her. She jumped backwards, barely missing the jagged barbs by a whisker. But there wasn't any time to pacify her throbbing heart. The Dragons had already begun to stir. She knew she had to find Draca's chamber soon.

Isabella found the Dragon king sprawled under a large pile of gold artefacts inside the topmost cavity. She moved past the other Dragons and reached his belly, covered with reddish golden scales which shone like fiery embers. The Sceptre of Attor was fixed on the front of his crown. But it sat upon his humongous head, almost fifteen feet above the ground. Isabella trod lightly up the gold until she was perched at the level of the sceptre. She slowly leaned forward, twitching her fingers as far ahead as her balance would allow. But it remained beyond her reach.

Isabella was about to hoist herself upon the crown when Draca let out a grunt, blowing wisps of smoke into the air. She scampered down into a dark corner behind the pile in a flash and remained motionless, listening. But the Dragon king had begun to move. Isabella clenched her fists and jammed them against her cheeks. The Sceptre of Attor had been within her grasp. Almost. She felt like beating someone with one of the goblets lying at her feet.

It was then that inspiration struck her. A few days ago, a similar instant of madness had consumed her. There was no other reason for her being in Sceadu. Her mind had been so clouded with rage it had compelled her to act against reason. And therein lay the solution to her dilemma. She would have to harness the power of anger, but not her own. Her eyes fell upon a gold blade, shining with a brutal intensity even inside the shadows.

Isabella scurried out and thrust the sword into a particularly fleshy part of the Dragon king's leg, twisting it hard before returning to her hiding place within seconds. A cry of anguish ripped through the chamber, followed by a deafening roar which thundered across Hatheartia. Draca, devoured by blinding anger, pounced upon the closest Dragon, slashing into his thick scales with his claws. In a matter of minutes, the entire chamber had turned into a small battlefield.

Isabella crouched petrified, watching the flames light up the chamber in violent bursts. The Dragons pounded with their bellies. They gored with their spikes. And they tore with their fangs. But she couldn't leave just yet. And then it happened. One of the Dragons swung his wing straight at the king's face, knocking off the crown. It flew through the air and landed with a thunderous crash just a few feet from her. The Sceptre of Attor splintered out and rolled towards her.

The ancient city of Helofor slowly unfolded before Isabella's eyes, nestled in a lush green valley suspended in mist. Although in ruins, the city still exuded a mystical charm, heightened by the exotic vegetation that had taken over. In the far distance, the frothing waves crashed violently onto the northern shores of Atolon. She removed her shoes and walked to the edge of the cliff, stirred by the picturesque tranquillity against the backdrop of the angry waves.

For a long time, Isabella remained still, savouring the cold wind coming at her in delightfully unpredictable bursts. But the weight in her right hand served as a grim reminder of the task she had yet to accomplish. She raised the Sceptre of Attor in front of her eyes, wondering how long it would take her to find the Shrine of Fordon.

The crimson stone which sat atop the carved Dragon's head gleamed like freshly spilled blood against the thin white mist.

Isabella clicked her tongue. Why had she just not asked Will to check on the location of the shrine earlier? She turned around with a sigh, but bigger problems awaited her. A troop of Ghouls had moved in stealthily and formed a barricade. She thought of the shoes. But alas, they were not on her feet. The only other option was a thousand feet plunge into the cold ruins of Helofor. She was trapped.

CHAPTER 25 – DASHED HOPES

"Don't draw blood!" the Goblin general shouted.

"Sorry, Ben," Will mumbled, trying to keep his chin from rubbing against the tip of the sword. "But we had to do what we did."

Ben twisted his eyes sideways. "It's not your fault. I checked with the marble as well. Could the problem have been in our execution?"

The general walked over and pushed the sword away from under Will's neck. "Did you really think you could just climb into Awestan?" he said, punching him in the ribs. "Those creepers had been disarmed for you. Otherwise, they would have eaten you alive."

Will doubled over. "What are you going to do with us?" he said coughing.

The general yanked his hair hard. "If it hadn't been for the king's direct orders, I would have separated your limbs from your body by now. Tie them up."

The Goblin soldiers pulled their arms back and bound them tightly. The ropes cut into their wrists, but the boys simply ground their teeth and stared ahead.

Ben tilted his head at Emilio. "Whichever way the prophecy plays out, it doesn't look like we're ever leaving Sceadu."

The general hauled them up the stone stairs of the fortress with the soldiers in tow. They had soon reached the roof of one of the towers where they were treated to the familiar sight of the Heorots.

"Were you expecting royal treatment again?" the general mocked, pushing the children roughly. "To the Temple of Fordon."

Ben twisted in his seat, trying to divert his mind from the ropes eating away into his chest. The vast expanse of the Mor Forest below did not offer any comfort either, constantly reminding him of the brutal killing of their friend just days before. But there was something important he had to tend to. And that was to somehow inform Isabella about their capture. There was only one way, a long shot, but worth the effort. The problem was that the effort involved theatrics, a field he was utterly ignorant about.

A few hours later, Ben spotted the Mælan, meandering around the edge of the forest under the familiar slopes of the Aglæca Mountains. That was his cue. He immediately began making moaning sounds and swaying in his seat, trying to emulate the actor from a stray episode of a television soap opera he had been forced to sit through by his mother. The Goblin behind had dozed off, but got up with a start after Ben raised the volume. "Stop making noises," he growled. "What's wrong?"

"Feeling… faint… water," Ben gasped, swaying dangerously on one side. He raised his head for a brief instant and fell forward in his seat, his torso swinging lifelessly in the air.

The Goblin panicked. The instructions had been clear. The Children of Leod were to be brought to the Temple of Fordon safely under any circumstances. The consequences of failing to do so would be severe. He frantically signalled to the general, pointing to Ben's slumped body.

Emilio and Will were jolted out of their disturbed slumber with the sudden descent of the Heorots. Will's gaze drifted to his brother. "Ben," he shouted at the sight of his brother lying unconscious in his seat. "What's happened to him?"

The Goblin general clipped him hard across the side of his neck. "Quiet, you fool. He's just fainted."

The Heorots had soon landed by the Mælan. The Goblin soldiers pulled Ben onto the riverbank and brought out a flask. They poured the water on his face and waited. Emilio and Will remained bound to their seats, throwing anxious glances at him as well.

After the slightest delay, Ben stirred a little, trying to remember the scene from the soap opera. He fluttered his eyes, showing as much white as he could muster. But there was only one thing he wanted. To somehow reach the Mælan. "Water… need water," he croaked, trying to make his throat sound parched and collapsed again.

"Take him to the river," the Goblin general instructed, glaring at Ben with disdain. If only the Children of Leod hadn't been so precious, he would have sealed their fate long ago. How humiliating that he, a great general, had been charged with escorting these scum. But he dared not disobey the direct orders of his king. "And don't untie his hands."

Ben plodded towards the Mælan, putting each foot forward limply and resting all his weight upon the shoulders of his captors. He was thoroughly enjoying his performance. But his eyes were fixated upon the river. Just a few steps more. And now. Ben collapsed in their arms, jerking his head towards the water. But the Goblin soldiers held him back firmly. One of them scooped up some water in his palms and held it to his mouth. Ben gulped it down with loud slurps, waiting. The moment the soldiers dropped their guard, he broke loose and plunged his face into the cold waters of the Mælan.

The soldiers dragged him out, but Ben had accomplished his purpose. Now all he could do was hope Isabella was somewhere near the whispering river.

The boys were dragged to the feet of King Mortuus, their hands and feet tied firmly behind their backs. "Grovelling won't do you any good now," he sneered, waving the Goblin soldiers away. His eyes hardened. "I offered you my hand of friendship. But you chose to ally with Egesa instead."

Ben twisted his body until his eyes faced the hideous enchanted, golden mask. "You surely can't fault us for that. After all, your hand, in the guise of friendship, would have still dragged us to our end."

The mask came closer. "You should be honoured to die for the great Mortuus, king of the Goblins."

"We know you're that loser who disappeared from our town four years ago," Emilio spat, struggling with the ropes.

Blake clapped in mock admiration. "And I know you know, chubby," he smirked, tapping him hard on the head. "You see, I didn't underestimate your intelligence. Such a pity, you did mine."

Emilio shrugged his head away.

Blake watched his subdued foes in amusement. "Why else would I set the trap at Awestan? I did send soldiers to the Gamol Forest, but I had this strong hunch the universe would deliver you at my fortress."

Ben coughed gently. "I suppose it wouldn't be too rude on my part to direct your attention to one tiny detail. If my memory serves me correctly, the prophecy mentions four children. But even with my spectacles at an awkward angle, I see only three here."

Blake glared at him. And then, the corners of his mouth slowly turned upwards, and he burst out laughing. "Did I forget to mention your sister's been captured as well?"

"You… you're a filthy liar," Will screamed. "Don't listen to him. He's just trying to mess with our heads." But the colour had drained from all their faces.

"Now why would I do that?" Blake teased. He brought out his sword and stabbed it into the sand beside Will's head. "I do want to crush your spirit though. She was trapped by the Ghouls in northern Atolon. And the looks on your faces say it all. It was a brilliant strategy,

I must admit. The three of you go after the pages, and even if you get captured, I still fall short. I do wonder how she, in fact, all of you, covered the distance you did."

"You shall never know," Emilio shouted.

"Sarcasm, you idiot. You forget my shadow was grey once. And yes, I have hitched a ride on a Griffin as well."

The boys slumped into the sand. What little hope they had harboured had been decimated. The enemy had defeated them comprehensively.

"Almost seven now," Blake continued. "Your sister should be reaching here in another five hours. And I have built a special cage just for her."

"You worthless piece of garbage," Will shouted, wrenching his arms again and again. "If you even so much as… "

Blake spread his palm over Will's face and slammed his face down. "Hush," he whispered, massaging the bulging veins on his neck. "I will need every ounce of your energy tomorrow."

"What if we reveal your identity to the other leaders?" Emilio said, looking at him defiantly.

Blake smiled back. "And what if I have your tongues cut out? I don't really need them."

The boys could feel their hair stand up, even in the blistering heat of the Drysmian Desert.

Blake put his hands around them and pulled them all closer. "Do you know where the other leaders are right now? Six feet under."

"You're nothing more than a cold-blooded murderer," Emilio said.

"Paying me compliments won't make things any easier." Blake got up and walked over to his throne. "All I needed was their sceptres. The fools thought they could rule alongside me, the great King Mortuus. That silly Færy queen really made me laugh. She wanted the diamonds in our world. The witch had no clue we would be turned into spirits."

"You know about that?" Will asked in surprise.

"It was all in the pages, you fool. That's why I was never really worried even when you reached the Eorls. The universe made sure you fell into my hands. Nothing can stop me now from becoming the supreme lord of the Hefigans."

"But if you knew we couldn't escape, why didn't you just wait until our shadows turned purple completely?"

"Do you see where you lie right now? So why would I even think of postponing my triumph by a year?"

Ben licked his upper lip slowly. Blake had thought of everything. It was still hard to believe that one of their own was behind the conspiracy. But he couldn't help but admire the planning. Their captor had outwitted them all. The only question that remained was why. "If you could humour a last wish, I'm very curious to know why."

"You'd like to know that, wouldn't you?" Blake said, taking a few sips out of the goblet. When he spoke again, it was almost in a whisper. "A deadbeat drunkard for a father. A mother who couldn't stand up to him. Surrounded by bullies. Do you know how that feels? To be punched every day? To be labelled as trailer trash? Do you? But of course, you don't. Why couldn't they just let me be? Now, they'll all pay for their sins.

"It does sound cruel, but don't you think your response is a bit extreme?"

Blake stared back with cold eyes. "They're getting exactly what they deserve," he said, through gritted teeth. "I had no hope before I came here. But after this, I will return triumphantly to our world."

Ben shook his head. "So it's the most common theme in history?" he sighed. "The quest for power."

"And revenge with a dash of immortality," Blake added, a maniacal look clouding his mask. He continued in a softer tone. "It was four years ago when the book found me. The moment I touched it, I could feel a connection, not with the book but with something greater. As if our destinies were intertwined together. Although I felt afraid, my fear was soon consumed by promises of untold power. It took almost five days, but I could resist it no more. I knew what I had to do. And I knew the universe would take care of the rest."

"Would it be correct to assume the book also instructed you to tear the last few pages?"

Blake spun around. "How dare you even suggest such a thing? But then, a feeble brain such as yours would do just that. So let me elucidate. I knew it would be me against the four Children of Leod. And if the book could lead me, I had a feeling it would do the same for you. So I selectively tore the pages that would aid you in any way and let the universe do the rest. A masterstroke, wouldn't you say?"

"I have to admit it was. This one simple act turned the entire game in your favour. But how did you manage the transition from a Leod to Mortuus, king of the Goblins?"

"It was a case of opportunity meeting decisive action. The verse transported me to the Drysmian Desert where I wandered for almost a day without any food or water. I could see my shadow turning purple slowly, but I always knew I could travel back at a moment's notice before it completely turned. And I almost did. But then, things suddenly started falling into place. I came across a stone structure which the carvings told me was the Temple of Fordon. The foolish Hefigan leaders thought I had used powerful magic to unearth it. And then, I met a Griffin. I told it to take me to the Mor Forest, which I figured would be the safest place to be in. As it so happened, I found myself in the middle of the battle between the Goblins and the Ghouls. I barely made it to a cave as Egesa battled Necrotus, my predecessor. They fought for hours, but it was Egesa who finally emerged victorious. However, here's a little secret. It wasn't he who killed Necrotus although that's what the Ghouls have always liked to believe. Egesa did grievously injure him and leave him for dead. But it was my hand that drove the sword through his heart."

The boys could feel a sickening feeling rising from the pit of their stomachs. Blake had been only slightly older than Will when he had committed the heinous act.

"I felt liberated." Blake threw the goblet at the tent wall. "That was the moment I knew I would only return to our world as its master."

"But how did you become king?" Will asked.

"With a little help from a Goblin named Manlice. He was the only one who knew everything about me. When Necrotus fell, Manlice was hiding nearby. As Egesa rushed to join the battle, we were left with the almost lifeless body of my predecessor. And we understood each other perfectly. He handed me a Ghoul sword lying nearby, and I did the rest. Manlice had been humiliated by Necrotus a few weeks before and had taken refuge in the Mor Forest. So he had his revenge, and I got the throne. With the Goblins left without a leader, it was actually quite easy."

Ben tightened his wrists to ease the ropes. "I couldn't help but notice you referred to Manlice in the past tense."

"I'm glad you did," Blake replied, a wicked glint lighting up his eyes. "Manlice was playing a game with me, staying in the shadows until it was time for the final move. He wanted to be the one holding Fordon's Ashes. And so he had to go. But I did make it quick. After all, I did owe him."

"You're inhuman," Emilio said, his lips trembling.

"I quite agree with you on that one," Blake beamed. "I must say you have a way with words. A pity you won't be alive to sing the praises of King Mortuus."

"Why did you kill Evan?" Will asked. "He had nothing to do with the prophecy."

Blake's mouth fell into a straight line. "The unknown always poses a threat," he said quietly. "I couldn't figure out why he was here. So the best option was to eliminate him. I would have done so much earlier had he not concealed himself so well. But I did make a mistake with you all. I should have taken you prisoners the old-fashioned way."

"But have you thought about the consequences? Your act will kill billions of innocent people."

"Is that the best you can do?" Blake snapped. He rested his head back and exhaled. "So naive, all of you. The universe has no time for emotional garbage. It's all about cause and consequence. And know this. The four of you are responsible for the fate your world shall suffer. I am but a tool to restore the balance."

The boys closed their weary eyes. There was nothing left to be said.

But Blake wasn't done yet. "By the way, a friend of yours is keen on meeting you," he said, parting the tent curtains and gesturing. He turned back and remarked, "He was the one who exposed Manlice's treachery."

"So we meet again," a harsh voice came from outside. It was their old friend turned foe, Beodan.

"No surprise there," Emilio smirked. "He's just the type who would betray his own. You both make a fine pair."

"I stand at the threshold of victory. Do you really think your empty words make any difference? But enough of this mindless chatter. Throw them in the cage. And tie them up well."

Beodan's fingers twitched. "With pleasure, your lordship."

"As for you all," Blake continued, patting their cheeks. "Don't try anything funny. I wasn't joking about cutting off your tongues."

The boys were bound and gagged and imprisoned inside an iron cage, suspended about fifty feet in the air from one of the few trees in the Drysmian Desert. They lay helplessly on the floor of the cage, communicating as best they could with their eyes and the occasional grunt.

With time, Emilio and Will both resigned themselves to their impending end. However, Ben's mind had thrown up another possibility. There did not appear to be any doubt about Isabella's capture; otherwise, Blake would never have been so confident. But she had been caught in Atolon. So it was logical to assume she had succeeded in getting the Sceptre of Attor.

But before his thought process could continue any further, the night was interrupted by the arrival of a platoon of Ghouls upon Brogas. The boys twisted their bodies and turned their eyes downwards. They could see some Ghoul soldiers leading Isabella towards Blake's tent. They tried catching her eye, but the darkness made it impossible.

Just then, the clouds parted and the moonshine fell upon Isabella's face. For the briefest of moments, their eyes met. In that instant, Ben finally accepted all was lost.

CHAPTER 26 – TRICKED AGAIN

When the boys awoke, the entire place was overcast with heavy clouds. They had spent the night drifting in and out of slumber, between dreams of despair and the harsh reality of the cold cage. To add to their woes, the skies had opened up in the early hours, giving way to torrential rain, and drenching them to the bone.

When they turned their gaze, they could see the Hefigans bobbing amongst the thousands of tents, eagerly awaiting the fulfilment of their destiny. The boys couldn't help but wonder how their end would come. That seemed to be certain now. But even the act of acceptance wasn't enough to quell the fear rising in their shivering bodies.

"Bring them down," Blake's voice boomed. The cage landed with a gentle thud on the damp sand. The gold mask approached the metal bars and whispered, "It hasn't rained here in over a century. And yet, the clouds opened up today in praise of King Mortuus. A sign of things to come."

The boys remained subdued.

"Are we feeling a little down today?" Blake asked, mocking his fallen foes. He clapped his hands. "Prepare them for the ritual. Make them worthy of King Mortuus."

The boys could feel their bones crackle when they straightened their limbs. But the moment his mouth was freed, Will spluttered, "Where's Isabella? You'd better not have harmed her."

Blake spun around. "Are you insane? Why do you think your tongues are still in place? I plan to use every drop of your blood to do my bidding."

"If only I could… "

"But you can't," Blake said, grabbing Will's jaw. "Because you're nothing. Just know this. If you jeopardize my plans in any way, I have your sister. You already know what I do to my enemies. The less said the better."

The boys left without a word. Their resolve had been completely shattered. All they wanted now was a quick end to the torment.

The children were taken to different tents and given an oil massage followed by a hot water bath. The water swept over their weary muscles, drawing away all the pain. But it was impossible to submit to the pleasure. After clothing them in purple robes, the children were once again held inside cages. The seconds passed slowly, stretching to unbearable lengths, until the appointed time was only a few minutes away.

The children were blindfolded and gagged and led barefooted towards the Chamber of Losian. A loud cheer rose through the air. Thousands upon thousands of Hefigans had been waiting patiently for the four Children of Leod who would pay with their lives to bring glory to the creatures of Sceadu. They parted swiftly to make four paths as the Goblin soldiers led them to the circular chamber.

The chamber lay embedded inside a crater in the desert. The Hefigans had removed all the debris accumulated over millennia and then demolished the ornate ceiling to open it up to the elements. The four sceptres had been placed in holes in front of the four pillars along the periphery. The final excavations had also led to the discovery of a groove that ran around the circular edge, along with four channels that started from each pillar and ended at the centre of the chamber. The entire structure had assumed a surreal look, glistening under the dull rays of Sceadu's five suns, almost perfectly aligned.

The children had deliberated over their fate for so long, it had almost driven their minds numb. But even under the thick robes, their bodies shivered from the gusts of the icy cold wind sweeping the desert. They were led to the pillars and thrust firmly inside the cavities. Thick clamps appeared around their wrists and ankles instantly. The Goblin soldiers pushed back the hoods and removed the blindfolds but left the gags. The first thing each of them saw was their sibling, and then their cousins on either side, imprisoned within the pillars. They could see the sceptres as well, each mounted in front of the cavities.

Isabella only glanced at the others once, her eyes wavering for a brief instant. And then, she turned her gaze downwards. Emilio pushed against the clamps when he saw her plight. She was only nine. How he wished he could give her one last hug. There were so many things he wanted to tell her. That he was sorry for all the times he had been mean to her. That he loved her. That it wasn't her fault. Why had he behaved like a jerk that day? Why had he let her go after the sceptre alone? Why? He couldn't hold back the tears any more.

Will was finding it hard to meet his brother's eyes. He had been ruing his decision to ignore Ben's warning ever since their capture in Awestan. But even before that, his actions had plunged them into untold dangers on so many occasions. He had also been the one, who in many ways had triggered this entire episode by refusing to believe Isabella. Poor Isabella. She had tried so hard. And Emilio. Although they had started off on the wrong foot, he had been a steady rock throughout their time in Sceadu.

One look at Will, and Ben knew exactly what was going on in his brother's mind. Although patience had never been Will's forte, he had more than made up for it with his courage and determination. How he wished he could tell his brother these things. Ben felt especially bad for Isabella. Sceadu had robbed her of her innocence. And now, it was ready to consume her spirit as well. He felt sorry for Emilio as well. What a stellar person he had turned out to be after all.

Blake slowly descended into the chamber, holding close the urn containing the Ashes of Fordon. A gold robe flowed over his armour, swaying wildly in the blustery wind. He threw back the hood with one hand while raising the urn high with the other. The Hefigans roared in unison. "My dear Hefigans," he said, as the onlookers fell silent. "Today is a great day for all of us. Today, we forget our rivalries and stand as one. Today, we reclaim a world wrongly taken away from us. And today, we become immortal. So tell me, are you with me?"

Another deafening roar went through the crowd.

Blake walked around the chamber, staring right into the eyes of the children. For all his wanton cruelty, he made sure each of his victims felt his loathing before the end came. He had neither respect nor mercy for his enemies. He derived his pleasure from seeing them squirm as he snuffed the life out of them, breath by breath. "You shall die most horribly," he smiled, saying each word slowly and deliberately, so that they would remain etched in their memories until their final living moment.

Blake pulled his hood down and walked to the centre of the chamber with soft steps. He closed his eyes and raised the urn to the skies.

When the alignment came, a deathly silence fell upon the entire site. At first, nothing happened. And then, a thick silvery black liquid began oozing from under the pillars and started spreading through the groove along the chamber and down the four channels that met in the centre. For a few moments, only the heavy swishing sound of the liquid could be heard. Before long, grey fumes began to rise out, covering the floor of the chamber completely within minutes.

The liquid suddenly started slithering up the pillars and seeping into the cavities holding the children. At first, they could feel a cold sensation, the kind that accompanies a fever. Their bodies began trembling. The liquid continued to swirl around them, clinging like a thirsty parasite, feeding on their fears and draining away their resolve. Slowly, the stones mounted upon the sceptres began emitting a mysterious glow.

The liquid had also crawled up their captor's robes, covering him from head to toe. But it moved around him gently, its poison nourishing the evil within, taking its potency to levels which would have consumed ordinary human beings. But for Blake, it was like ambrosia, every touch growing his power, every drop pushing his soul to escape from the physical confines of his weak body.

Without warning, the chamber started shaking, sending everyone scurrying for safety. Seconds later, massive cracking sounds rumbled through the desert, and the entire structure broke away from the crater and rose almost fifty feet into the air. The stones burst open, sending out violent beams. The Imp's sceptre gave out a brown beam, the Ghoul's, a grey one, the Færy's, a yellow one, and the Goblin's, a black one. The beams crashed into each other above Blake.

The resulting beam, a deep purple in colour, gurgled furiously and shot upwards into the dull skies. Lightning bolts hurtled around the edges, illuminating the vast expanse in violent bursts. The clouds broke away slowly, turning a dark grey, even as the beam continued to pound mercilessly. Moments later, it finally ripped through the cover with a thunderous sound, throwing open the portal to the world of the Leods.

Blake's body began to tremble, unable to withstand the ruthless assault of the evil from within. It began rising above the chamber floor, the golden robes shimmering brilliantly under the purple onslaught. There was a loud shattering noise as the urn in his hands splintered open. A mighty wind blew from beyond the Hefig Mountains and caught the ashes, carrying them all over Sceadu. The moment they came in contact with the Hefigans, their spirits tore out of their bodies, sending them lifeless to the ground.

The spirits of the Hefigans were whisked away into the purple beam from the farthest corners of the land. Last of all, Blake's soul was wrenched out of his being. The next instant, his body dropped upon the cold grey stone with a dull thud, the maniacal expression frozen on the gold mask forever. He could feel infinite power surging through. Blake turned his gaze upwards, breaking through the hordes of Hefigans floating towards the portal.

As for the children, they had almost been sucked dry by the evil. What had started as a sickening chill had soon turned into excruciating pain. The liquid had clasped their skins like burning plastic, needling away into their flesh for every last drop of energy. It had travelled down their throats, poisoning their insides like the venom of a thousand snakes. Their screams had died in their throats, even as their veins bulged out with the pain. The children's bodies soon collapsed, hanging limply upon the shackles inside the pillar cavities.

The purple beam continued to pummel the skies, growing wider and wider. At first, the Hefigans had been bewildered by the sudden transformation. But when they realized they had been returned to their true form, that their spirits had been released from physical confinement, they began to scramble towards the portal. At a subconscious level, the Hefigans had been preparing for this moment for thousands of years. And it was all about to come true.

The Hefigans were ready to reclaim their lost dominion. And it seemed like the age of the Leods was approaching an abrupt end. But just as the first Hefigan was about to cross over, a different beam erupted from the Shrine of Fordon in the northern part of Sceadu. Dark red in colour and quivering with an intense fury, it cut through the disturbed skies and smashed into the purple beam. The force that accompanied the collision shook the desert for a few seconds, sending shock waves as far as Fyren. The red beam continued to batter its purple nemesis above the chamber until it finally breached its boundary.

The anger poured in, slashing repeatedly at the very fabric of the purple beam. The Hefigan spirits suddenly found themselves drowning in an uncontrollable fury. They scrambled towards the portal only to be dragged away in a whirlwind of inescapable rage and into a large jar inside the Shrine of Fordon. Blake's spirit tried to claw its way out, tearing fiercely at the red beam. But the more he tried, the more it consumed him. When the last spirit had been transported inside, the lid slammed shut. The universe made no exceptions.

The clouds barged in, assuming dark hues of red, rumbling over each other until the portal ruptured and closed with a massive clap. The purple column began developing gigantic fractures along its length, beginning at the top and spreading downwards like termite lines, under the relentless pounding of the red beam. Unable to withstand the force any longer, it ripped apart into a million beams. They struck the lifeless bodies of the Hefigans, turning them to ashes, never to rise again.

The Chamber of Losian descended back into the crater it had left behind in the desert. A sudden lull fell over Sceadu.

Will blinked slowly. The drops of water felt cold on his cheeks. He wiped his face wearily and opened his eyes. The sky was still slightly overcast, but it had lost its dismal aura. He felt confused. What was he doing lying inside what appeared to be an ancient temple? And why was he feeling so drained? He turned to one side with great effort and was about to push his palm to the ground when his eyes fell upon a gold sceptre with the carving of a Goblin's head. He fell back and clutched his head, trying to block the deluge of painful memories that had surfaced. Was he still alive?

Will rolled over and moved his eyes around. He could see Ben lying under the pillar directly in front of him making groaning noises. Emilio was sitting on one side, a dazed look clouding his round face. But Isabella's body was slumped inside the cavity on his right. He dragged his arms out and crawled towards her. "Bella," he croaked. "Milo, I need you here."

Emilio forgot his troubles the moment he saw his sister. He stumbled towards them as fast as he could.

Will placed Isabella's head gently on his lap. "Quick," he said, pointing to the water accumulated in the groove.

Emilio scooped the water and sprinkled it on her face. "Open your eyes, Bella" he cried. "Look, everything's fine. We're all fine."

Isabella slowly opened her eyes. She smiled weakly at her brother and cousin. The evil had affected her small body the most.

Tears streamed down Emilio's face. "Don't give up," he pleaded. "You can make it. Please."

"She's fading fast," Will whispered, feeling her brow. "Splash more water."

"Perhaps this will help." Ben came running over from the tent and squeezed the dark red tendril over her lips.

Isabella's eyes rolled back in her head and her hands thrashed around a few times. The next moment, she flipped over and coughed out a thick grey liquid as the others watched anxiously. "I'm okay," she said, after a few minutes.

Emilio rushed at Ben and held him in a bear hug.

"A simple word of thanks would have sufficed," Ben gasped. He bent over and wheezed a few times as Emilio dropped him back on the ground. "The person who deserves all our gratitude though is Isabella."

But Isabella staggered to her feet. "We must proceed to Atelic immediately," she said, leaning upon the Færy's sceptre and spitting out some more of the liquid. "Only a few hours before we get trapped here forever."

The boys peered at their shadows in horror. They had almost turned purple once again.

"Let's get out of this chamber first," Will said, helping Isabella up the steps.

Below, the Chamber of Losian stood frozen in time. The pillars had cracked in several places. The sceptres remained, but their tops were bare. Broken pieces of the urn lay scattered near the centre. And a solitary gold mask gleamed ominously, a grim reminder of what could have been.

"It's the only chance we have," Isabella said, setting down her shoes upon the table inside Blake's tent.

"But can you make it back in time?" Will asked. "We have less than five hours left."

"I know I can."

Emilio chewed on his lips. "And if you can't for any reason, you promise to return home."

"But I shall."

"What's that?" Will whispered, pushing his finger to his lips. They could hear soft tapping sounds from outside. He slowly drew Blake's sword out of the sand and parted the tent flap. "It's the Griffins."

And indeed it was. Four Griffins stood upon the sand, gleaming brightly under the sun's smouldering rays. They swished their bushy tails furiously, as if urging the children to make haste.

Emilio threw a few punches in the air. "Now that's what I'm talking about."

Moments later, the Griffins flapped their mighty wings and leapt into the clear skies over the Drysmian Desert. The children were almost out of breath by the time they reached Atelic. With no Hefigans around, the Griffins landed right inside the courtyard of Awestan.

"Here it is," Will said, emerging out of the ghost tower. He opened his palm to reveal the golden box.

Ben ran his slender fingers over the intricate design. "I still can't come to terms with the role these torn pieces of paper have played in creating the chain of events that have brought us thus far."

"Just open the damn box," Emilio cried, prancing around them.

Will flipped the delicate latch. The lid flew open, causing the pages to jump out. He began turning them, slowly at first and then frantically, his excitement changing to bewilderment and then to anguish.

"What's the matter?" Isabella asked.

Will started to say something but finally shook his head and handed the pages to the others with trembling hands. They had all been blacked out.

CHAPTER 27 – FINAL PROPHECY

milio slunk to the ground. "It's all over," he sniffed. "I'm sure Blake must be laughing his head off inside that jar right now."

"At least our world is safe," Will said, putting his hand upon his cousin's shoulder.

"But what about our parents?" Isabella asked in a small voice.

"It's just not fair," Emilio cried. "We did everything asked of us, and it's still not enough. I want to go home."

"Yet again, I feel like I've been downgraded from a knight to a pawn in this game," Ben said.

Emilio glared upwards. "It's the fault of this stupid universe. Someone messed up thousands of years ago and guess who has to bear the consequences?"

Ben peered at Isabella's watch. "With only half an hour to go and our final option exhausted, I would peg the probability of our return at exactly… "

"There," Isabella said, running ahead and pointing at the sky. The others looked upwards. It was the Eorls, descending into Atelic upon the magnificent Unicorns.

"My dear Children of Leod," Halig said. "Let me be the first to congratulate you. You have vanquished the Hefigans and in doing so, saved your world from a great evil force."

"Thank you," Will said quietly.

Ben fidgeted a little, wondering whether to speak up. "I'm certainly pleased to see you all," he said finally, "but I must say I'm surprised as well."

"The Hefigans were creatures of Fordon. We were made by Mundbyrd, remember."

"What about Blake though?" Isabella asked. "He wasn't a creature of Fordon."

"But when he became a part of their destiny, he also had to share their fate. Do you remember the last line of the original prophecy? But 'tis clear, one will be dead. His spirit now finds itself confined to the jar in the Shrine of Fordon."

"Is this even the time?" Emilio wailed, pushing past his sister and cousin. He gave them a stern look and faced Halig. "The torn pages were all blacked out. Can you please help us return home?"

"When the last of the Hefigan spirits was banished into the jar, a lightning bolt struck the spherical ball on top of the fountain in the Fælsian Lake. The ball shattered, echoing with what I believe is the final prophecy. We started for Atelic knowing it would be your obvious destination."

Isabella couldn't resist herself. "But how did the unicorns come all this way?" she asked, sliding behind Will before her brother could direct another look at her.

"Sceadu has been rid of all evil."

"So let me get this straight," Emilio jumped in before any more questions came up. "There is a way back home. Please say there is."

Halig nodded at the eager faces of the children. "But it's not that simple. Mildheort, please narrate the last prophecy."

Mildheort bowed.

> *"The Hefigans have lost, once and for all*
> *Sent to their fate, great was their fall*
> *The Children of Leod have triumphed thus far*
> *The door to their home lies slightly ajar*
> *But unless each finds a Fordon's Tear*
> *Their destiny is Sceadu, they remain here*
> *Stand in a circle, closed right fist*
> *Blow upon twice, release the mist*
> *Your shadow beckons you through the door*
> *Grey once again, purple no more."*

"A simple task but for one minor detail," Halig said. "You each need to find a tear of Fordon."

Emilio let out a low whine. "Now where are we going to get these things? What are they anyway?"

"Legend has it that when the divine voice first spoke about the prophecy that would seek to bring together the Hefigans and the Leods, Fordon was so saddened he wept tears of blood. The moment these tears touched the ground, they turned into red stones. Unfortunately, it's not easy to find them."

"The telescope," Will cried, pushing his hands into his right pocket and then his left and then his right again. "It's… it's not there."

Ben chewed on his thumb, pointing to their shadows. "Even if the telescope showed you where the stones were, we only have five minutes to find them."

"That is way too long," Isabella said, reaching inside her left pocket. "I suppose you wouldn't be looking for these."

The boys gaped at the four crimson stones sitting upon her tiny palm, unable to decide whether they were looking at an illusion.

"But how?" Will asked. "I mean… I thought… how?"

"Don't you remember? I picked them up in the Gamol Forest."

"We're going home, we're going home" Emilio sang, suddenly springing to life. He hoisted Isabella up and swung her around, amidst cheers from the others.

Halig closed his eyes. He had always known they would find a way. But the ways of the universe never ceased to amaze him.

The children quickly formed a circle, each holding a red stone tightly in their right fist.

"Hold on," Ben shouted, before any of them could blow. The others twitched their limbs impatiently. But he was back within seconds, clasping his precious backpack. "I didn't want to make a trip back for this. Here we go."

The children nodded at each other and blew upon their right hands twice. A cold sensation hit their palms almost instantly, with red mist slowly escaping through the gaps in their fingers. It twirled around their bare arms and then their bodies, moving in feathery wisps that had soon enveloped the complete circle. Slowly, they began to feel drowsy. The last thing they saw was the Eorls waving at them and then everything went blank.

The children woke up to the familiar feel of the soft, worn-out carpet in the living room.

"My shadow is grey," Emilio shouted, pouncing upon it and trying to hug it. "We're really back. I need food."

Will sat up and pushed his back against the couch. "I wonder if my phone's working again. I wonder what day it is here. I think I need to lie down before I do anything else."

"Sounds like a good plan," Ben sighed. "I wonder if there's any strawberry yoghurt in the refrigerator."

"Do you think it was all a dream?" Isabella asked, looking around. "I mean, now that we're all here… it all seems so distant, as if it never happened."

"Unless you guys beat me in my sleep, I think these bruises say a lot," Will grinned.

Emilio ran over to the window. "And look," he laughed, throwing open the curtains. "Just one sun. What a beautiful sight!"

"I propose we start thinking about damage control," Ben said. "We need a believable story, one where…"

Will goggled at him. "Now? I don't think so. I'm off to take a nice hot shower."

"That does sound good," Emilio said, "but only after a few slices of pizza."

"Don't even think about it." Isabella ran after him into the kitchen. "That pizza's over a week old."

"After eating with the Imps, do you think I even care?"

Isabella came back with a pot of strawberry yogurt. "Here you go, Ben," she grinned. "And don't worry. Our mothers won't be back until tomorrow."

"For once, I don't detest the feel of this plastic," Ben said, peeling away the top. He picked out a strawberry chunk and placed it on his tongue. "Heaven."

"We're home!"

Emilio almost tripped while slipping into his trousers. He knew that voice. It was his mother. But why were they back a day early?

"I've missed you all so much. Where's Milo?"

Emilio rushed out and leaned across the banister. His mother was giving a tight hug to Isabella, who had shrivelled up like a mouse. His cousins were there as well, perched upon the couch like mannequins.

Just then, the front door opened and Aunt Sarah walked in. "Hi guys," she smiled. "It's good to see everyone. So what have you all been up to?"

Emilio could see Will beginning to splutter. He ran down the stairs and interrupted. "Hi, mom. We've had a great week. I hope gramps is feeling better."

"He absolutely is." His mother stared at him. "That's some tan you've got there. And I must say you're looking quite lean and fit."

"Will's been making us work hard. And he took us camping as well."

Aunt Sarah sat beside Ben. "This one came camping?" she said, tousling his hair. "Frankly, I'm surprised your house hasn't burned down yet. I'm just kidding."

"Ben's been awesome," Emilio said. "He even got us to do some bird watching. So how was your visit?"

"Grandpa's stable now," his mother replied, squeezing her sister's hand. She closed her eyes momentarily and took a deep breath. "But you have no idea what we've been through. A massive thunderstorm hit the town after we had landed. We had so much difficulty reaching Grandpa's place in the mountains. There was no reception there, and after that call I made, the phone lines suddenly went dead. We decided to leave the moment he got better. But the storm had caused a landslide upon the only route that led to town. It got cleared only this morning. You have no idea how worried we were about all of you."

"Aren't you glad you didn't come with us?" Aunt Sarah said, bringing out her compact. "You wouldn't have lasted for a day."

Emilio suppressed a smile. "Mom, can you please make us something to eat? If you're not tired, that is."

"It's almost half past eight, but I suppose I could. How about some enchiladas?"

"You're the best, Mom."

The lawn carried a dull sheen from the moon, cocooned amongst the silhouettes of the surrounding trees. The children lay sprawled upon the cool grass, enjoying the soft touch of the breeze.

"That was a meal to remember," Emilio said, patting his stomach.

Ben nodded. "It indeed was. For the number of helpings you had. I now see the reasoning behind wearing those elastic trousers."

They all had a good laugh.

Will turned to Emilio. "Thanks for covering for me back there. You really held the situation together."

"That's why everyone should eat pizza."

"What?"

"I checked the messages when I had the pizza in the microwave," Emilio winked. "So I knew our parents hadn't called. "

"Isn't it strange how the phone lines went dead?" Isabella said.

"Don't forget the landslide," Emilio interjected.

"The universe works in mysterious ways," Ben sighed, pressing his palm gently over the blades of grass.

Will chuckled. "Look at you, talking about the universe and its ways. Are we looking at voodoo or crystals next?"

"You might just feel a sharp pain in your ribs tonight."

"What if we hadn't made it?" Emilio asked suddenly.

Ben shrugged. "With the Hefigans gone, I do believe we would have had access to the choicest real estate in Sceadu. I can already see Isabella laying claim to Gifredia."

But Isabella didn't reply.

"I hope I haven't offended you with my poor attempt at humour."

"Eh… no, it's not that at all. I just remembered Evan. I really miss him."

Will held her hand. "We all do. It was the only thing that didn't work out. But if it hadn't been for him, we wouldn't be here right now."

"The world will never know of his contribution."

"I just wish we could have seen the look on Blake's face as he was getting sucked into the jar."

"And we mustn't forget out good friend Beodan," Emilio added.

"There's only one question I have," Ben said, facing Isabella. "And I can't hold back my curiosity any longer. How did you orchestrate Blake's fall?"

Isabella swallowed hard. "I'm so sorry for keeping you all in the dark. I must have told you a million times in my head. I really wanted to, but there was too much at stake. If Blake had suspected anything in the slightest, he could have destroyed our only chance. So I had to act as if I was in distress. It wasn't easy keeping up with the pretence though."

"You did the right thing. And I can attest to your marvellous acting skills. They really had everyone fooled."

"So what happened?" Will asked.

"You'll never believe it in a thousand years."

Isabella narrated her journey to Helofor as far as the moment where she had found herself surrounded by the Ghouls.

"And then?" Emilio asked, pushing his nails to his teeth.

Isabella gently pulled his hand away. "I thought all was lost. But suddenly, the Ghouls fell upon their knees and started praying. For a moment, I wondered if they had gone insane and decided to worship me or something. And then, I heard a familiar voice behind me. It was Egesa on his Broga. The Ghouls probably thought it was his ghost, I suppose. I quickly hopped on, and we were off."

Will gave a low whistle. "So Egesa did manage to take out the entire platoon of Goblins back in the Gamol Forest. But what was he doing in Helofor?"

"If you recall, Helofor lies in northern Atolon. Egesa knew he couldn't return, back to the Ghouls, but he wanted to spend his remaining days in his own kingdom. The largely deserted Grymetiana was the ideal hideout."

"Did you tell him what you were out to do?"

"I couldn't deceive him. But all he wanted was an escape from the life that had been forced upon him."

"What happened next?"

"Once I reached the Shrine of Fordon, I thrust the Sceptre of Attor into the eye of Fordon. But nothing happened. That's when I remembered what Halig had said. Although the outcome had yet to be determined, the prophecy would be fulfilled. So it meant that for the second prophecy to work, the conditions of the first prophecy had to be satisfied."

Ben leaned forward. "And that's why you had to get captured. I have to commend you for this brilliant deduction. I suppose that's also the reason the marble directed us to scale the walls of the Goblin fortress."

"I wasn't sure if my reasoning was correct," Isabella replied, blushing slightly. "But I had to take my chances. So I made sure I ran into a group of Ghouls, pretending to be scared and lost."

"I wonder why the Eorls never mentioned this to us."

"I'm not sure how my resolve would have fared had they told me I had to get past the Dragons, pierce Fordon's eye and then get deliberately captured."

"You may have a point there," Ben said. "But how could you be sure the rest of us had been captured as well?"

"I almost forgot. Egesa got your message. It so happens that a small tributary of the Mælan does flow through Grymetiana. I knew it had to be you. And it was quite obvious you all had been captured and were being taken to the Temple of Fordon. That was very smart."

"You really had me worried back there," Will said, feigning a punch at his brother.

"The book," Isabella said, sitting up with a jerk. "Where's the book?"

Emilio patted her hand. "Don't worry. It's locked away in a safe place."

The children inhaled deeply, savouring the silence of the starry night. For the past week, they had been carrying the burden of the entire world upon their shoulders. It felt really good to have their load reduced to a few household chores.

Will suddenly clicked his tongue. "You know something. I still can't get over those Færy wings."

"What?" Ben and Emilio cried together.

The next moment, Will found himself being chased around the lawn as Isabella burst out laughing.

Epilogue – Pandora's Jar

A massive stone jar lies precariously balanced inside an underground chamber of the Shrine of Fordon. It is home to the spirits of the Hefigans, physical manifestations of negativities that had made a futile attempt to claim another world as their own. A prophecy made thousands of years ago had promised to unleash their wrath upon the Leods, plunging their world into the Dark Ages, reminiscent of the times when it was first ruled by the ruthless and callous Firas. A traitor from among the Leods had led the Hefigan forces, only to be thwarted by four Children of Leod. The result: the spirit of the Leod traitor also languishes inside the jar. But can the spell that protects the jar withstand the fury of this maniac? His spirit only seeks one thing. Revenge. How long will the jar hold its prisoners? Only time will tell.

www.ingramcontent.com/pod-product-compliance
Lightning Source LLC
Chambersburg PA
CBHW011602210726
48287CB00012BC/2740